D0114480

NEVER AFTER

NEVER AFTER

REBECCA LICKISS

ACE BOOKS, NEW YORK

NEVER AFTER

An Ace Book / published by arrangement with
the author

Copyright © 2002 by Rebecca Lickiss.
Cover art by Judy York.
Cover design by Judy Murello.
Text design by Julie Rogers.

ISBN: 0-7394-2853-5

ACE®
Ace Books are published by The Berkley Publishing Group,
a division of Penguin Putnam Inc.,
375 Hudson Street, New York, New York 10014.
ACE and the "A" design
are trademarks belonging to Penguin Putnam Inc.

PRINTED IN THE UNITED STATES OF AMERICA

For Seth, Benjamin, Majel, Jacob, Kayleen.
Go for it.

ONCE UPON A TIME . . .

❦

VERDANT FORESTS GREW up and around the mountains, covering most of the low foothills. A few scattered cleared patches indicated the locations of small farms
or villages. A treeless plot of oddly shaped green hillocks
tucked themselves out of sight and away from the rest of
the world in a valley between the foothills and the mountains.

Up close, the odd hillocks could be seen to be, in fact,
a covered castle. Its turrets and towers standing defiant
though surrounded and overrun by herbage. Vines grew up
around the stone walls, hiding them as effectively as grass
hides dirt. Thick, thorny briars grew round the base of the
castle, defending the vines from any predators larger than
mice.

A small path, just wide enough for a man to pass, had

been recently cut through the decidedly unpicturesque
bramble. The pungent fibrous cores of recently slashed
branches defined the limits of the path as pragmatically as
the exposed soil. Still-green vines clung to the open iron
gates, with exposed roots withering in the sun, trailing
over the gashes in the earth caused by the swinging open
of that portion of the gate.

In the outer courtyard, spring flowers fought for light
and space with the vines and briars. The cherub fountain
had long since clogged, and scum-covered water filled the
pool at its base. The castle lacked any sort of fortresslike
feel: no stone projections calculated to provide maximum
cross-fire coverage, no dark entrance tunnels with murder
holes, no heavy portcullis. The castle had been a peaceful
place, secure in its power and privilege, until overcome by
a massed attack of the tranquil, bucolic herbage around
and in it.

A pigeon came to rest on the head of a guard, sleeping
at his post beside the iron gates, as he had been for gener-
ations. A whitish sort of gray plaster covered the guard,
giving him the look of a statue and possibly forming as
hard an armor as any he had started with.

Should he ever be relieved of his post, he certainly will
never take it up again.

⚜

PRINCE ALTHELSTAN LEANED against the wall, eyes
open, as he stared unseeing at the room around him.
He'd fought nearly every inch of the way here, dulled two
axes and a sword hacking at the briars, brambles, and
thorns that grew around the castle, protecting it. Once inside, he'd discovered thousands of rooms . . . thousands.

His systematic search had led him through nearly all of them, and through the better part of a month, before he found this one. And, since he hadn't known which one was the sleeping princess, he'd kissed hundreds of unconscious women. To no avail.

Here at the end of his systematic search, in the topmost room of the tallest turret, three biers held three sleeping forms in their well-preserved, elegant, old-fashioned nightshirts and coronets, each under its own thick, quilted blanket, under another thick layer of dust. Three sleeping princes. Althelstan supposed they might be considered handsome by some interested woman, but right now he found them hideous and wanted to strangle them.

Althelstan had come here to kiss a princess. He needed a princess, not three more rivals. And he wasn't about to kiss those three.

It had to be a transcription error. A sleeping princess, 3 sleeping princes. Althelstan could see that in a moment of hurried copying, hunched over a clean sheaf of paper with only a candle for lighting and a blotched original to work with, someone might transform the number 3 to an a. Of course, then it would only make sense to add the extra s on princes. But, right at this moment, he didn't have much sympathy for the harried copier.

He surveyed the room again. A simple, square, stone tower room; with arrow slit windows to the east, south, and west; a narrow wooden stairway heading down along the north wall; three wooden biers with three sleeping male figures; and lots of dust.

Fists on hips, Althelstan strode through the room, kicking at the decayed rushes on the floor, though he really didn't expect any answers there. Caution made him stop. He didn't want to repeat whatever had caused this disaster, or get caught in it. There really wasn't anything for him here. He decided it was high time to leave.

At the bottom of the stairs, he stopped. There, in what he'd dubbed the waiting room, sat eight people on a series of beautiful, well-cushioned lounges, all asleep, a few snoring briskly. An older man, whose gray hair nearly hid his small gold crown, was dressed from chin to toe in extremely expensive, old-fashioned finery. Two guard types, holding swords across their laps, slept on either side of him, in probably the same slumped positions they used when sleeping on duty. Another lounge held two middle-aged couples, leaning husband-to-wife, with hands clasped.

The object of Althelstan's fascination was a young woman sitting off by herself in a chair. Her tiara and elegant, expensive, old-fashioned clothes had at first led him to mistake her for the sleeping princess and to make several unsuccessful but not unpleasant attempts at a cure. He still believed she was a princess. Her beauty drew him to her again. He took her warm hand in his own, stroked her long, thin fingers, then raised them to his lips. "I shall release you from this curse."

He had to find a way to lift the curse. His father insisted he marry only someone of the same or higher rank. All the queens he knew were married or too old, and the only real princess, from a neighboring kingdom, was two years old. He had no intention of waiting the fourteen or fifteen years it would take the toddling Princess Caryl to grow up. Let some other, more patient prince marry her.

The dearth of princesses in this generation had seemed a blessing until Althelstan had reached a certain age. All the various royal families had welcomed their sons, rejoiced over all the extra, spare, sons. None had stopped to wonder or remark on the lack of young royal females.

Other princes had simply made do with less royal women for their wives. Althelstan suspected his father, the king, wouldn't be so picky over Althelstan's younger brothers' wives. But for him, Crown Prince Althelstan, only the daughter of a king would be accepted. Surely this beautiful woman was the daughter of a king. All Althelstan had to do was wake her and prove her a princess to his father.

Althelstan set the sleeping young woman's hand gently back into her lap. He smoothed a curl of dark hair back from her cheek, while he thought. He needed someone to kiss the princes, probably a princess. He doubted Caryl's mother would allow her out here into the wilderness for that purpose.

If there was ever a woman who could finesse her way through the labyrinth of this curse and place, it would be his cousin, Vevila. She was, without a doubt, the most conniving, manipulative, beguiling, crafty individual ever born. Quite possibly she was also why the king had been set against anything but a real princess for the son who would inherit the throne.

Althelstan sighed. Vevila would want something out of this, though there was no telling what. She made little sense to Althelstan. Though princes were a dime a dozen, perhaps she'd be more intrigued with someone she hadn't known all about since her childhood. Perhaps the allure of the mysterious princes trapped in this insidious spell would appeal to her.

If nothing else, Althelstan could guarantee her a few weeks away from home.

Ꮳ❧Ꮳ

L ADY VEVILA HELD her wine goblet in a tight death
grip, wishing it were a good solid red rather than the
weak white. If she stood up from her seat on the padded
wooden bench, the oaf, Lord Osric, standing by her right
shoulder, would undoubtedly ask her to dance. If she
didn't, he would continue to stare down at her cleavage,
thinking she didn't know he was staring. White wine
would only make him temporarily wet; a good full-bodied
red would make a beautiful, permanent stain on his pale
yellow tunic.

She stood.

"Would you honor me with this dance, milady?" Lord
Osric asked.

"No."

Men. Ask them if they'd like to spend the rest of their
lives embroidering and caring for babies, and every one of
them would be horrified at the thought. But they never understood why a woman wouldn't want to do that. What
truly infuriated Vevila was that many women didn't understand either. Such as . . .

Her mother, Princess Lucilla, intercepted her before she
could reach the door. Her mother's strongly floral perfume
stopped her squeezing past more effectively than a strong
arm. "And just where do you think you're going?"

"Nowhere," Vevila answered truthfully. How much she
desperately wanted to go somewhere.

Princess Lucilla smiled, a practiced smile that Vevila
recognized as false, and plucked at the white silk sticking
through the slashes in the blue velvet sleeves of Vevila's
uncomfortable dress. "Dear heart, you will stay here in the
ballroom, and you will dance with the fine gentlemen. One

of them will one day be your husband. You do remember that?"

Vevila smiled, her own rehearsed false smile. "Yes." *Over my dead body.* Which, unfortunately, could be arranged.

"At least Lord Osric is young. You need not fear being married off to some old geezer." Princess Lucilla's attention was on her husband, Vevila's father, Prince Bernard, sitting in the near corner. The aged Prince Bernard, brother to the previous king and uncle to the current one, rested in his large chair, his gouty foot on a stool. "You will have some choice."

But not enough, Vevila thought, *not enough of a choice.* She'd seen what happened to her older half sisters, daughters of her father's previous marriages. "Yes, Mother," she said dutifully.

"For pity's sake, at least pretend you are interested in the dance. Flirt with someone."

Batting her eyelashes at a servitor carrying a tray of glasses, Vevila managed to bring him to heel and exchange her nearly empty goblet of white wine for a full goblet of red. She waggled her eyebrows as she took in the fine figure he presented in his subdued gray tunic and green tights.

A ghost of a nervous smile flickered on his face, and he passed on with his tray.

"Vevila! That is not what I meant." Princess Lucilla leaned close to her daughter's ear to whisper harshly, "Dance with him."

Lady Vevila blinked, thinking her mother meant the servant. But Lord Osric stepped into her field of view.

"Your Highness." He bowed.

"We were just speaking of you," Princess Lucilla said. "You must dance with my daughter, you dance so well."

"Only if she wishes it," Lord Osric said gallantly.

Laughing, Princess Lucilla took Vevila's hand and put it in Osric's. "You mustn't take to heart what the young ladies say these days. They think it the height of wit to say no, when they really mean yes." She managed to glare at Vevila while simultaneously smiling at Osric.

"So what other witticisms may I look forward to?" Osric led Vevila onto the nearly empty dance floor. Most of the guests were Vevila's father's cronies, who took little interest in dancing, preferring instead to rest gouty feet by roaring fireplaces. A few had brought their children or grandchildren. These were twirling about the dance floor.

Vevila ground the heel of her shoe into Osric's big toe, then stepped away in mock surprised horror. "Pardon me. I'm so very sorry." She fluttered her eyelashes and said coyly, "I'm not a very good dancer."

"Quite all right," he whispered, as he limped through the next steps of the dance. Osric's sweaty palm clamped down on hers to guide her through a series of turns. "Do you enjoy dancing?"

Seeing a way out of this, Vevila leaned closer to him. "Not tonight; it's so very warm in here. I begin to think I might need some fresh air."

Lord Osric's eyes lit up with whatever reptilian plan his feeble brain was forming. "Of course, milady, of course."

He steered them through the dancers to an open doorway. Outside, the crisp nighttime air felt like a brisk slap. They stood on a small semicircular balcony, only half a story up from the ground below. She smiled at him and looked significantly at the door.

When he turned to close the door, Vevila swung over the balcony railing to drop to the ground below. Quickly and quietly, she ducked under the overhanging balcony, effectively disappearing.

"Lady Vevila?" Lord Osric whispered fiercely. "Lady Vevila!" She heard him step up to the rail. "Lady Vevila?" He was quiet for a long while. "Whatever shall they think?" he moaned. "What shall I do?"

It wasn't that she hated Lord Osric or in any way blamed him for her predicament . . . Well, yes, she did hate him and blamed him, but not him in particular. He was no worse than any of the other suitors her parents had inflicted on her. And certainly no better.

Waiting until she was certain he'd gone back inside, Vevila ran along the edge of the mansion, slipping into the back servants' entrance and up the stairs. She hurried down the hallway and to her room.

To find her mother waiting for her, standing by the bed with arms crossed, her perfume filling the room. "Back to the ball, young lady. You frightened poor Lord Osric nearly out of his wits."

"It didn't take much," Vevila muttered.

"It's a good thing your father and I know what to expect from you. Otherwise, Lord Osric or—no I should say *and*—you would now be very deep in trouble." Princess Lucilla paused. Vevila knew it was for some response, preferably remorse, but just couldn't find it in her. Her mother's frown deepened. "Now. Back to the ball."

Lady Vevila behaved herself for the rest of the dance and took the lecture her mother gave her afterward. When finally alone, she slipped out of her nightgown and into a tunic and trousers she'd acquired not long ago. She packed a few things in a small bag she could carry, strapped a long knife at her waist, and slipped out the window on a line of tied bedsheets.

She'd run away from home before. Practice runs, she thought of them, since she always had to return before. However, now she was almost of age, had enough cash to carry her for a few weeks, and generally knew more of what she was doing. It was high time she took her life into her own hands and steered her own course.

Let some other fool woman marry those idiot lords and princes. She'd had enough of them. Enough of dancing with nitwits and conversing with dunces, enough of sewing and proper ladylike behavior. She wanted adventure and excitement. Surely out there somewhere was a man who'd understand her, who wouldn't want to force her into a role she hated. Though he'd have to be very different from any man she'd ever met before.

Resting her hand comfortably on her knife, she smiled to herself. This time she'd get adventure and excitement, and woe be unto any who got in her way.

❧

MAZIGIAN WATCHED THE road from where he stood leaning against the outer wall near the doorway of the tavern. He was impatient to be on his way. Impatient to be seen and hailed as a great wizard. Impatient to be of some use to someone.

Puffed up with the power of magic and wizardry inside him, Mazigian wanted nothing more than to make the world better, use his talents for the greater good of all, to bring peace and prosperity to the world. He could see himself already, humbly accepting the gratitude of everyone everywhere he went, the subject of numerous bardic sagas, and paraded and feted and beloved.

He glanced inside the tavern to confirm that his com-

panions were still there. Unfortunately, they were. Rueberry sat, nearly reclining on the wooden bench straining
to support his large frame, clutching his tankard of ale,
having finished off the fowl, ham, roast, bread, and cheese
the ale man had brought them. Zenpfennig leaned on the
table, like a half-forgotten, lost-to-the-wind scarecrow in
the fall. His long, bony hands steepled, one eyebrow up
and the other down, as he frowned at something off near
the fire, while lecturing Rueberry.

As wizards, they, of course, commanded the best table,
comfortably far from the fire. The late-spring-day sun
streaming in through the open door kept the inn warm
enough, but the fire was kept going through the day to heat
the tavern at night.

Mazigian had thought that with the status that wizards
had, he'd have no problem securing a position after grad-
uating from the Recondite University. He'd been wrong.

The University's Board of Directors had given him a
position with one of their crack investigative teams at the
urging and recommendation of the Chairman of Fire and
Explosives, who had become particularly doting after
Mazigian had demonstrated a talent for rebuilding and but-
tressing, after the distressing demolition of the Adminis-
tration's Dining Hall.

The culprits had never been caught, and Mazigian
rested easy in the certainty that by now nothing could ever
be proven.

He sighed, remembering fondly his old college days,
just last Tuesday. How he and Ordred and Thornside had
used to toss aside their robes and run across campus in
their underalls, snatching the pointed hats off of the pro-
fessors' heads. How he'd fooled the entire class, even the
professor, in Illusions 101 with his Illusion of a Perfect

Student. How he could, with a few gentle marks here and there, change the Runes textbook into a step-by-step instruction on welding.

A young peasant boy stepped up to him, bobbing a series of bows and clutching his hat to his chest. "Sir. Excuse me, sir. Not to bother, sir. But . . .."

"Speak, child," Mazigian said in his best patronizing tones. Here, perhaps, was the opportunity to demonstrate to the world his power and magnanimity.

"Oh, sir. Grand, wise, and fearsome." The child looked like his eyes might pop out of his head in fear. Mazigian suspected it was an act. Children that afraid tended to save their breath for running. "Our well has run dry, and try as we might, we can't find the right spot for the new one."

"And you were wondering if I might help?" Mazigian finished for him. So much for his great opportunity. Still, it couldn't hurt to do the poor boy a good turn.

The boy nodded fearfully.

"Of co—"

Mazigian was pushed aside by a sharp, bony elbow. Tall, thin, white-haired, and sporting a perpetually constipated expression above a long, scraggly beard, Zenpfennig looked the part of an experienced wizard. "There is our fee, of course."

The boy backed away, truly scared. "I, I, I have no money."

Zenpfennig made a tisking sound. "Magic is not a thing to play with. It takes time and effort to learn, patience and finesse to accomplish, and is an exhausting and exacting science. An enterprise of skill and a straining exertion. We who have sacrificed so much to acquire it cannot afford to give it away without recompense."

Having heard all this before, Mazigian sighed in frustration. Zenpfennig rewarded him with another sharp elbow in the ribs. The boy looked from one to the other of them, then bowed his head and slowly walked away.

The old wizard returned to the tavern with a sniff. Mazigian waited a moment, then sauntered after the boy. It didn't take him long. The boy wasn't moving fast.

Grabbing the boy by the shoulder, Mazigian concentrated a moment. Then he leaned down and said, "Up the hill, by the withered plum tree."

The boy grinned and took off running.

Returning to the tavern, Mazigian found Zenpfennig waiting for him. "That's coming out of your share of our profits."

Mazigian nodded. He'd heard that before, too.

❧

PRINCE ALTHELSTAN RODE on through the capital. He had no intention of stopping in at the palace to give his parents, the king and queen, a chance to try to talk him out of his quest to find a princess. The king just didn't seem to understand that there weren't hundreds of unmarried princesses waiting for a husband, like there'd been in the king's heyday. Althelstan kept his hood pulled over his head, hiding his face. He hoped to get through town anonymously.

At the edge of town, he saw a familiar figure leaning against a tavern doorway. It was a young wizard, complete with pointed hat and light tan robes. It took him a moment to recognize Mazigian. It was the robes. The last time Althelstan had seen Mazigian, he'd been wearing white robes. With the accrual of age and experience, the wizard would change to darker-colored and more spangly robes.

Mazigian showed no sign of recognition when Althelstan waved. Throwing back his hood, Althelstan waved again. This time, Mazigian responded promptly.

"What are you doing here?" Mazigian demanded. "I'd heard you were off on some quest or other."

"I'll tell you over a drink."

Inside, two other wizards in dark brown robes and pointed hats sat near the bones and crumbs of a finished meal, actually several finished meals. Mazigian introduced them to Althelstan, the tall, bony one as Zenpfennig and the short, fat one as Rueberry. Althelstan bought a round of drinks and told them about his adventures so far.

"Do you mean to say there really is a castle full of sleeping people? It's not a myth?" Zenpfennig asked.

"I've been there. It's real," Althelstan assured them.

"Sounds like the work of an evil witch." Rueberry patted his large stomach knowingly. "That's the sort of thing they get up to, whenever they can."

"Perhaps we should investigate," Mazigian said.

Zenpfennig frowned deeply. "The Recondite University frowns on evil witches."

As far as Althelstan could tell, the Recondite University frowned on witches of any kind. They could do just about everything a wizard could and had a distressing tendency to also take soup to sick people and the suchlike. And they did it cheaper than wizards, which was the university's main objection.

"We should help him," Mazigian said enthusiastically.

Rueberry shifted on his bench. "Not much we could do. His cousin kisses the princes, and everything is back to normal. It sounds like he has the situation perfectly under control."

"But an evil witch?" Mazigian griped. "What if she's still lurking around? She might do Our Prince harm."

Althelstan hadn't thought of that, or at least had tried to avoid thinking about it. Perhaps having three wizards on his side would be a good idea. However, the only thing he knew of to motivate a wizard was money, and the king had made it clear that if Althelstan wished, he could waste his own money on this quest but not one copper halfpenny would be forthcoming from the royal treasury.

"He's a big lad," Zenpfennig said stoutly. "He can take care of himself."

Mazigian leaned back. "Well, yes, but those poor people, sleeping by their golden goblets, silver trays, all their treasures, completely helpless."

Zenpfennig's bony fingers steepled on the table, each tapping its opposite number in turn. "I suppose their treasury has already been raided."

Shrugging, Althelstan said, "I hadn't located their treasury. I was looking for a princess. But I shouldn't think so, if there'd been any path to the place, such as someone raiding the treasury might make, I'm sure I would have found it." He glanced at Rueberry. "I do know all of their belongings appeared to still be with them: clothes, furniture, tapestries, food. There were huge hams and enormous cheeses in the larder, wines that have to have been sitting for a hundred years in the cellar."

Rueberry looked thoughtful.

"A bramble-covered castle, with vulnerable people sleeping through it all. A tragedy, a tragedy," Zenpfennig mused. "Perhaps we should investigate."

Mazigian grinned at Althelstan, who tried to look only mildly relieved. Althelstan nodded to the older wizard and said, "If you would go on to the castle, I will bring my cousin, Lady Vevila, and together I'm sure we can straighten this out."

❧

LADY VEVILA SIGHED. It had been a long day, especially since it had started the night before and was still going. The sun hid itself in the westering forest, sending dark shadows across her path. A little farther down the road was a small village where she planned to spend the night. But there was this problem.

Three grubby men with battered, blunted swords faced her on the road. They were actually gloating with glee. She debated whether to be merely moderately annoyed or if she should just go ahead and take all her frustrations out on these poor, innocent bandits.

"Lady Vevila, how unusually you're dressed today," the lead bandit said.

"Go away." Vevila leaned on her walking stick. Earlier in the morning it had been a tree, but she'd used her knife on it, and now it was a walking stick, a little taller than she.

"Worry not, fair lady," the leader said sarcastically. "We won't harm you. You're far too valuable unharmed."

Vevila leaned with both hands on her walking stick. Frustrations it was; that would teach them to threaten to return her to her parents and marriage to some lord or prince. "Come closer."

The lead bandit stepped forward. Vevila swiftly swung her stick, catching him in the stomach and doubling him over. She looked at the other bandits. "Next?"

The next one had the foresight to keep his sword up defensively. She jabbed her stick into his foot. He tried to move his foot at the last moment, and the stick tore into the old, rotting leather of his boot, separating it from his foot.

"Hey! My boots!"

"Sorry. That's not what I meant to do." Vevila struck his head with the other end of her stick. "I hadn't meant to do that, either, but you're giving me no choice." She pulled her knife out and lunged at the third bandit.

As he dodged, Vevila became aware of the sound of a horse's hooves galloping toward them.

"Leave that boy alone!"

She recognized the voice, and turned on her cousin, Prince Althelstan. "Who are you calling a boy?"

The bandits scattered in three different directions.

"Lady Vevila?" Prince Althelstan dismounted his horse. "What are you doing here?"

"Frightening bandits." She leaned on her walking stick, wondering if she'd really be charged with treason for using it on him as she had on the bandits. "What does it look like?"

Prince Althelstan's gaze took in her grubby tunic and trousers, the walking stick, and the pack slung over her back. His expression seemed unable to decide exactly what to convey: puzzlement, amusement, concern, dismay, and, strangely, relief. It settled into a mildly surprised look. "Actually, I was looking for you. I'd hoped to be able to get your parents' permission to allow you to accompany and assist me."

"Accompany and assist you?" Vevila asked skeptically. "On your quest for a princess?" She'd known Althelstan a long time. He meant well, but he really didn't understand why she couldn't seem to fit into her lot in life. "What exactly were you looking for?"

He explained about the sleeping castle and the curse,

dwelling particularly on the handsome princes and what a catch they would be.

"Well, if they're sleeping, they can't be that hard to catch. Good luck to you." She started walking down the road the way she'd been going and he'd come.

"No. I need a princess to kiss the sleeping princes and awaken the castle." He fell into step beside her, leading his horse. "Technically, as the daughter of a prince and princess, you do qualify as a princess."

"And what do you get out of this?" Vevila asked.

"Well. There's this woman . . ."

There always was when he was involved.

"I'm sure she's a princess. If you awaken the princes, she'll awaken, and then I can marry her."

"And what do I get out of this?"

Prince Althelstan frowned, obviously puzzled. "You get your choice of the princes."

"What, not all three?" she asked sarcastically.

"Lady Vevila!" he said, shocked.

"Forget it. I don't want one prince. What would I do with three?" She had no interest in the princes, but she could see the possibility of adventure and excitement in this. A bit of company on the road wouldn't hurt, either. Best of all, if she could somehow get a reputation as a swordswoman or an adventuress, if she could rescue someone or something, perhaps she wouldn't have to marry a prince or a lord after all. She could spend her days happily, instead of sewing and breeding brats.

He walked silently beside her for a moment. "I won't feel obligated to try to take you home or turn you over to the palace guards to take you home."

"What, here in the darkened woods?"

"If you come with me, I'll send word to your parents so

no one will be looking for you, and you'll probably spend a month or more away from home."

Althelstan might not understand her weaknesses, but he knew where they were. Vevila stopped. "I'll agree, but this is what I want. I want you to buy me a horse, and it will be mine, not one you've loaned me. And saddle and tack for the horse. And I want walking boots. And three pairs of trousers, a good cloak, and a real sword."

"The horse, saddle and tack, boots and cloak. Or I ride to the palace and rat on you."

"Agreed."

❦

RUEBERRY CONTEMPLATED THE sky as he lay in the hay in the back of the wagon. He ignored Zenpfennig and Mazigian, who sat on the front seat, Zenpfennig lecturing Mazigian on how to drive a wagon team and Mazigian doing the opposite of whatever Zenpfennig told him merely because Zenpfennig had said it.

The hay was thick and cushioned Rueberry nicely against the jolts and bumps of the wagon. This certainly beat horse riding, though it wasn't quite as nice as a fancy carriage.

He picked up an apple from beside him and bit into it, licking the juices before they could run down the side of his face. This mode of travel wasn't half bad.

"There, that has to be it," Zenpfennig said.

"Yes. I told you that at least an hour ago," Mazigian muttered.

"That was something different entirely."

The wagon stopped.

"Wake up." Zenpfennig prodded Rueberry with one

bony, weirdly stained finger. "Oh, you are awake. And eating our supper, I see."

Mazigian helped Rueberry down from the wagon, and the three contemplated the bramble, briars, and forest around the castle.

"This must be the place," Zenpfennig said.

"Yes," Rueberry agreed. "But where is the path Prince Althelstan said he hacked in to the castle?"

Zenpfennig and Mazigian walked along the edge of the bramble. Rueberry elected to stay with the wagon.

"Here!" Mazigian called. "I can see where the scrub was cut and where there's now new growth."

The other two wandered over to examine what he'd found.

"Definitely magic," Zenpfennig declared after analyzing a few cut branches some two feet apart and the briars and thorns growing between them. "This isn't a natural growth."

He stood up straight, head back, a serious look on his bearded face. Rueberry pulled Mazigian to the rear. When Zenpfennig did magic, it was with a grand and imposing flare, generally to impress the unmagicked, but Rueberry had found it convenient warning to get out of the way ahead of time.

After a few passes of his hands and some arcane words, Zenpfennig pointed at the plants now growing in the path Prince Althelstan had cut. Flames shot out from his crooked finger, turning the bramble to instant ashes. Zenpfennig started walking along the path, so Rueberry and Mazigian followed.

They walked at a fairly normal pace, with some quick stepping around particularly hot spots, to the front gates of the palace. Zenpfennig flamed the vines covering the closed gates, so they had to wait for the iron to cool before they could enter.

An old, stooped woman wearing a tattered black dress, with only a few wisps of gray hair to cover her head, a hooked beak of a nose, and no teeth, tottered through the courtyard inside the gate. She glared and shook her trowel at them.

"What do you think you're doing?" the old woman shouted. "You can't come in here like that. You're exactly the wrong sort. Go away." She began muttering, "Worse than that fool prince. He shouldn't have been here either, but once the story is warped you can't keep them out, I suppose."

"Madam," Zenpfennig said with distaste, "we have only recently learned of the existence of this castle and heard of the terrible tragedy that befell its occupants."

The old woman cackled. "They've been saved from evil, and he calls that a tragedy."

Mazigian strode forward, opening the gates to get at the woman. "Some evil spell is upon this place, robbing its denizens of their will and animation, leaving them helpless prey to any passersby."

"Helpless prey to any passersby?" the old woman asked incredulously. "I'd never allow that, young man. Why do you think I put all that bramble out there? Why do you think I made it so hard for anyone to get in? Why do you think I've stretched my own life to guard them and protect them?"

"You're the evil witch who's imprisoned them?" Mazigian loomed over the tiny, stooped woman.

"Evil witch!" she shouted, nearly jumping up and down in rage. "I'm no evil witch. I'm the prince's fairy godmother, Urticacea. I've been preserving the prince's peace and protecting him from evil since his mother died birthing him. And this is the thanks I get!"

"The prince?" Zenpfennig asked condescendingly. "We understood there were three princes."

"No, no, no. There's only one prince. I divided him into three when he was a baby. That way, an assassin would have to get all three bodies to murder him."

"Was there much concern about that?" Mazigian asked.

"One never knows," Urticacea said cryptically.

Zenpfennig held his hand up to stop Mazigian's next ill-thought and sarcastic question and asked, "Why put everyone to sleep?"

"That was my spell to protect him from evil." Urticacea tried to stand straight and proud, hampered by her hunched back. "He and all who lived in the castle will sleep until a true princess can be found to love him honorably, make her way in here, and kiss him. So he can live happily ever after, as it should be."

"You expect a princess to wander in through that bramble?" asked Mazigian.

"A true princess, lovely and honorable and pure, will come. Someday, some faraway day." The old woman brushed at her tattered clothing. "Until then, I will protect them all and preserve them from evil."

The three wizards stared at her. Rueberry took a prudent step backward so that he was, more or less, behind Zenpfennig.

A tear ran down her cheek. "I cast spell after spell over him, to protect him from harm, any sort of harm or evil I could think of that might hurt him. His sweet mother had been so kind to me. I did it for her." She glared at the wizards. "I did it for his own good. He's safe now, preserved from evil. Especially the likes of you. Go away."

Mazigian looked at Zenpfennig and Rueberry, tilting his head toward the old woman. "We're not dealing with a full spell book here."

"I don't like your tone, young man. Or your manners. Or your character."

"Well, I don't much care for you, either."

"This is my home, my castle, my people. You will speak respectfully toward me."

"Beg your pardon," Rueberry began, hoping to stop the explosion before it happened.

"You don't own those people. You have no right to restrict their lives like this. And I'll speak any way I want," Mazigian said.

Urticacea frowned at him. Her hand shook as she twisted the point of her trowel through the air between them. "Speak as you want, you never shall, your tongue will always your thoughts befoul. Unsimple quotes stand in the stead, of what it was you wish you said. The words of the bard of another place, dropping trippingly from your face. Until you've learned humility, respect for others, and docility." She paused a moment with the trowel pointing directly at Mazigian. "The better part of valor is discretion, educate yourself upon this lesson."

Mazigian folded his arms, obviously unimpressed. "I will not hear thee speak: I'll have my bond, and therefore speak no more. I'll not be made a soft and dull-eyed fool, to shake the head, relent, and sigh, and yield." His eyes grew wide. He touched his lips and gasped.

"Now see here!" Zenpfennig said. "You can't just go around cursing people like that!"

"What? You mean for free?" the witch sneered. She turned the point of her trowel upon Zenpfennig and Rueberry.

Rueberry remembered the time he'd spent as a frog during his first term at the Recondite University and hastily threw a spell to protect himself and his fellow wizards.

"Worry not, you'll understand, every word he can command. And in addition . . ." She frowned at the trowel, then at Rueberry. "Well, at least one of you has some sense. I suppose there'll be no additional curse. Though you may find understanding him to be enough of a curse."

❧

THE WAGON WAITED with its patient oxen outside the bramble surrounding the castle, so Prince Althelstan knew the wizards had arrived. He found the path they'd taken though the bramble by the black smell of soot. The ground no longer smoked, but Althelstan could tell the fire had been recent. He also knew it was wizard-wrought, by the way it had burned away only the scrub in the path.

Dismounting his horse, he told Vevila, "We'd best lead the horses through. They might spook at the smell of smoke."

Vevila jumped to the ground. "Wizard fire. Finally we're getting somewhere."

"What do you mean?"

"Are all your adventures this uneventful?"

Prince Althelstan shrugged. "Uneventful? I've tried to make the journey as easy for you as possible. We've scared off two bandit attacks and have finally come to the enchanted castle, where we'll disenchant it. Isn't that enough?"

He didn't hear her reply, as he was too busy calming his skittish horse and leading it into the path burned by the wizards. He caught the sound of the wizards' voices, echoing down the confines of the path, before he could see them. They were talking with someone who sounded female. Had they managed to remove the curse without having a princess kiss the princes? Had he brought Vevila for nothing?

At the gate, with Vevila holding her horse beside him, he saw the old witch curse first Mazigian, then the other two wizards. He started to reach out to Vevila, to warn her to stay behind him, but she'd already started forward.

"Good morning to all," Vevila called. "Have we arrived too late?"

"Too late for what?" Zenpfennig muttered.

Prince Althelstan hurried to catch up to her. "We've only just arrived. Have you roused the castle then?"

"No," Rueberry said. "We found the prince's fairy godmother, Urticacea," he waved at the old woman, "and she cursed us, like she did the castle."

So paying Vevila's price hadn't been in vain. Althelstan sighed inwardly. He didn't mind his cousin, but he didn't want to have spent his allowance like water for nothing.

"It's not a curse! I'm preserving them from evil. Like you." Urticacea frowned particularly at Vevila. "What do you want?"

"Princess Vevila," Althelstan half bowed to Vevila, "having heard of the plight of the princes herein, and her tender heart swooning with charity and sympathy for the princes, such that she is nearly heartbroken with love, has journeyed long and far to partake of their goodness and kindness."

Vevila glowered at him. The old witch, Urticacea, merely frowned. "She wants to kiss my sweet prince, and bring him back to the sordid, evil world."

"Yes," Vevila said dryly. "Though truly, I'm only here

for the adventure, not the princes. You can have them. Actually, he's pining for some princess who's asleep."

"You're not a true princess!" Urticacea accused. She shook a bony finger at Vevila. "You must be a true and honorable, a real princess to wake the prince."

Seeing Rueberry wave his fingers in an arcane movement, Prince Althelstan rushed to Vevila's side. "Madam, I assure you she is a real princess. I am the son of a king, and she is my first cousin once removed, and the granddaughter of two kings, her mother's father and her father's father. Indeed she is a princess."

He wished Vevila would swoon, or faint, or do something to act more like a traditional princess, rather than grasp the handle of her long knife and appear as if she wanted to slit the witch's throat.

"Dressed like that?" Urticacea oozed scorn. "Traipsing about out here in the wilds? Acting like a hoydenish bandit? No real princess could ever—"

"Truly, I assure you," Althelstan began.

"This is all very much beside the point," Zenpfennig said, seething, and surging forward. "You cannot curse everyone who comes to this castle. It's a blatant and egregious abuse of magical talent that will not be tolerated."

"Oh?" Urticacea asked. "I don't curse everyone that comes to this castle, just those who deserve it."

"What judgment shall I dread, doing no wrong?" Mazigian said.

Vevila smiled at Althelstan and whispered softly, "Now, this is fun."

"You are very wrong, all of you, coming here to disturb the quiet rest of my sweet prince, to doom him to be the prey of every evil of the world." Urticacea's eyes watered, threatening to spill over.

"This isn't protection!" Zenpfennig waved his hand toward the gray-covered guard sleeping and still at the gate. "This is the usurpation of their rightful will. This is torture, madam, nothing less."

Mazigian nodded. "Thou mak'st thy knife keen; but no metal can, no, not the hangman's ax, bear half the keenness of thy sharp envy. Can no prayers pierce thee?"

Urticacea made shooing motions at the wizards. "You three have no part in this. No part in this at all. It's not your business, nor is it the University's business. You should not be here, not at all. Go your way and bother someone else."

"We will not go," Zenpfennig declared.

"Any abuse of magic reflects badly on all users of magic," Rueberry said calmly. "We do have a reason to be here."

In an aside to Althelstan and Vevila, Mazigian said, "She seeks my life, her reason well I know. I oft deliver'd from her forfeitures many that have at times made moan to me; therefore she hates me."

"What?" Vevila said, as Althelstan tried to sort that one out.

"He means," said Rueberry, "that the witch wishes us all dead because we're here to undo her work."

"And vile work it is," Zenpfennig announced loudly. "To rob people of their lives, even if only by sleep, is a kind of murder." He began pacing back and forth across the courtyard.

"Thou call'dst me dog before thou hadst a cause, but, since I am a dog, beware my fangs," Mazigian said.

"You set upon us as soon as we arrived," Zenpfennig said. "Before you even knew anything of us. Deciding we were evil, I suppose, by the way we stood."

Althelstan hoped it was an interpretation of Mazigian's

strange utterance, otherwise none of this made any sense. He looked to Vevila, who seemed to have no trouble following this.

"We should go survey the castle," Rueberry suggested. He half bowed to Althelstan. "If your highness would lead the way, we shall follow."

The dusty castle showed his trails through it as if preserved for posterity. Unfortunately, his trails crossed over each other, wandered here and there, and generally covered the entire castle. Prince Althelstan had some trouble remembering the route.

"I'm sure I remember this stairway," he said, as he mounted yet another spiraling staircase, listening to catch the gentle echo of snoring from above.

"The problem is, you remember them all," Vevila muttered.

Mazigian turned to the witch, who brought up the rear, and said, "I pray you, which is the way?"

"I won't help you," she spat, "find your own way, or find none and leave my prince alone."

Shrugging, Mazigian said, "In the end, truth will out."

This time, though, Althelstan had remembered, and at the top of the stairway, they discovered the waiting room. The dust had been stirred about but still covered the old king with his small gold crown, the two guards on either side of him, the middle-aged lords and their ladies, and the fair princess.

Prince Althelstan walked directly to his ladylove, taking her hand and kissing it in greeting. "Fair princess, I have returned."

"Ha!" barked Urticacea. "She's no princess. She's Lady Jaquenetta, bastard daughter of Claudius, duke of Salsifry."

"She's a princess to me." Althelstan kissed her hand once more and sighed.

"Yes, yes, but where are the princes?" Zenpfennig asked.

"Up those stairs."

"Are you certain?" Rueberry asked from where he leaned against the wall, panting.

"Come with me."

Upstairs, the room was unchanged. The decaying rushes crumbled beneath their feet, and the dust swirled up to tickle their noses. Urticacea moved to position herself between Vevila and the nearest prince. She moved whenever Vevila moved, blocking Vevila's access to the princes.

Vevila sighed and surveyed the three sleeping princes. "They look awfully young."

For the first time, Althelstan gave the princes more than a glance. They did indeed look younger than Vevila, though not by that much to his eye. "How old are they?"

"A hundred and thirteen," Urticacea said with pride.

"They were thirteen when you bespelled them?" Zenpfennig asked incredulously.

"No. Oh, no. They were sixteen, almost seventeen," Urticacea said.

Vevila sneezed, bringing Urticacea's attention back to her. The witch spread her arms out to herd Vevila back to the stairs. "You shall not kiss my sweet princes, not until you've proven you're true and honorable, a real princess." A sudden, crafty look took over her wrinkled face. "You must pass a princess test."

"What is a princess test?" Vevila asked.

"A test to prove you are a princess. A real princess would have no problem passing; only a girl pretending to be a princess would have anything to fear." The witch smiled, showing a mouth missing several teeth.

She managed to force Vevila down the stairs. Althelstan followed behind them, with the wizards behind him.

"What exactly is this test?" Vevila asked.

"Oh, nothing much, you just have to spin. Women are always spinning or sewing. Turning ugly, coarse wool into glorious yarn. And, of course, princesses can spin the best of all. So you shall spin straw into gold."

"What?" Vevila shouted.

"You do spin, right?" Althelstan asked nervously. He knew she wasn't very good at most womanly pursuits.

"Yes, but there's a difference between wool and straw!"

"My mother used to spin all the time," Rueberry said reminiscently. "She made the most pretty cloaks."

"Yes, yes," Zenpfennig said impatiently. "And she made stockings that would last longer than the person wearing them." He shuddered.

"But to spin straw into gold, that would be magic, and that I don't know," Vevila said.

Urticacea said, "I don't see that much difference between spinning wool, such as is pulled off a sheep from the field, into a fine silken thread to make a prince's doublet with, and spinning straw, such as grows out of the earth, into thin ribbons of gold, such as is dug out of the earth."

Zenpfennig stroked his long, thin beard with his bony hands. "Well, I suppose if sheep's wool can become a silken doublet that straw from the earth could become gold from the earth." His eyes gleamed as he stared, unfocused, at the witch. "It would certainly be worth a try."

"That's impossible," Vevila cried. "You can't spin wool into silk!"

"But where else would it come from?" Urticacea's voice was smooth as silk.

Mazigian patted Vevila on the shoulder and said to Urticacea, "She is not yet so old, but she may learn; happier than this, she is not bred so dull but she can learn."

"Bring her," Urticacea ordered, hooking a crooked finger at them to indicate they should follow her. "You'll have to get her clean straw from the cold room beneath the cellars, for her to spin into gold. Only the best, mind you."

She led the way through the dusty castle's corridors and out to vine-curtained breezeways and balconies that showed glimpses of the sun setting redly in the dense bramble around the castle. She led them to a corner tower far from the sleeping princes.

⚜

VEVILA LOOKED AROUND her small prison: no windows, one door, four flaming torches in peg holders on the stone walls, a small pallet to sleep upon, and, next to the pallet, a spinning wheel. Most of the room was taken up with piles and piles of straw. The door to this prison room hadn't been fashioned with convenient hinges that could be easily dismantled. Oh no, the door was as thick as the width of her hand, solid oak, and the very functional iron hinges had a long iron bar of a pin that ran from the stone ceiling to the stone floor. Outside the room, where she couldn't reach it, a thick oak slab barred the door. The walls were made of large, square stone slabs, connected with mortar, and she'd bet they were at least as thick as the door.

They'd brought her some bread to eat and wine to drink when they'd brought the straw. Not enough wine for her to drink herself to oblivion, of course. She had to spin straw into gold. And that nasty, devious, evil witch had forced her to change out of her trousers and tunic and into an exceedingly old-fashioned dress.

"Men!" she shouted.

Picking up a handful of straw, she threw it at the door. "Of all the blithering idiots!"

She threw herself on the straw, kicking and clawing and screaming. Bits and pieces flew through the air, caught in her hair, and clung to the old dress.

The thunk of wood against wood caught her attention. A portion of the old witch's face appeared in the little square peephole in the door. "Tisk. Tisk. Such an unladylike way to behave. You haven't any manners at all. You're not a princess. You're merely spoiled and selfish."

"You miserable, lying cheat!" screamed Vevila. "When I get out of here—and I will!—I'll make sure everyone knows what an ugly, miserable, foul, nasty, horrible crone you are. How you cheat and lie and steal and rob. All about your evil, wicked spell casting."

"Oooh, temper, temper," Urticacea said. "It would appear that if you aren't a princess, I'll just have to turn you into a toad. Can't have liars wandering around loose."

Vevila flung herself at the door, trying desperately to reach through the peephole and strangle the witch, but the peephole door shut before she could reach it.

"You'll pay for this, you . . ." Vevila slouched slowly down the rough wooden door. She vowed to get them all, somehow. Especially her stupid cousin.

A strange voice said, "You seem to be in some sort of fix, but what is it? I can't quite figure that out."

She turned to see a very short man standing beside—well, actually leaning upon—the spinning wheel. His out-

fit was a strange mixture: crisp new green trousers, battered muddy brown boots, shiny gray shirt, thick red vest,
long light blue jacket, and a sensible black hat of the sort
young children were told to wear by their mothers because
it would "keep your head warm and cover your ears."
Vevila stared a moment and asked, "Who are you? How
did you get in here?"

The odd little man shook his finger at her. "No. No. No.
That would be telling."

"If you don't tell me, I'll never know." Vevila stood and
carefully, cautiously approached him. When he stood up
straight, his eyes were about level with her waist. Which
he seemed to be staring at a bit too much for her taste.

"I'll keep my secrets for now. Until I know more." His
face finally turned up to look at her. "That's a very . . . un-
usual sort of dress you're wearing."

Looking down, Vevila realized the old dress had begun
to tear at the weak points, probably from all her flailing
around in the straw. The side seams were torn in spots, and
the skirt ripped. She growled, and he took a quick step
back, returning his gaze to the sash at her waist, the only
spot without a tear.

"I never quite know what to say to damsels in distress,"
he muttered. "And I always seem to pick the wrong thing.
I'm very sorry." He glanced back up at her face. "I thought
women liked being complimented on their clothes."

"Forget it." Vevila brushed at the straw on her dress.
"I'd like to get out. That's what I'd like."

He motioned to the door.

"I know about that," Vevila said testily. "But they've
locked it. I can't get out that way."

"Surely they'll let you out eventually."

"After I turn all this straw into gold."

The odd little man gave her an even odder look. "Are you a witch? An enchantress? A sorceress? A magician?" She shook her head no to each of these.

Looking puzzled and picking up a bit of straw for closer examination, he asked, "Then how are you going to turn this straw into gold?"

"I'm supposed to spin it into gold." Vevila motioned to the spinning wheel and flopped down to sit on the straw.

"That won't work," he said, looking from the straw in his hand to the spinning wheel. "How's that supposed to work?" He tentatively tried putting the straw in the wheel and giving it a good spin. Bits of straw flew through the air.

"Oh, it won't work," Vevila said bitterly. "It's supposed to be my princess test. That witch Urticacea just wants to keep me from kissing the princes and waking them up. She wants to turn me into a toad."

"Okay. Let me see if I've got this straight. You want to kiss the princes. So this witch Urticacea wants you to spin straw into gold, so she can get you before morning to wake the princes up. It seems a bit of a strange way of deciding who gets to give the princes their wake-up call."

"No." Vevila picked at the straw around her, tossing it away. "I have to prove I'm a princess. Then I can kiss the princes and remove the curse."

"Spinning straw into gold proves you're a princess?" he asked, scratching his beard. After she nodded, he said, "But I thought women were born princesses. Like your mother's a queen, your father's a king, sort of thing."

"My mother is Princess Lucilla, my father is Prince Bernard. My grandfathers were King Ambrose of Portula and King Otto of Regenweald. I should be a princess," she said stubbornly.

"Oh. I understand. In some systems of titles you are; in others you're not." The odd little man climbed up onto the spinning wheel's seat to sit, letting his feet dangle down. "All right. Start at the beginning, and explain it all slowly to me. Perhaps I might be able to help you."

Vevila, having nothing better to do, did as he asked, starting with her reservations about helping her cousin and going right up until the witch threatened to turn her into a toad.

Idly sharpening a straw point by turning the spinning wheel, the odd little man said, "Neither your cousin nor those wizards are very bright, are they?"

"No." Vevila frowned at him. "So, I suppose now you'll offer to help me in return for my firstborn, or some such thing."

"I'm on to that one." The odd little man tossed the straw away so he could shake his finger at her. "Those nasty little buggers cost a fortune in nannies and diapers and clothes. And I don't think he's ever going to be of any use to anyone, assuming he survives all the idiot things he comes up with to do to himself. And I've heard that when they're finally old enough to be of any use, they just run off. Ungrateful wretches."

"You could just take him back to his parents, you know."

His finger stopped midshake, and a surprised expression stole over his face. "Just . . . take him back?"

"Yes," Vevila said patiently. "If your supposed reward is costing you more, then just take him back."

Pulling his hat off his head, the odd little man ran his hand through the wild tangle of brown curls revealed and looked chagrined. "Just take him back," he murmured in the surprised tones of one finally discovering that the answer to the complex riddle was really very simple.

"Now, maybe you could do me a favor. Hmm? Like help me get out of here?"

He sighed. "I'm sorry. I'm afraid I'm constrained in other ways and cannot do that."

"What do you want as payment?" Vevila knew she sounded cynical and pessimistic, but couldn't help it. How many times had her mother told her that being sweet and nice and innocent would get men to help her without requiring something in return? Funny, Vevila didn't know anyone who actually got something for nothing just by being nice.

Shaking his head, he said, "You'll have to pass this princess test, I'm afraid."

"But I can't spin straw into gold!"

"Ah!" he said. "There I can help you."

"You can spin straw into gold?" Vevila asked doubtfully.

"No." He paced around the edges of the straw, as if measuring it. "But I can replace this straw with an equal amount of gold." He looked at her. "All you have to do is be in here with the gold in the morning, correct? And then they declare you a princess, and you can kiss the princes and remove curses?"

"That's what they said."

"Very well." The odd little man strode over to her, hand outstretched. "I will replace the straw with an equal amount of gold if you will promise me," he paused, appearing to think carefully, "that I may claim a favor from you, any favor of my choice, at some time in the future."

"What favor?" she growled.

"Just a favor," he said irritably. "Not 'favor' as in 'your favors,' just a favor. A good deed, so to speak."

"Uh-huh." Vevila frowned at him as she thought this over. "A good deed? How disgusting is this good deed?"

"Well, I don't know." He tried to look wounded but couldn't hide his amusement. "It might be something that some people would consider disgusting. But for a princess who can kiss princes and remove curses, it shouldn't be too bad. I will remember your station in life."

"Doesn't everyone?" she asked bitterly.

"Now what?"

"Nothing!" Vevila stared at him, wishing she could divine what he was thinking. She didn't want to be a princess. She didn't want to marry a prince. She certainly didn't care for her station in life. Making such an open-ended promise was a stupid thing to do, generally. It was well known that royalty did this sort of thing all the time, much to their detriment.

But, then again, a nebulous promise would make a good excuse for anything she wanted to get out of. What prince would want to marry her, knowing she owed an odd, ill-dressed, little man an unnamed favor?

"All right." Extending her hand to shake his, Vevila said, "You change the straw into gold, and I promise you one favor."

They shook hands.

"If we could gather the straw up," the little man said, as he started picking up stray stands of straw and putting them back in the pile. "We want to be sure to get all of it."

They gathered the straw into one large mound.

"You might want to . . ." The odd little man waved vaguely at her. "Get the straw out of your hair, and, uhm, uh, dress."

Vevila looked down at herself. Straw clung in the gaping seams and tattered shreds of her dress. When she plucked some straw from her left shoulder seam, the whole sleeve came away. "Perhaps not."

"Wise decision," he murmured. He took off his blue jacket, flung it over the spinning wheel's seat, and started rolling up his long sleeves. Motioning to her pallet, he said, "Sit down, and stay back."

⋙⋘

ZENPFENNIG PRODDED RUEBERRY away from the rough table in the kitchen they had been dining upon. "You've had enough for now. Let's find the library and get the counterspell. I could hardly stand him before; this is unbearable."

"How shalt thou hope for mercy, rendering none?" Mazigian said.

"Until this curse is lifted," Zenpfennig laid his gnarled, bony hand less than gently over Mazigian's mouth. "Don't talk."

Mazigian pushed Zenpfennig's hand away. "On what compulsion must I? Tell me that."

Rueberry stepped between them quickly. "This way," he said, grabbing Mazigian by the arm and leading off.

They passed through the dining room, where two scullery maids slept hunched over one end of the table and the wine steward snored loudly at the other. They carefully skirted the scum-covered puddle of drool collecting on the floor at the steward's end of the long table, and entered into the maze of castle corridors.

Dust and cobwebs clung everywhere, defending the castle as thoroughly as the bramble outside. Luckily, Althelstan had fought most of the old webs back out of the way on his travels through the castle. Even so, the three wizards touched nothing except the floor with their shoes as they passed.

Following Rueberry's locate spell, they quickly found the library. Inside was hushed, full of books, and empty of any sleeping people.

"There must be spell books here somewhere." Zenpfennig stroked his thinning gray beard with his gnarled hand. "First we find the spell she used on Mazigian and us and remove it. Then we'll see about this sleeping castle."

The spell books were on the second floor, in a small nook, off by themselves. Zenpfennig distributed the tomes, pamphlets, and boxes of scrolls amongst the three of them. Rueberry lit the candles about the nook with small, sulfurous taps of his finger, and they began their evening's work.

Finishing it without success. As Zenpfennig frowned over his last tome, Mazigian tossed aside another scroll and said, "Men that hazard all do it in hope of fair advantages. A golden mind stoops not to shows of dross; I'll then nor give nor hazard aught for lead."

"He's right," Rueberry moaned. "I don't think the spells are here. But if not, how did she do it?"

Zenpfennig slowly, carefully set his tome down. Rueberry's fuzzy, chubby face and Mazigian's unbearded one both looked to him for guidance. Zenpfennig sighed. "She must have learned her magic on her own, as it were. Her talents, as such, unbridled by formal education."

"A wild witch?" Rueberry said in horror. "That would explain a lot." He looked thoughtful. "Though she'd have to be a very good poet to come up with such rhymes off the cuff."

"Just because it's wild, tempestuous, feral, and amoral doesn't mean it's unpracticed." Zenpfennig stood up from his chair and began to pace. "Even animals practice their crafts: hiding, stalking, hunting, running."

"I am the unhappy subject of these quarrels," said Mazigian.

Covering his eyes, Zenpfennig said, "I'm already tired of that."

Mazigian nodded sympathetically. "It wearies me; you say it wearies you; but how I caught it, found it, or came by it, what stuff 'tis made of, whereof it is born, I am to learn; and such a want-wit sadness makes of me, that I have much ado to know myself."

Covering his ears with his hands, Zenpfennig began to pace the small nook. "Let me remember what she said." He spoke softly to himself. " 'Speak as you want, you never shall, your tongue will always your thoughts befoul. Unsimple quotes stand in the stead, of what it was you wish you said. The words of the bard of another place, dropping trippingly from your face.' That was the curse." He took his hands off his ears, his face lighting up. "Aha! And then the key to the curse's undoing: 'Until you've learned humility, respect for others, and docility.' Even the untutored know there has to be a release."

"Well, yes," Rueberry said. "Otherwise the spell will drain all their power." He patted his stomach. "There was something else. 'The better part of valor is discretion, educate yourself upon this lesson.' "

They both looked to Mazigian, who slowly shook his head and his fists. "Did I deserve no more than a fool's head? Is that my prize? Are my deserts no better?"

"There must be a way to break this curse other than the simple expedient of the release," Zenpfennig said. He leaned down to whisper in Rueberry's ear. "Humility, docility, and discretion: I doubt he could ever learn those."

Rueberry sighed. "We might be able to find someone else who could lift the curse. Someone else not formally trained yet knowledgeable and skilled might know of a way to break the spell."

"Waste no time in words, but get thee gone; I'll be there before thee." Mazigian rushed over to pull Rueberry out of his seat.

Zenpfennig stopped them by putting his hand on Mazigian's shoulder. "I doubt we have the fee on us."

Shifting angrily from under Zenpfennig's hand, Mazigian said, "Therefore haste away, for we must measure twenty miles today."

"Besides," Rueberry added as he reseated himself. "We don't know of any other wild magician. All our acquaintances learned at the Recondite University."

Mazigian threw his hands up in furious surrender as he stalked away. "You may as well go stand upon the beach and bid the main flood bate his usual height. You may as well use question with the wolf, why he hath made the ewe bleat for the lamb. You may as well forbid the mountain pines to wag their high tops and to make no noise when they are fretted with the gusts of heaven. You may as well do anything most hard, as to seek to soften that." He flung himself onto the bench he'd been using, knocking all the scrolls and pamphlets he'd read onto the floor. "I do beseech you, make no more offers, use no further means, but with all brief and plain conveniency, let me have judgment and the witch her will."

"Wait! That's a little off." Zenpfennig rushed over to pull Mazigian up to sit on the bench. "Say that again."

"You may as well—"

"No, no, no. That last part."

"Let me have judgment and the witch her will?"

"In the original it's not a witch!" Zenpfennig shook Mazigian in his bony clasp. "If there's a way to warp them, maybe we can stop them."

Rueberry sat up straight. "You may be on to something."

"Say something," Zenpfennig commanded imperiously.

Mazigian opened his mouth, but no words came out. He shrugged and waved his hands in the air.

"He might have to have something to say in order to speak," Rueberry said.

"'Tis very true!" Mazigian said. "O wise and upright judge!"

"Say it again!" Zenpfennig shook Mazigian again. "Only change it this time."

Obviously concentrating hard, with beads of sweat breaking out on his forehead and teeth clenched, Mazigian said, "'Tis very true! O wise and upright . . . wizard."

"Not easy, eh." Zenpfennig let go of Mazigian, and resumed pacing. "This may well take time." He glanced out at the library proper and the windows, with their draperies still pulled back as they had been for almost a hundred years now, shadows flickering in the guttering candlelight, the darkness outside giving the library a gloomy, evil cast. "We should get some rest. Tomorrow, we can try again."

"I wonder," said Rueberry. "Perhaps it's not important, but I just couldn't help wondering. Where is Venice? And just who is this merchant?"

"It's not important." Zenpfennig walked out of their little alcove into the library.

The other two wizards followed him.

"I don't trust that witch," Rueberry said. "We should

sleep near Princess Vevila's cell. I'm afraid that witch, Urticacea, may try to sabotage her."

They found a room down the hall from Vevila's cell, obviously intended for use by the guards who attended the cells, and bunked there for the night.

Strange noises disturbed their slumber occasionally, and one or another—Zenpfennig or Mazigian, Rueberry could sleep through almost anything—would go see what the fuss was. However, Urticacea never showed, and, when they checked through the peephole, Vevila would be sitting at the spinning wheel, claiming to be at work.

❦

PRINCE ALTHELSTAN KNELT at the feet of the beautiful lady in the waiting room, holding her hand in his. "Jaquenetta. Lovely Jaquenetta. Princess Jaquenetta. My darling."

He kissed her hand. "The witch must be wrong. You couldn't be the bastard daughter of a Duke. You're far too beautiful to be anything but a princess."

Laying his head on her lap, his eyes closed, he whispered, "I'll find the castle's records." Yawn. "There must be proof somewhere."

Soon Althelstan's snores joined those of the king and the king's guards.

❦

URTICACEA TIPTOED THROUGH the garden to the gate. "Grow and tangle, briar and thistle." She took a breath to continue, but nothing had happened yet, so she just let it out. Crouching down, she pinched the dirt in the burned path between two fingers, rolling it, sniffing it, tasting it.

Slowly, with a good deal of creaking, popping, and snapping, she stood up. "Blasted wizards."

The path remained open and inviting. Unfortunately, there was nothing she could do about it now. The castle would probably be overrun with people in a few days. However, Urticacea knew how to handle any women who showed up purporting to be princesses. She hadn't worked this long and this hard to be thwarted by a fool prince, three idiot wizards, and that mere slip of a girl.

She glared back at the castle. "Butting in where they don't belong. Why can't people just leave well enough alone?"

༄

D ARLING, DON'T WORRY SO." Queen Tarax patted her husband's left arm, looped in her right, as they walked down the corridor to their bedchambers. "Althelstan is perfectly capable of taking care of himself."

"It's not Our son We're worried about." King Abelardann took a deep breath. "It's Vevila. You heard the wizards' report; she's joined him on this fool quest."

"Althelstan and Vevila can handle whatever trouble comes up," Queen Tarax said soothingly.

"Vevila *is* the trouble. She's been nothing but trouble since the day she was born."

"She's just high spirited. There's no sense trying to make her something she isn't. If everyone would just let her be, she'd soon settle down." Queen Tarax smiled up at her husband. "And Althelstan is a fine young man. He'll find his princess."

"Yes," said King Abelardann bitterly. "And that stupid quest is all Vevila's fault."

"Isn't some of the guilt yours, dearest?"

King Abelardann patted his wife's arm. "Yes, We know. But We wouldn't have made that stupid pronouncement about Althelstan having to marry a princess if We hadn't feared he would marry Vevila."

Queen Tarax giggled. "Vevila wouldn't have Althelstan, not even for all of Portula and Regenweald."

"Are you certain?"

"Unless We threw in a dragon she could slay into the bargain." Queen Tarax snorted. "Even heroes only demand a princess and half the kingdom, but that wouldn't suit Vevila. Not at all. Trust me."

"Is it too late to revoke that pronouncement?"

❧

PUTTING HIS EAR to the rough, heavy wooden door of Vevila's cell, Rueberry motioned for silence. "Not a sound," he muttered. "Do you think she's dead?"

"I don't know what you think you might hear through solid oak," Zenpfennig sneered. "Check the peephole."

Reaching for the little latch that held the peephole door closed, Rueberry heard swiftly approaching footsteps. His hand recoiled from the latch as if it were scalding, and he stood with his hands behind his back, endeavoring to look as innocent as possible.

Prince Althelstan strode into view. "Aha, you're awake. How is everything?"

"We were just about to ascertain the facts of the situation," Zenpfennig said.

Mazigian nudged Rueberry. "I am sure you are not satisfied of these events at full. Let us go in."

Zenpfennig thumped Rueberry's shoulder with his gnarled hand. "Open the peephole."

"Hurry, man, before the witch gets here," said Althelstan.

The four huddled close as Rueberry reached for the latch again. As he opened the peephole, all four heads bumped together as they all tried at the same time to see into the cell.

Behind them, someone cleared her throat and said, "Just open the door."

Rueberry slammed the peephole shut, nearly catching Zenpfennig's nose. "Open the door," he murmured.

"Yes." Urticacea stood, hunched over, arms folded, glaring at them. "Open the door. Let's have an end to this nonsense."

Zenpfennig stepped aside, motioning for Rueberry to open the door. Mazigian and Althelstan huddled forward. Rueberry opened the door a crack, peeked in, then flung the door wide.

Off to one side, away from the rumpled pallet and the spinning wheel, was a small pile of gold nuggets. Lady Vevila sat on it like a smug dragon waiting to flame anyone who came within reach. The tatters of her skirt had been arranged to cover as much of her legs as possible while still allowing a good view of the heap of gold.

"Would you just look at this!" Vevila smoothed her frayed skirt. She glared at the witch. "These old dresses just don't hold up the way they should. This is a disgrace."

The witch paid her no mind, being mesmerized by the gold.

"Gold," murmured Zenpfennig. "She's sitting on a pile of gold!"

"Yes. I spun the straw into gold, as ordered."

Vevila cautiously stood up, taking care not to hurt herself on the sharp edges of the rocks. No one helped, no one moved from the doorway. She edged away from the rocky heap to her rumpled pallet.

The others walked, as if in a dream, toward the gold.

Seeing an opportunity, Vevila stepped over the pallet and edged along the wall toward the still-open door.

Zenpfennig picked up a nugget and carefully bit it. He frowned at the bite marks on the nugget and said to Rueberry, "Stay with the girl. She's had a hard night of spinning. We wouldn't want anything to happen to her."

Shaking the tatters of her skirt, Vevila said, "I just wanted to get something decent to wear. I'm perfectly capable of taking care of myself."

Rueberry managed to pull his gaze away from the pile of gold to actually look at her skirts. "You poor thing." He hurried over to put his arm around her shoulders and, coincidentally, block her access to the door. He certainly didn't want anything happening to someone who could spin straw into gold.

Urticacea stirred the pile a bit. "What have we here?" She pulled a small rock out of the pile. "This isn't gold." She hobbled over to a torch to get a better look at it. "This is quartz!" Turning on Vevila, she shouted, "You're no princess!" She held out the quartz rock, shaking it. "This isn't gold. Not that good a spinner, eh?"

Pulling herself up to stand straight and pushing away from Rueberry, Vevila said, "Not everything you sent up here was straw. Some of it was merely hay. The best I could do with hay was to spin it into quartz. I'm not a witch."

"You're no princess!" the witch said.

"Now, now." Zenpfennig put himself between the two women, facing the witch. "You did say that if she spun the straw into gold, that would prove she was a true princess. The straw is gone. There's the gold. She has to be a real princess."

"How do you explain this?" Urticacea shoved the rock under Zenpfennig's nose.

"All that glisters is not gold, often have you heard that told," murmured Mazigian.

"Well, hay." Zenpfennig shrugged. "Straw into gold, hay into quartz. It's a well-known phenomenon."

Mazigian and Rueberry hastily nodded.

"I didn't see any hay," Urticacea said. "Did you?"

"Uhm," Zenpfennig said, looking to Rueberry and Mazigian for help. They shrugged, so Zenpfennig turned back to Urticacea as haughtily as he could. "No. But, I'm a wizard. We're not all that involved with straw and hay."

"Ha!" the witch shouted. "You don't know the difference."

Rueberry glanced around the room, hoping to find something, and he did. "Prince Althelstan." Rueberry waved a hand toward the prince. "It stands to reason that princes and princesses would know more about straw and hay than mere wizards, since, after all, princesses spin the stuff."

"Prince Althelstan." The witch made a creaking, joint-popping, and yet taunting curtsey. "Perhaps you can tell us the difference between straw and hay."

"Well, straw is . . ." Althelstan pulled a piece of straw from the seam of Vevila's sleeve, causing the sleeve to fall to the floor. "Oh. So sorry." He held the slim, tan shoot out for examination. "Straw is straw. While hay is merely, well, hay."

Urticacea shook her head. "That's the best you can do?"

After a moment's thought, Althelstan added, "Horses eat hay and bed down in straw. Horses don't eat straw." He glanced at Vevila. She frowned at him. "Well, unless they're very hungry."

"There you are," Rueberry said, glad that was over with. He put his arm back around Vevila and started herding her toward the door.

"Wait!" the witch shouted. "There wasn't any hay here last night."

Althelstan glanced at Vevila, appearing to gauge which was the most dangerous female in the room, and said stoutly, "Of course there was. There almost always is hay mixed in with straw."

"Well-known fact." Rueberry gently squeezed Vevila.

"She is not a true princess!" Urticacea screamed.

"She passed the princess test." Zenpfennig picked up two handfuls of gold.

"No she didn't. Some of that is quartz!"

"It was hay!" Vevila shouted back, nearly deafening Rueberry.

"Seven times tried that judgment is, that did never choose amiss. Some there be that shadows kiss, such have but a shadow's bliss; there be fools alive, I wis, silver'd o'er; and so was this." Mazigian snatched up the rock from the witch's hand and threw it at her feet.

Urticacea stepped back, looking small and hunched and old and confused.

"Vevila is a princess," Althelstan said.

"Not yet." Urticacea shook like a tree against a great wind. "Some of this is not gold."

Zenpfennig put one thin, gnarled finger to his lips and frowned thoughtfully at the witch. "Either she is a princess, or you are a liar."

"Not necessarily," Urticacea said quietly. She paced the room a moment. "I can't be certain, because of the hay. Maybe she is, maybe she's not." The witch gave Althelstan a creaky, creepy, smile. "We wouldn't want to be mistaken on this, would we?"

Turning smugly to Vevila, the witch said, "If she can do this two more nights, then I'll be certain."

"Two more nights!" Vevila shouted. "I'm leaving now!"

"Wait, wait," Zenpfennig said, eyeing first Vevila then the pile of gold. "She may have a point. We do want to be certain here. There is all that gold, I mean people, slumbering away. We wouldn't want them to start sleepwalking or wandering around only half awake."

The witch grinned evilly at Vevila.

"Of course," Rueberry said, "You'll have to allow that the hay will be quartz instead of gold."

The witch growled what could have been a yes.

"I'm leaving!" Vevila shouted.

Easily blocking the doorway with his bulk, Rueberry said with deep feeling, "Sorry." He knew that once Zenpfennig had found a source of gold, no one would leave until Zenpfennig had acquired as much of the gold as possible.

"I need a dress," Vevila said.

"We'll bring you one." Zenpfennig pulled Vevila away from the doorway. "But first we must find some sacks or a wheelbarrow to get all this gold out of your way."

Rueberry stood guard in the doorway, letting the others

out one by one. Mazigian whispered to Vevila, "He would detain you here some month or two."

"I believe in the original, it's 'I would,' " Rueberry said. Mazigian shrugged.

They closed and barred the door, as Vevila screamed and shouted in a most unladylike and unprincess-like way. The door shook as she flung herself against it, and they could hear her fists pounding the other side.

"We'll return presently," Zenpfennig shouted. "And remove the gold."

Rueberry added, "And bring a dress. And breakfast. And another torch."

⁂

F AR AWAY, A long, deep, blue lake nearly filled an almost triangular valley. Several small streams fed into the lake from the surrounding mountains, but only one stream emptied out. The point across from the longest side of the lake was really more swamp than lake, and as such had a more varied inventory of plants, fish, amphibians, and insects.

A quaint, odd, little man in rumpled green trousers, battered muddy brown boots, shiny gray shirt, thick red vest, long light blue jacket, and a sensible black hat sat down at the base of a willow tree near the edge of the swamp. He looked across the vast expanse of the lake and said, "Well, that's one problem I won't have again."

A moment later, he turned toward the swamp and said, "That firstborn boy I acquired accidentally. He's gone now. Not my problem anymore."

A short pause.

"No, no, no. I just gave him back to his parents. I didn't hurt him."

In the quiet of a much longer pause, only a distant splashing and the buzzing of insects could be heard.

"Weren't you watching?" The odd little man picked up a clear crystal ball that rested in a smoothed-out hollow of a nearby, exposed, twisted tree root. "I left the thing on so you could follow along. I think I may have found the key to the problem."

He contemplated the depths of the ball. "Not only have I finally found a princess, I think I might know why there aren't that many princesses anymore." He turned the ball, caressing it with his hands. "It seems this witch has a castle under a spell, keeping everyone in the castle asleep. She thinks she's protecting this prince, who she's already split into three princes."

Looking up from the clear ball, he said, "Urticacea."

Close by, a series of splashes brought a sprinkling of water close to his feet.

"Well, you don't have to carry on like that. I can handle her. If I have to." The odd little man held the crystal ball up to stare in fascination at it. "The only way to wake the castle is for a princess to kiss the princes. I think Urticacea has done something to limit the number of princesses born, although the sheer amount of power and will required would be formidable. I just don't know if she has it. Or if she does have it, if she can maintain it."

The insects buzzed undisturbed for a few minutes.

The odd little man sighed and set the clear crystal ball back into the hollow of the exposed twisted root. "It would appear that the lady is not a princess yet. It may be that Urticacea has grown too powerful."

He pulled his hat off and scratched his head, shaking

out his long, brown curls. "I suppose it all depends on the amount of power and will that those wizards and prince and princess can bring to bear on that ugly old witch." He smiled. "And, of course, myself."

The insects buzzed a bit more.

"That's nothing new." He leaned back against the tree. "I've been in over my head since I was born."

Abruptly, the odd little man stood up. "Oh, that was a joke, was it?" He reached down and grabbed a twig as a splash interrupted the buzzing of the insects. He tossed the twig at the center of the spreading ripples in the swamp's water, and shouted, "Well, ha, ha, ha."

❧

ALTHELSTAN STRODE DOWN the quiet, dusty castle corridor, grumbling. That tall, gaunt wizard, Zenpfennig, had ordered, actually ordered him, a prince, and not just any prince, the crown prince of Portula, to find Vevila a dress, while they, the wizards, took care of the gold. As if he, Prince Althelstan, were nothing more than a simple valet, or in this case, a lady's maid.

Where in the world were ladies' dresses kept, anyway?

Bedchambers perhaps? In his experience hitherto, ladies' dresses were found on the floor of their bedchambers.

While Princess Jaquenetta undoubtedly knew where he could find an appropriate dress for Vevila and also undoubtedly had better taste and discernment when it came to choosing such things, Althelstan feared she'd be of no help currently.

He searched through several dusty, cobweb-filled bedchambers and threw open the doors to numerous disused

garderobes, without success. Most of the clothing had
fallen to the ravages of moths and time. Althelstan closed
the door of the garderobe he'd just finished checking.

If all the clothing had rotted or been moth-eaten over
time, how come all the slumberers were still well clothed?

The majority of the castle's sleeping residents were in
the servants' areas, so Althelstan headed for the main dining hall.

Althelstan surveyed the long table, the two scullery
maids sleeping at one end, and the wine steward snoring
loudly and drooling at the other. Their clothes were in fine
condition. Gently stepping around the scum-ridden pool of
drool, Althelstan tried tugging on the steward's sleeve. The
old steward snorted, nearly lifting his head off the table before settling back to his rhythmic, atonal snoring. However, the seams held beautifully, and the heavy woolen
cloth felt thick and strong.

Strange.

He headed back for Vevila's cell. The wizards weren't
there, the pile of gold remained untouched, but Althelstan
could see Vevila fuming and cursing through the peephole.

"Excuse me," Althelstan said. "But I'm having problems finding you a dress. Moths seem to have gotten to
most of the dresses I can find. The only ones in good shape
are on the sleeping women."

"Well then, why don't you give me the dress from off
that woman you've been admiring," Vevila snarled.
"You'd have so much more to admire then."

"Vevila!"

She looked up at the peephole from where she'd been
sitting at the spinning wheel. "I'm sorry, Your Highness.
Did you check any of the cedar boxes?"

"Cedar boxes?" Althelstan was confused by the difference between her contrite tone and the sharp look on her face. "What cedar boxes?"

"No, I suppose you wouldn't know about them." Vevila stood up and slowly approached the door. "Fetching me a dress is not the sort of thing a prince should be doing. Why isn't that old hag out scaring up something for me?"

"They told me to. As if I'm some sort of lady's maid." Althelstan couldn't help complaining. He leaned against the door. "It's not right."

"You bet it's not right." Standing very close to the door, Vevila whispered through the peephole, "I don't understand why I can't just go look for a dress myself. I'd know what to look for and where to look. I don't think you even know what size I wear."

"Size?" Althelstan said.

"There, you see, it's not right that you should have to do this. Why don't you open the door and let me have a look around."

"Well." Althelstan contemplated the heavy square oak plank barring the door. "I think the others want you locked in."

"But why?" Vevila asked in a smooth, reasonable voice. "I volunteered to accompany and assist you. Haven't I helped you wherever and whenever I could? What exactly do they think I'm going to do if I get out of here? Destroy the castle?"

"Well." Althelstan turned this over in his mind. What could she do? Find her own clothes? Wander around the castle? Fix their meals? "I'll have you out in a minute."

The bar was heavy to lift without assistance, but Althelstan managed it. He opened the door, and Vevila stepped out, clutching her dress to keep it on.

"I'd better find something quick," she said.

"That way, take the second corridor on the right to the east wing, take the stairs up one story, and that whole corridor is bedchambers."

"Thanks." Vevila patted his arm quickly. "You're a real treasure." She ran off, one hand still clutching her dress.

Althelstan slowly walked down the corridor after her but didn't head for the east wing. His destination was the waiting room.

On his way there, he wondered about the clothes the sleeping people wore. He also wondered what he was going to do to fill up the rest of the day.

❧

THE CEDAR CHEST in the second room Vevila found had women's clothes in it. These dresses had been made for someone shorter and fatter than Vevila, but she didn't much care about size. She selected a plain pale blue chemise and a strong wool and linen overdress, belted with a good long length of rope. She tied her hair back with a bit of ribbon and started toward the door to the corridor.

Somewhere in the depths of this castle, the three wizards and that ugly witch were going about their profane occasions. Vevila didn't wish to encounter any of them on her way out. Knowing her luck, they'd all four be just down the corridor.

Vevila went back into the bedchamber. The room consisted of a dust-covered, moth-eaten bed; the cedar chest; moth-eaten, dust-covered, embroidered wall hangings; a window with rotting shutters; and a small door. Dust had settled everywhere, covering everything like democratic dirt. Single motes and congregations of dust danced in the sunlight streaming in through holes in the shutters.

Nothing much to help her sneak out of here, and nowhere she could hide, not in this room. Vevila checked the small door. It opened up to a small semicircular balcony with vines growing up around it and sheltering it. She stepped out, parted the vines, looked down, and lurched backward with vertigo.

The main problem with this castle was that most of it was vertical. As if someone had told the architect that here was a small kingdom with only a tiny plot of land on which to build the entire castle, and since no defense was possible, none would be attempted, but the castle needed to be large enough to host grand parties of neighboring kingdoms' envoys, and the whole thing was built around the idea that there was no such thing as too many towers and turrets. The east wing was really nothing more than a tower with more branches than a tree, and each branch sprouted several gables and turrets.

Taking a deep breath and pulling her courage around her, Vevila stepped out again onto the balcony. Just below her were the vine-covered, cracked, red and yellow tiles on the pointy cone roof of another branch's turret. Off beside her, covered in more spring-green vines, was a protruding pale blue gable that contained the room next door. Above her was another vine-covered semicircular balcony, then another pointy cone roof.

Far, far below were the grounds and the walls and the gates, looking very, very small.

Just like climbing a tree, Vevila tried to convince herself as she swung a leg over the balcony's railing. Lots of green stuff to grab onto, loads of branches beneath her. Probably she could make it to the ground. Most likely.

It was either that or go back to her cell and wait for more straw.

Hanging down while clutching the base of one of the railing's uprights, Vevila kicked and prodded with her foot, trying to find the roof below her. Her skirt swirled around her legs, hampering her, but her toe came in contact with something hard and sloped. She risked a glance down.

The point of the roof was off to her left, so if she fell straight down—well, just a little to the left—she should be able to grab the roof or at least a goodly number of vines, and halt her fall.

"One," Vevila whispered to herself, as she swung her legs toward the roof below her. "Two. Three."

She let go, dropping rapidly onto the hard, tile roof beneath her and flinging her arms around the cone. Her hands met and clasped on the other side, tearing some of the vines loose, but she stopped. Vevila rested her head against the roof, reveling in the pungent, moldy green scent of the tiles and vines.

Using the vines as hand- and footholds, Vevila worked her way down to the vine-sheltered balcony below the roof. She dropped into the balcony and sat for a moment, enjoying the way her heartbeat moderated to a more leisurely pace, and the way she continued breathing.

The best part of adventuring was the way it provided you with opportunities to feel really alive and be properly grateful for that feeling.

Parting the vines to look down again, Vevila discovered nothing but air between the balcony and the distant ground. Looking up, she could see an ever-receding line of turret towers. The vines covering them made it difficult to judge just how many were above her, but she estimated at least three, stairstepping to the topmost tower.

By standing at the side of the balcony, leaning out, clutching the railing and the vines on the wall of the castle, Vevila determined that the branches and turrets beneath her position receded back to the main portion of the castle like the underside of a staircase. She would have to climb both down and sideways on the vines from here on, almost all the way to the ground.

There was no help for it, and standing around wasn't getting it done. Vevila reached out and pulled on the thickest vine she could find to test how well it was anchored to the castle. It seemed sturdy enough. She climbed over the railing to stand on the very edge of the balcony and jumped over to grab the thickest vine.

For a few seconds the vine held; then, in a horrible series of snaps and jerks, it pulled away, and Vevila found herself swiftly swinging out and down, away from the castle wall.

Vevila gritted her teeth to keep herself from screaming and alerting anyone to her predicament, and clung tightly to the vine as she gathered speed.

❧

RUEBERRY WADDLED RAPIDLY through the warm kitchens and down the rough stairs to the cool cellars and pantries. He estimated he had only a few minutes before Zenpfennig realized he'd ducked out on the argument with Urticacea.

There on a shelf, a round wheel of cheese waited for him. Rueberry glanced around, but no one was there to see or stop him. He picked it up and stashed it in a pocket in the depths of his robe near his stomach. Any difference in his appearance was indiscernible.

He relieved other shelves of cured hams and dried fruit

before ducking into a wine cellar for a couple of bottles. All the loot disappeared into his robes.

As he hurriedly waddled his way back, he wondered about the way certain portions of the castle seemed well preserved, and others falling to ruin. Dust, cobwebs, and rot had taken over in rooms, halls, and corridors; plants had taken over the exterior; but the people and their personal items, along with the foodstuffs, were well preserved. It certainly indicated something about the witch's spell.

They'd have to look into it and see if there was a wedge they could drive in to break the spell on the castle, if not the spell on themselves.

In the dining room, over the roar of the steward's snores, Urticacea and Zenpfennig were shouting at each other.

". . . And we all know about wizards and gold." Urticacea stood with her fists on her hips, her head upturned over her hunched back to glare at the tall, bony, haughty Zenpfennig.

"The wizards weren't the ones insisting on testing her princessliness by having her spin straw into gold." Zenpfennig looked down his nose at her. Though really, with as tall as he was and short as she was, there wasn't any other way he could look at her.

Mazigian motioned to Rueberry from his seat at the middle point of the long table. "Go to thy fellows; bid them cover the table, serve the meat, and we will come in to dinner."

Rueberry emptied the food he'd scrounged onto the fine cherrywood table, in front of Mazigian. Seating himself in the tall chair across from Mazigian, Rueberry planned the course of his snack to tide him through the argument.

Urticacea sputtered, and Zenpfennig added, "Nor did we insist that she continue spinning for two more nights." He smirked. "It seems to me that the witch is the one greedy for gold."

"I am trying to protect the castle," the witch shouted. "That's all I'm trying to do."

"By luring princesses here to spin gold?" Zenpfennig murmured. "Are you certain it's the castle you're protecting?"

"I have no interest in that gold!" Urticacea shook a crooked finger at Zenpfennig. "You're the one that wanted to claim the gold."

Zenpfennig sneered down at her. "I merely wish to put it into safekeeping until such time as its owner can be determined properly."

"The gold belongs to the prince."

"I'm not sure how you figure that," Zenpfennig said in an extremely reasonable tone. "Wouldn't the straw have belonged to the king, the prince's father? And wouldn't Princess Vevila be entitled to some of it for her pains?"

"That wretched slattern has no portion of it!" The witch was nearly jumping up and down with anger. "It's rightfully the prince's. Everything here is rightfully the prince's."

"It must not be." Mazigian picked up a bottle and saluted Zenpfennig with it. "'Twill be recorded for a precedent, and many an error by the same example will rush into the state. It cannot be."

"My esteemed colleague is correct." Zenpfennig's gaunt gnarled fingers waved toward Mazigian. "You cannot claim the entire castle for the prince without allowing others' claims to themselves or their portions."

The witch fumed and glared. Rueberry expected smoke

to curl out of her ears, or lightning to bolt from her fingertips, or fire to flash from her eyes. But she merely growled.

"Very well. Very well. You take charge of the gold." She
pointed a crooked finger at each of the wizards in turn.
"But every bit of that gold had better be accounted for
when it comes time to judge who it belongs to. I intend to
make certain that it goes where it belongs."

"As do I," Zenpfennig said.

"And the quartz?" Rueberry heard himself asking. He
was certain he would never have said such a thing. Whatever could have come over him?

"Nobody cares about the quartz," Zenpfennig said.

"Let that wench keep it." Urticacea waved one old-age-
stained hand regally as she hobbled out of the room.

Zenpfennig strode over to stare disdainfully down at the
food. "I don't suppose you fetched some sacks or wheeled
carts for the gold."

Rueberry chewed his mouthful of ham.

"I suppose one of us will have to go get the sacks."
Zenpfennig looked meaningfully at Mazigian, who broke
off a large hunk of cheese, stuffed it in his mouth, and tried
to look innocently stupid.

"Go get us some sacks," Zenpfennig said, pointing a
gnarled finger at Mazigian. "And no backchat."

Mazigian opened his mouth as if to say something, but
stopped when Zenpfennig's fingers started an arcane motion.

"Just get some sacks," Zenpfennig said. After Mazigian
left the room, Zenpfennig seated himself next to Rueberry
and picked up the bottle. "Is this the best you could do?"

Shrugging, Rueberry said, "I don't know. I just grabbed
and hurried back."

Putting the bottle back, Zenpfennig picked up a circle of dried apple. "I suppose we shall have to make do."

They ate quietly for a moment. Mazigian returned and threw a pile of sacks onto the table. Zenpfennig stood to leave, but Mazigian sat and reached for the ham.

"Very well, eat." Zenpfennig sampled a few more pieces of dried fruit, then impatiently paced the room.

Rueberry refused to be rushed and continued to calmly eat his way through the food on the table before him. Even after Mazigian finished, Rueberry continued.

"Watching him's worse than watching a cow graze," Zenpfennig whispered loudly to Mazigian.

Pretending not to hear, Rueberry picked up what remained of the joint of ham.

"If we grow all to be pork eaters, we shall not shortly have a rasher on the coals for money," Mazigian said impatiently.

Rueberry sighed and set aside the bone. "Oh, all right. Let's go get this gold."

All was quiet in the hallway outside Vevila's cell. The three wizards couldn't help noticing that while the door was closed, the stout square oak bar leaned upright against the wall.

"What mischief is this?" Zenpfennig asked.

They rushed to the cell, flinging the door open.

Zenpfennig sighed, apparently in relief. "The gold is still here. Nothing to worry about."

"But where is Vevila?" asked Rueberry.

"She'll be around somewhere," Zenpfennig said negligently. He took a sack from Mazigian. "Come, let's get the gold."

"But do you think Vevila is safe and sound?" Rueberry

asked nervously as he took a sack and joined the others gathering up the nuggets of gold.

"Undoubtedly." Zenpfennig tied his sack with a length of thick thread pulled from a loose end. "She's the sort that can take care of herself."

"But isn't she supposed to spin straw into gold again tonight?" Rueberry discarded several chunks of quartz. "How can she spin if she isn't here?"

Zenpfennig stood abruptly. "We must find her." He looked down at the bulging sack in his hand. "After we stash the gold somewhere safe."

⟨ℰℐℰ⟩

ALTHELSTAN KNELT AT the sleeping Jaquenetta's feet, taking her soft, warm hand in his. He told her all about finding Vevila with the gold, and how the witch had refused to pronounce Vevila a princess.

"So, my sweet, lovely princess, we must wait yet another two days." He stroked her hand. "Soon, soon, my love."

He looked up at her face. Her soft brown hair curled around her face, slipping from its pins. He wondered what color her eyes were. Gently, gently he reached up and pried one eye open.

Gray. She had gray eyes the color of shadows against stones in the late sunset.

Hearing footsteps on the stairs, he hastily stood and began to pace. He wasn't sure how the others would take his talking to a sleeping woman.

The three wizards hurried into the room, robes fluttering around them, boots pounding the stone floors.

"Lady Vevila is missing!" Zenpfennig said.

"Oh no. No, no, no." Althelstan waved his hands at them. "She's not missing. I let her out to go find a dress. I couldn't find one."

"So, where is she?" the chubby Rueberry asked.

Shrugging, Althelstan said, "Looking for a dress?"

"But where?" Zenpfennig demanded. "We have to find her so that she can spin straw into gold again."

Althelstan patted Zenpfennig's thin, bony shoulder. "Not to worry, she'll show up when she's hungry. She's already promised to help me with my quest, and she wants to kiss the princes. Get herself a husband, you know. She'll need some exercise after spending all her time in that cell. So she may take a tour around the castle."

Rueberry and Mazigian seemed content with that answer, but Zenpfennig frowned.

❧

LADY VEVILA STRUGGLED to get air into her lungs, past her aching ribs. Spitting out strongly sour bits of leaves helped. Coughing and sputtering, she tumbled the rest of the way through the vines and over the balcony's railing, and lay in an aching heap on the floor. Now that the adrenaline rush had ended, she trembled with the delirium of survived terror.

As she tried to get up, hysterical laughter gripped her, squeezing her bruised sides painfully. She'd heard of people swinging from balcony to balcony on vines or ropes, but she'd never seen it done. Truth be told, she hadn't seen it this time, either, since she'd spent most of the time with her eyes closed.

Ah, the thrill of adrenaline, the sound of hysterical

laughter, the taste of fresh leaves. Vevila marveled that more people didn't follow their adventurous dreams.

She staggered to the balcony railing, looking out through the vines torn by her abrupt passage into the balcony. The ground was much closer now. There was another tower with one balcony and two gables back below her, then below that the riot of weed-choked grounds.

Some of the vine-covered trees and shrubs looked soft and cushiony. Vevila eyed the vines climbing up the wall next to the balcony. Looking back down, she tried to gauge the distance and softness of the ground.

Perhaps she might try using the vines to go all the way down this time, rather than swing into the lower balcony. The vines on the right-hand side of the castle looked long and sturdy enough. As she recalled from her previous go, she'd jumped to the vines, they'd pulled off the castle, and she'd swung down and out, under the balcony she'd left, before swinging back into the lower balcony.

If she could catch a tree on her outward swing, she could skip the rib-slamming stop on the railing of the next balcony.

Vevila searched the tall, vine-strewn and weed-choked trees below her and picked out a likely one to aim for. Carefully, she climbed up onto the slippery, vine-covered railing and jumped toward the thickest vine she saw.

Grabbing the vine tightly with both hands, Vevila waited for the cracking sound of the vine pulling loose. And waited. After a minute, she concluded that this vine was far too sturdy for her purposes and began climbing down and sideways toward the castle, expecting with each new vine she grasped to feel the jerk and hear the pop of tearing vine. She'd worked her way along for several minutes before a vine gave way.

The vine looked far too thin, and it was all Vevila could do to keep her eyes open. Knowing where she was going and how she would arrive didn't seem like such a good idea now.

⤖

WHEN I SAID, 'Why don't we just work in the cellars,' I was being sarcastic." Zenpfennig drummed his fingers on an empty shelf and glared around the gloomy, candlelit reaches of the cellar's shelved walls.

"I thought it was a grand idea," Rueberry said around his mouthful of ham.

Zenpfennig tried a withering glare but could see no visible withering of Rueberry's abundant flesh.

Mazigian, looking very young in the dim candlelight, slammed an earthen jug down on the coarse table in front of Rueberry. "The curse never fell upon our nation till now; I never felt it till now."

"Oh don't carry on so." Zenpfennig stroked his beard. "We are going to do something about it. I have no intention of letting the witch get away with this."

Rueberry waved a long loaf of fine white bread around before breaking it into several pieces. "We know that she's maintaining several difficult spells on this castle to keep everyone asleep and to keep everything from rotting."

"Yes." Zenpfennig's eyes narrowed, and he ran one long thin finger over the shelf in the manner of someone's mother-in-law searching for dust. His expression on discovering his finger was clean was along similar lines. "And we know she has at least one other spell to keep the weeds and vines growing beyond the realm of their ordinary spheres."

"Perhaps she's at her limit, magic-wise. Perhaps if we pushed her now . . ." Rueberry looked from Zenpfennig to Mazigian, then shook his head. "Perhaps not."

"No." Zenpfennig paced along the walls of the cellar, running his finger along the shelves at his shoulder height. "However, since she obviously has many spells to maintain, and since Mazigian can warp the quotes, perhaps he can break the spell himself."

"Good news, good news!" Mazigian sat on the edge of the table. "Ha, ha! Where?"

"Try saying *how*," Zenpfennig said.

Rueberry picked up a bottle and washed down his mouthful with a goodly amount of wine. "Perhaps if he were to repeat or at least paraphrase her curse."

"What says this?" Mazigian asked.

"You must try to repeat or at least paraphrase her curse. Sometimes simple curses can be removed simply by repeating them." Zenpfennig stood as if at an oration. He cleared his throat, blinked twice. Suddenly, he hunched over, twisted his head slightly, tried to straighten one gnarled finger at Mazigian, and said in a cracking alto, "Urticacea said, 'Speak as you want, you never shall, your tongue will always your thoughts befoul. Unsimple quotes stand in the stead, of what it was you wish you said. The words of the bard of another place, dropping trippingly from your face. Until you've learned humility, respect for others, and docility. The better part of valor is discretion, educate yourself upon this lesson.'"

"Now you try it." Rueberry pointed at Mazigian. "Paraphrase the curse."

Mazigian hesitated as Zenpfennig stood straight. Mazigian's brows drew together as he concentrated. "Speak not so grossly."

"Not bad, not bad," whispered Rueberry to Zenpfennig. "There is no power in the tongue of man to alter me."

"Try a different one," Zenpfennig said.

"Thou shalt not know the sound of thine own tongue."

"Ooooh, better, much better." Zenpfennig nodded. "Now, 'Unsimple quotes stand in the stead . . .' "

"To fill up your grace's request in my stead." Mazigian smiled.

"You wish you said?"

"To wish myself much better."

Rueberry saluted Mazigian with the bottle. "Oh, very nice. Better and better."

Zenpfennig waved at Rueberry to hush him. "The words?"

Mazigian grinned and bowed. "Madam, you have bereft me of all words."

A nod of approval escaped Zenpfennig. "Dropping trippingly from your face?"

A moment's frowning concentration passed before Mazigian said, "Thou mayst with better face exact the penalty."

Rueberry and Zenpfennig exchanged a look. Zenpfennig shook his head. "Keep trying. Now *humility.*"

"What is his humility?"

"Respect?"

"Talk with respect and swear but now and then."

"Docility?"

Mazigian frowned and chewed his lower lip, but not until he began to pull his bright red hair out by the roots did he say, "Moved with the concord of sweet sounds?"

"No," said Zenpfennig. "Try again."

"A gentle riddance?"

"No."

Raking his hands through his hair and dropping strands on the floor, Mazigian paced from side to side. Finally, he looked up triumphantly. "Happiest of all is that *my* gentle spirit commits itself to yours to be directed."

"Very good," Zenpfennig said. "Now, 'The better part of valor is discretion."

Mazigian smiled. "O dear discretion, how his words are suited!"

"Educate yourself upon this lesson?"

Bowing, Mazigian said, "I am to learn."

"Try it all together," Zenpfennig commanded.

"Speak not so grossly. Thou shalt not know the sound of thine own tongue. To fill up your grace's request in my stead. To wish myself much better. Madam, you have bereft me of all words. Thou mayst with better face exact the penalty. What is his humility? Talk with respect and swear but now and then. Happiest of all is that *my* gentle spirit commits itself to yours to be directed. O dear discretion, how his words are suited! I am to learn."

For a moment, all was silent in the cellar.

Rueberry picked up a piece of cheese. "Perhaps if it rhymed."

"I don't think that would help," Zenpfennig said. "Individually, each sentence isn't bad, but together they are nothing."

"Loss upon loss!" Mazigian cried. He slumped to the floor, covering his face with his hands. "The thief gone with so much, and so much to find the thief; and no satisfaction, no revenge; nor no ill luck stirring but what lights on my shoulders; no sighs but of my breathing; no tears but of my shedding."

"Stop it!" Zenpfennig shouted. His hand shook as he first held it out toward Mazigian, his fingers moving in the first dance steps of a spell; then he pulled it back to himself. "We'll find some way out of this. We are stronger than her. We are better than her. We are more educated than she is. We can break this spell."

"Now what?" Rueberry surveyed the scattered remaining crumbs of his snack.

"Now we leave these cellars and see what we can spy above ground." Zenpfennig started immediately for the stairs, his dark brown robes flapping around his ankles.

☙❦❧

P RINCE ALTHELSTAN CAREFULLY brushed the dust from another book. The king's clerk's office had books in stacks and on shelves and covering desks to the point that Althelstan guessed there were nearly as many as in the library, in about a third of the space.

The windows opened onto the east side of the castle, and a good deal of morning light illuminated the dusty, neglected tomes detailing the running of the kingdom. It was as good a place as any for Althelstan to while away the remainder of the morning and stay out of the way of the other conscious miscreants and malefactors in the castle.

With a bit of luck, he might actually find out something helpful about the history of the castle and its denizens.

He opened the book and discovered to his surprise that it wasn't another account ledger with neat columns of spare black ink totaling up how many hogs, chickens, pheasants, lambs, and ducks were consumed. It appeared that Althelstan had in his hands a record of the genealogy of the current king.

It put him in possession of the sleeping king's name: Lazare. King Lazare. By the Grace of God, His Most

Royal Imperial Majesty, King Lazare of Chateau-Arbre, Guardian of the Law, Defender of the Truth, Protector of the People, Gardener of the Soil, Carver of the Meat, Keeper of the Guest List, and Bouncer of the Unruly.

As always, the smaller the kingdom, the larger the list of credits after the king's name.

Althelstan read the fine print at the bottom of the page, "Five-Time Winner of the Chateau-Arbre Grand Prix, and Undisputed Champion of the Quaff."

Oh yes, he knew the type.

A few more pages were taken up with listing Lazare's other many interests, including and especially the queen. Then a whole page was devoted to the birth of the royal prince, Lucien, and all his many titles, awarded shortly after birth. The next page could barely contain the sad news of the queen's death. Several hastily scribbled pages followed, chronicling the spells imposed on the prince by the witch Urticacea.

From this Althelstan gleaned that the three boys actually went by the names Un, Deux, and Trois, to avoid confusing their names with dead ancestors.

After a sufficient mourning period, the king had remarried, but unfortunately, the marriage was a complete disaster. No official reason was given for why the marriage failed, but Urticacea received implied credit. The new queen had produced a child and run off, leaving the child behind.

The baby's name was recorded only in a tiny, backwards, scribbled footnote.

Jaquenetta.

Althelstan scooped up the record. He had proof now. She wasn't the bastard daughter of some duke. Jaquenetta was a princess.

And all that was needed was a princess to kiss the princes and lift the curse.

There was no rule that said the prince had to marry the princess or even love the princess. And vice versa.

That was why all the castle was asleep, rather than just the princes. If Urticacea hadn't put them all to sleep, Jaquenetta could, and—from the way the family had gathered in the waiting room—probably would, have awoken her half brothers.

Althelstan strode out of the room, carrying the records with him, bound and determined to rub Urticacea's nose in it.

☙❧

LANDING IN A tree had not been as soft and cushiony an experience as Vevila had hoped. However, even crashing through the leaves and branches of a tree, and breaking boughs on the way down, had been much easier and gentler than her final landing in a vine-covered clump of sweet-smelling, brightly colored, thorn-covered rosebushes.

Vevila tried moving her head, hoping to dislodge the thorns in her hair, but managed merely to scratch her scalp. Usually at this point she liked to stop her mad rush, relax, breathe, and, as the saying goes, smell the roses, but on this occasion, she desperately wanted to be somewhere else. Anywhere else.

Well, not anywhere else. Come to think of it, being trapped in a rosebush certainly beat being trapped in a small cell in a high tower in a castle.

She wrenched her right arm away from the rosebush. Free! Her arm was free. Her sleeve was shredded ribbons, but her arm was free. Wrenching her other arm served only to prove that the rose's thorns weren't going to let go. Vevila tried rolling onto that side, ignoring the thorns scraping into her side, putting more rips in her dress, and pulling a few branches of the rosebush with her.

Getting her feet under her, Vevila stood upright, putting more tears in her dress, and breaking off a branch of roses draped across the back of her shoulders. She could feel twigs and thorns and blooms in her hair also.

Her left sleeve and the hem of her skirt were still trapped. Very cautiously, she plucked the thorny branch from her sleeve, then started on her hem.

Finished and finally free, Vevila sat on a vine-covered stone bench to catch her breath. She glared balefully at the fragrant, blazing roses and vowed that forever after, any man who besought her with roses would find himself pulling thorns from his nose.

Vevila stood and, finding her legs still shaky, stomped off through the weeds and vines, determined not to let anything get in her way. Several times she had to back-track to find an overgrown path or a better way through the weeds. The vines and weeds gave a monotonous green color to everything, but she fancied she was learning to see beyond the weeds to the grass, stone, or wood underneath.

Until she discovered that the hill she had been climbing was in fact a half-rotted, tumbled-over shed, when the wood gave way under one step and she fell in to her waist. Vevila tried to pull herself out without success. Now that a portion of it had broken, none of the moldy, rotting wood would hold her weight, and more and more of it broke and fell around her. It reminded her of thin ice cracking on a lake as winter turns into spring.

In the dark, dank decay, something small and furry crawled over her ankle. Vevila shrieked and discovered she was capable of a very long, high, standing leap out of the rotten shed to the safety of a weed-covered path.

She dashed along, determined more than ever to escape this place. Luckily, the path took her right to the front gate.

The gate's iron doors were still open. The wizard-burned path still there, just beyond the gray-covered, sleeping guard. Vevila sighed with relief and walked steadily to the gate.

"Wait right there!" the old witch cackled from behind her.

Vevila turned. "What do you want?"

"I knew you'd try to escape. Your kind's all the same. You know you aren't good enough." Urticacea stood on the bruised vines of the walkway, looking smug and superior.

"You want me to stay, pass the princess test, and kiss the princes?"

The smug look disappeared from Urticacea's face.

Vevila walked back to the witch, folded her arms, leaned over so they were nose to nose, and whispered, "So why are you stopping me?"

The witch frowned.

Before Vevila could turn and walk away, Althelstan bounded into the courtyard, followed by the three wizards.

"Too late," she whispered so softly only Urticacea could hear.

"You!" Althelstan shouted, running toward them. "Witch, Urticacea, whatever your name is. I've found proof she's a princess."

"She was trying to run away," Urticacea accused.

"How can she run away? She's asleep." Althelstan opened the book he was carrying and thrust it under the old witch's nose. "See, right here." His finger thumped the book several times. "Jaquenetta is a princess."

"Not her," Urticacea shouted. She pointed to Vevila. "Her. She was trying to run away."

"I was not!" Vevila did her best to look offended.

"Then why are you out here by the gate?" Urticacea's smug look had returned.

"I fell out of a balcony while I was getting dressed!" Vevila sneered at the witch as she pulled the remaining branch of rosebush from her shoulders. "I was trying to get back in, and the only way I know to get in is through the front gate."

Apparently this argument would pass with the wizards, though Althelstan was oblivious and still pointing to the page in his book.

"Poor thing." The short, fat one, Rueberry, put his arm around her and plucked at her tattered left sleeve and scratched arm. "Are you quite all right?"

Mazigian, the young wizard, leered. "I would outstare the sternest eyes that look."

The witch grimaced. "Perhaps we should take her safely back to her room."

"But my dress," Vevila wailed to the three sympathetic male wizards.

"And what of Jaquenetta?" Althelstan shouted. "She's a princess!" He closed his book. "I'll bet that's why you put the castle to sleep. Because if you didn't, she would have kissed the princes, and then where would you be?"

"Don't worry." Rueberry patted Vevila's arm. "We'll find you another dress." He glanced at Zenpfennig, who wore his customary frown. "Though I hear slashes are in fashion."

Zenpfennig shook his head. "I understand they prefer to put them about more artistically, rather than slapdash all over."

"I say! Have you been listening?" Althelstan shook Mazigian. "That witch is doing everything she can to keep those princes and this castle asleep."

"Nay, that's true, that's very true," Mazigian said.

"Oh, for pity's sake!" Urticacea shouted over the hubbub, as she jumped up and down. "Jaquenetta isn't a princess. If you check the rest of the records, you'll see that she arrived here as a babe, already born. I'm sure she's the duke's get." Calming down and looking sly, she added, "And anyway, look at her. Does she look younger than the prince?"

Althelstan paused, looking at Mazigian, who shook his head sadly. Althelstan tucked the book under his arm. "We'll just see about that," he said and stalked off.

"Poor, poor thing," Rueberry murmured as he gently led Vevila inside. "How did you fall out of a balcony?" After glancing up at the towering castle, he added, "How high up were you?"

"Oh, it was awful," Vevila whispered, trying not to laugh.

Mazigian, walking on the other side of her from Rueberry, took her hand as if escorting her and patted it gently in a "there, there" sort of way.

Glancing back, Vevila saw Zenpfennig walking directly behind her. His rail-thin body couldn't shield her from Urticacea's glare, but, though thin, he made an unfortunately effective barrier between her and the open gate.

Z ENPFENNIG AND MAZIGIAN put the bar carefully
down across the stone wall and heavy door of Vevila's
cell, while Rueberry wrung his hands.

She'd seemed happy enough while they were helping
her find another dress. But from the time they'd found her
again, after she'd lost her way coming back after dressing
in private, she'd been very quiet and subdued, almost sad.

Rueberry felt quite sorry for her. It had to be difficult to
spend all day and night locked up in a cell with very little
food and no company. As Zenpfennig and Mazigian
stepped away from the door, he moved between them and
opened the peephole door.

"Will you need anything else?" he asked. "Perhaps a
book or something?"

Vevila frowned at him from where she sat on the floor.
"Sure, a book or something."

"When we have time," Zenpfennig said sternly as he
closed the peephole door almost on Rueberry's nose.

"No need to be so rude," Rueberry muttered as he was
elbowed away from the door.

"We have work to do." Zenpfennig started walking
briskly down the corridor. "We have to find a way to lift
the curse on our young colleague."

Waddling in the rear, Rueberry complained, "But it's
past noon, and we haven't even had our midday meal!"

"We've eaten enough this morning." Zenpfennig sailed
down a flight of stairs. "I've had another idea for lifting the
curse from Mazigian. We'll get him all settled, then we'll
find you more food."

He led them to a large ballroom. The parquet floor had
cracked in places, and the small, new-green, tendrilling

shoots of vines could be seen peeking out of them. One whole wall was made of broken, empty windows, with glittering shards of glass scattered near their base. The vulgar weather breezed on in, unwelcome and uninvited, to stir the spotted and faded remnants of the once colorfully embroidered tapestries hanging on the walls.

Zenpfennig kept going until he'd reached almost the exact center of the room. He turned to Mazigian and pointed toward a spot away from the open windows. "Stand there."

One stained, gnarled finger curled at Rueberry to beckon him over. He leaned down to whisper in Rueberry's ear, "Stand behind me, and don't interfere."

While this was Rueberry's standard position, having Zenpfennig order him there boded ill. Rueberry scuttled behind Zenpfennig, taking the brunt of the ill-mannered spring breeze from the open windows. He tried not to glance at Mazigian, knowing Mazigian would look to him for reassurance and support. He couldn't give any this time.

Starting, as always, with long, bony hands working through an arcane dance in the air, Zenpfennig's spell took shape. When the chanting began, Rueberry closed his eyes, wishing fervently that this was over.

When the drone of Zenpfennig's chant quickened, and an odd smell of cabbage soup drifted in the air, Rueberry knew it was close to the end of the spell. The hairs on his arms and head stood on end, and the oppressive feeling of a storm coming in made him wince.

The echoing sound of a cannon shot was followed by something rather like the thud of a quarter side of beef against a table.

"I don't think that worked," Zenpfennig said.

Rueberry opened his eyes.

Mazigian lay flat on the floor. Zenpfennig stood over him, frowning and stroking his long, white beard.

"Well, as long as he's out, there are some other spells I'd like to try." Zenpfennig returned to Rueberry. "He wouldn't stand for it if he was awake, so I'd better take the chance I have now."

Rueberry sheltered his eyes in his hands, wishing he could block out the rest of his senses, too.

❧

PRINCE ALTHELSTAN KNELT at the feet of the lovely Princess Jaquenetta, stroking her hand and admiring the way she sat so elegantly.

"None of that now," Urticacea said.

He whirled around, surprised to see her. He hadn't heard any footsteps on the stairs or in the room. How had the old bat gotten there? "None of what?"

"None of that." The witch shook her finger in his face. "You know, *that*. None of that."

"There hasn't been any *that*." He stood up to get his face higher than her hand could reach. "*That* never occurred to me." He gave her a stern and suspicious look. "Until you brought it up."

The old witch snorted and began hobbling around, pacing the room nervously. "I'm protecting everyone in this castle. Even her, though she doesn't deserve it. So I'll know if you try anything naughty."

"Oh, for pity's sake!" Althelstan placed one hand on Jaquenetta's head, as if bestowing a blessing. "I was just thinking how elegant she looked, even in sleep. What with all the snoring and everything else going on." He waved at the king and guards.

"Still think she's a princess, do you?" Urticacea sneered.

"Yes. I do." He leaned close so he was nose to nose with the witch. "And I'll prove it." His stomach chose that moment to growl and ruin his stern image.

The old witch laughed at him.

"When is the noon dinner going to be ready?" he demanded.

"I don't know," she snarled. "I have enough to do keeping this castle up, protecting the people in it, and keeping the larder stocked and fresh. Especially with those hungry wizards about. I'm not cooking also."

"I'm a prince!" Althelstan said horrified. "I'll be king someday. I'm not cooking."

"Surely an experienced adventurer such as yourself is capable of making his own meal from the raw materials at hand."

Althelstan frowned a moment. The witch frowned back.

He smiled and said, "Well, if you're just not capable of handling that many spells, then I guess you're just not capable. I'll have to shift for myself."

Expecting to be hit with a spell or at the very least to see smoke come drifting out of her ears, Althelstan sauntered down the stairs. Nothing happened, and she didn't follow him, leaving him wondering if maybe he hadn't been right.

Right or wrong, he figured it probably wouldn't hurt to leave the castle for a while and let the old bag cool off. So he picked up a few things in the pantry and left through the front gate, down the wizard-made path, to have a picnic in the countryside.

The sun shone brightly. The cool breeze blew briskly.

And away from the overgrown green vines of the castle, wild flowers dotted the countryside with pinks, reds, yellows, oranges, and purples. Their scents drifted away on the wind; here sweet, there tart, here soft, there strong, and everywhere pleasant. In the distance, birds chirped and twittered. Althelstan hadn't realized how tired he was of monotonous green, the choking smell of old dust, and the aggravating sound of snoring.

He lounged at the top of a hill of grass, dotted with small, dainty purple flowers, overlooking a series of hillocks in a valley below. He picnicked while watching birds soar and wheel above him, below the slow-moving, fluffy white clouds. He tried to find shapes in the clouds.

As he was finishing the last of the bread and cheese, he looked down into the valley. There was something about the hills there. It took him only a moment to recognize the castle; the tree shape of several towers gave it away.

While wrapping everything up in his blanket, he tried to think of something else to do for the rest of the afternoon. He really wanted to spend the afternoon with Jaquenetta, but undoubtedly the witch or the wizards would interrupt him.

Poetry. With all the beauty of nature around him, surely he could compose some poetry for Jaquenetta. Surely this much inspiration would overcome his inherent lack of talent.

Sitting on the green hill overlooking the castle, with the bundled remains of his picnic beside him, Althelstan opened himself up to inspiration.

"Roses are . . . No. No, that'll never do." His fingers drummed on the old woolen blanket. "There once was a princess from . . . No."

"Excuse me," a delicate, high, feminine voice said. "Could you tell me where the sleeping castle is?"

Althelstan turned around. A young lady stood, smiling tentatively. Her long blonde hair fell in thick curly locks to her waist, framing her pink face, blue eyes, and slim figure. She wore a pale blue, almost white silk ball gown and carried a large, battered, brown leather bag.

"Who are you? Why do you want to know?" he asked.

"I've heard that the tale of a sleeping castle is true," she said in her high, childish voice. "That it was found by a prince, and there are three sleeping princes that need to be kissed by a princess to awaken." She looked shyly at her feet. "I'm Princess Berengaria of Perideridia. I've come to kiss the princes and awaken them."

"I didn't know Perideridia had a princess," Althelstan said.

"Yes. Not many people know." Berengaria looked sad. "It's a very sad story."

"I've got nothing better to do."

She glowered at him. "I need to find the castle."

"As it happens, I'm the prince who found the castle." He stood and bowed to her. "Prince Althelstan of Portula. And I'm still trying to get the castle awakened."

"Oh, uhm." Berengaria looked confused. "I thought there were princes needing the kiss of a princess. Why are you still here?"

"I'm here for the prin*cess*. My father has commanded that I marry only a real princess, and I fell in love with the one in the castle. So, I brought my cousin, Princess Vevila, here to kiss the princes, because the only way to awaken the whole castle is to awaken the princes."

"So the princes have already been kissed?" Berengaria asked disappointedly.

"No."

"No?"

"No." Althelstan motioned to the strangely shaped hills in the valley. "Why don't I tell you about it on the way to the castle."

❦

T HE WALLS WERE closing in on her, and there was nothing in the cell that Vevila could use to stop them. She looked frantically around. The dark, gloomy cell was empty except for her and a cold mist. She put her hands against opposite walls but couldn't stop them. The ceiling touched the top of her head, pushing inexorably downward.

Sitting up, Vevila awoke, panting.

Around her, the stone walls remained as they were when they were first mortared into place. The pallet under her was hard, but at least it kept the cold stones from leeching warmth from her. The spinning wheel sat idly in its corner. A few scattered stones remained from the pile she'd had this morning. At the foot of her pallet sat a tray with fine elegant china, a crystal goblet, a silver serving knife, and the crumbs and dregs of her meal.

Her short rest hadn't made up for a night's sleep lost, but it helped some. Vevila slowly stretched, making sure she got each and every part of her involved. She idly picked up a stone that had rolled under her pallet. This one was actually gold. She figured only its hiding place saved it from the wizards.

Gold was a metal. Vevila wasn't too certain of the fine points of metallurgy, but knew that swords and picks and shovels and such were made of some sort of metals. And such tools could be used against stones or mortar.

Vevila scrapped the nugget against the mortar. Only a close examination showed scratches on the gold and extremely fine lines of gold on the mortar.

Pocketing the nugget, Vevila reached for the silver knife. It worked somewhat better against the mortar, but quickly dulled, and she wasn't at all sure she could explain away the scratches on it.

The wooden tray was the wrong size and shape and undoubtedly far too soft. She doubted the china or crystal would make an appreciable dent, even if she smashed them and used the pieces. That left her with the pallet and the spinning wheel.

Since she had no plans for actually using the spinning wheel as intended, Vevila saw no problem with appropriating judicious portions of it to escape confinement. She looked it over but could see no easily detachable part. Pushing it away from the wall to get a better look at the thing, she stepped on a sharp piece of quartz.

Hopping back to her pallet, she determined that the rock had drawn no blood, but it had left a deep gouge in the bottom of her slipper.

"This wouldn't have happened if you'd let me keep my boots," Vevila shouted.

No one replied.

She glared at the rock. It continued to sit quietly on the stone floor, the pointy end toward the spinning wheel.

Snatching it up, Vevila tried it against the mortar. It worked much better than the gold and even possibly better than the knife.

She was about to start digging in earnest but realized she should think this through before starting.

Whatever she did, she had to be able to hide it some-how. Not only that, but it would be nice to pick a spot where the mortar was likely to be soft, or perhaps not as well mixed, or not as thoroughly applied. She'd have to pick her spot carefully. Vevila looked at the stone walls around her.

Near to the floor would be easier to conceal. She could roll up her pallet and put it in front of her work. But most likely the mortar would be strong and solid there, in antici-pation of escape attempts. Perhaps the mortar wouldn't be as carefully applied higher up. If she stood on the spinning wheel, she could work above eye level. People rarely looked up when searching for things.

However, the spinning wheel was in the wrong spot. Vevila guessed it to be near an exterior wall, and she'd had enough climbing for a long while. So. . . .

Vevila quickly rearranged her cell, kicking all the quartz into a pile and moving the spinning wheel and pal-let so they exchanged places.

Standing on the seat of the spinning wheel, Vevila began scraping at the mortar on the side of one stone. The dust fell such that it was nicely hidden by the base of the spinning wheel.

It might take a while, but Vevila would never give up. She would get out.

❧

RUEBERRY WONDERED IF Mazigian had been putting on weight. The arm draped across Rueberry's shoul-ders certainly was heavy, and he was convinced Zenpfen-nig wasn't straining as hard under the weight.

Mazigian stirred. His eyes opened momentarily, blinking in surprise, then closing. The soft rumbling sounds issuing ominously from his mouth gave warning of what his insides thought of the treatment they'd received.

"There, there." Zenpfennig patted the portion of Mazigian nearest his hand as he staggered under the load. "You'll be fine. Just relax."

They scooted him into a small receiving room and allowed him to fall onto a small gold couch. A cloud of dust rose from the cushions, leaving all three coughing and choking.

Zenpfennig waved his hands unmagically through the air, stirring the raised dust. "Blasted witches!"

Helping Mazigian up to a seated position, Rueberry asked, "Are you all right?"

"Yes, yes." Zenpfennig pushed Rueberry out of the way. "Say something. Let's find out if this worked."

"My little body is weary of this great world." Mazigian rubbed his head, with his eyes tightly closed.

"Not very helpful," Zenpfennig grumbled. "Say something more. Make it longer so we can tell if the curse is gone."

"I am a tainted wether of the flock, meetest for death; the weakest kind of fruit drops earliest to the ground; and so let me." Mazigian sagged back to recline on the couch, raising another cloud of dust.

"Not still!" Rueberry said.

"Apparently." Zenpfennig drummed his fingers on his bearded chin. "We'll have to think of something else." He glared down at Mazigian and said, "Don't say anything unless you absolutely must."

"Hello!" Prince Althelstan called from down the hallway. "Is anyone around?" He appeared in the doorway with a pretty, blonde refugee from a fancy-dress ball. He motioned to the young lady. "This is Princess Berengaria of Perideridia. She's here to kiss the princes."

"What about Princess Vevila?" demanded Zenpfennig.

"Well." Althelstan shrugged. "The witch won't let Vevila kiss the princes, so let's try Berengaria."

"What about the straw and the gold?"

"We won't be needing that if Berengaria can wake the princes," Althelstan said.

"We could at least try," Rueberry said, as Zenpfennig continued to frown.

"Very well." Zenpfennig led the way to the royal tower.

Urticacea stood in the waiting room, blocking the doorway to the upper stairs. She looked them over, frowning intently at Berengaria, and growled, "Now what?"

Althelstan waved to the princess. "This is Princess Berengaria of Perideridia. She's here to kiss the princes."

"Perideridia has no princess! She's a fraud," Urticacea shouted.

"She says there's a long story that clears all that up." Althelstan abandoned Berengaria to go stand beside the sleeping Jaquenetta.

Snorting, Urticacea approached Berengaria. "So, tell us how you're a princess, when Perideridia has no princess."

Berengaria's hands shook as they clutched the brown leather bag to her. Her high, sweet, childish voice filled the room as she repeated, as if by rote, "My father was king of Perideridia, before the present claimant usurped the throne."

"I'd heard all the family was murdered," Zenpfennig said.

"I alone escaped."

"Ha!" shouted Urticacea. "The last king had no daughters."

"Yes, he did!" Berengaria looked indignant. "The queen had just given birth to a baby daughter, me, hours before the usurper murdered almost the entire royal family."

"Hm," Rueberry mused. "Could be. She was expecting. And, as I recall, King Verill took the throne seventeen years ago."

They all looked at the girl, who smiled faintly.

"You have no proof!" the witch shouted.

Rueberry watched Althelstan grimace in a "here we go again" look.

"I am Princess Berengaria. I am." Berengaria had begun to shake all over now. "If you just let me kiss the princes, you'll see."

"Oh, no!" Urticacea was jumping up and down with anger.

Berengaria stepped backward, looking scared, and accidentally stepped on one of the guards' feet, losing her balance, and sitting down on the sleeping guard. The guard snorted, pausing momentarily in his snoring to smack his mouth open and closed twice, wrapped his arms around Berengaria, and snuggled back into sleep. Berengaria screamed.

Rueberry and Mazigian rushed to her aid, prying the guard's arms open and assisting her up. Once they'd loosened the guard's grip, he again snorted, turned, put his arms around the king, and, laying his head ever so gently on the king's shoulder, resumed snoring.

Mazigian opened his mouth, but Zenpfennig shook a finger at him and said, "Don't say a word."

Patting Berengaria's arm, Rueberry said, "Don't be afraid. We'll watch over you." Strangely, she didn't seem comforted.

"She can't kiss the princes," the witch said, pacing in

front of the doorway to the upper stairs. "She has no proof she's a princess. We can't risk it."

"I am!" Berengaria sobbed in a high-pitched shriek.

"Would you have a handy birthmark or some such thing?" Rueberry asked.

Mazigian leered, and Berengaria cringed against Rueberry, her skirts rustling. She whispered, "No. I don't."

"Another princess test," Zenpfennig said with relish. "We'll just have to gather more straw."

"No!" screamed Urticacea. "No more straw!"

"We have to find a way to determine if she's really a princess," Rueberry said reasonably.

"There's another test," the witch said firmly. "She'll have to take it."

"Oh? And what's this test?" Zenpfennig looked disappointed.

"I . . . I can't tell you about it in advance," the witch muttered.

"Then how will we know if she's passed?" Althelstan asked.

"I'll know." Urticacea nodded to herself. "I'll tell you. In the meantime, you can make yourselves useful. Bring me . . ." Her mouth twisted a moment as she thought. "Bring me twenty mattresses and twenty feather beds and twenty silk blankets."

"Here?" asked Althelstan incredulously.

"No, no, no. I'll have to find a room." For once Urticacea looked tired and worried. "I'll have to find a room." She started toward the stairs, while shooing Berengaria in front of her. "Go on. Down the stairs. The rest of you go find the mattresses."

"But it's nearly supper, and I haven't had lunch yet," wailed Rueberry, rubbing his stomach.

"I think you'll live," Urticacea said.

"Perhaps." Althelstan approached the witch. "Perhaps someone could show the princess the kitchen, and she could prepare something for us."

"A princess cook? A real princess? For us?" Urticacea said scornfully.

"Princesses are very accomplished," Rueberry said. "They can do practically anything."

"Certainly they are accomplished in all the feminine arts." Zenpfennig smiled happily. "If they can spin, surely they can cook."

Mazigian smiled evilly down on the witch. "She is fair, and, fairer than that word, of wondrous virtues."

"If even I, a lowly prince, can cook," Althelstan added, "Berengaria should have no problem whatsoever."

"Very well." Urticacea pushed Berengaria ahead of her down the stairs. "Someone take her to the kitchen, and we'll all get to work."

꩜

WHEN ALTHELSTAN SAW the room the witch had picked, after he left Berengaria in the kitchen, he decided it was time he put his royal foot down. "Lower," he said. "Much lower."

"What? Don't you think it's a princess' room?" Urticacea said.

"I have no problems with the room itself." In fact it seemed a very royal room to Althelstan. High, cobwebbed ceiling, large gilded windows with a fine view of the green, trespassing vines, sturdy dusty tall four-posted bed, though there was nothing in the room to indicate who had inhabited it previously. But the thought of carrying twenty mattresses and twenty feather beds and twenty silk blankets up to the top of this tower's staircase left Althelstan cold. "I will only carry mattresses downstairs, not up."

The wizards, silhouetted by the evening sun streaming in the windows, nodded their agreement.

"The other rooms aren't tall enough," the witch said.

"You honestly expect us to carry up here, and stack on that bed, twenty mattresses and twenty feather beds and twenty silk blankets?" Althelstan shook his head.

"Be in peril of my life with the edge of a feather bed!" said Mazigian.

"I've checked the other rooms. None of them are tall enough." Urticacea balled her fists, as if looking for something to hit.

"Perhaps," Rueberry said as he walked away from the window to the bed, "we could bespell some mattresses up here."

"And waste our magic on her silly princess tests? I think not." Zenpfennig looked haughtily down his nose at the witch. They glared at each other, each trying to outfrown the other, neither winning.

Mazigian stepped forward from the window to stand beside his mentor. "Go draw aside the curtains and discover the several chambers to this wicked witch."

"What?" Urticacea shrieked, her face turning bright red.

Rueberry smiled. "You're the one who cursed him. He can only change bits of the quotes, with substitutes that fit the circumstances."

She turned on Rueberry. "Why you—"

"Come," Zenpfennig said, pushing Mazigian ahead of him and pulling Rueberry behind. "Show us these rooms."

At ground level, Mazigian ushered them into a small ballroom. This room still lay intact, the vines not having breached the floors or walls. It was smaller than the one where the wizards had spent the afternoon practicing, but with a ceiling even higher than the bedchamber's. A layer of dust lay undisturbed, graying the dark parquet floor and leeching the colors from the bright embroidered tapestries hanging on the walls. The chandeliers hung empty from the ceiling, with cobwebs dangling and swinging jauntily like the leftover decorations of some long-ago party. Two small windows in one wall faced away from the setting sun, lending a gloomy cast to the abandoned room.

Althelstan sneezed.

"This will do nicely," Zenpfennig said.

"How can we guard it, to make sure she doesn't cheat?" Urticacea asked.

"The door swings outward." Zenpfennig demonstrated his point on the carved wooden door. "We'll block it from the outside."

"And the windows?" the witch demanded.

"Probably stuck fast." Zenpfennig turned to Mazigian. "If you would please."

Mazigian tried the windows, making a great show of not being able to open them.

"Very well." The witch's eyes narrowed, and she smiled slyly. "You'll need to bring a bed along with the twenty mattresses and twenty feather beds and twenty silk blankets." She hobbled out of the ballroom, cackling.

Althelstan sighed. "I suppose we'd better get to work."

Mazigian laughed. "No bed shall e'er be guilty of my stay, nor rest be interposer 'twixt us twain."

"What?" Althelstan asked.

Flinging his arms out, Mazigian shouted, "Here an angel in a golden bed lies all within. Deliver me the key."

A gilded bed appeared momentarily, only to be covered

as mattresses and feather beds and blankets stacked themselves high as a hill upon it. The stressed wood groaned beneath the weight but didn't break.

"I distinctly remember saying that we weren't going to waste our magic on arranging her princess tests." Zenpfennig glared down at Mazigian, who grinned impudently.

Leaning out the door, Althelstan called to the retreating figure of the witch. "It's ready."

Urticacea hobbled quickly back. She looked at the bed, horrified. She marched over and pushed against one side, trying to topple the straight, tall heap. "No, no, no. You can't have all the mattresses on the bottom, and then all the feather beds in the middle, and all the silk blankets on top. You have to alternate them."

She took charge from there, ordering them about, deciding exactly which mattress had to be on the bottom, and what feather bed should come next, and arranging the silk blankets by color, and so forth. She rejected one mattress and two blankets outright as being the wrong sort for this princess test. The mattress ended up staying, since none of the men would fetch another, but Althelstan found himself hunting up silk blankets in dusty bedrooms. He pulled one pale pink one from off a couple sleeping back to back in one room, and another from a box at the foot of an empty bedroom.

In the ballroom he found the old hag bustling about, getting in the men's way, and generally irritating them. Finally they had the stack piled to suit her.

"Now what?" Zenpfennig asked.

The witch frowned at him. "Now we see if the princess can cook."

Frankly, Althelstan didn't care. Tired, worn, and hun-

gry, he knew he'd eat anything gladly. And he bet Rueberry would, too.

⚜

THE SUN HAD nearly set behind the mountain just beyond the swampy point of a blue, triangular lake nestled in a long valley. A quaint, odd little man held two hats
in his hands, considering. Should he wear the red knit, or
would the befeathered brown felt be better?

"No, I don't want your opinion," he said.

Insects whined as they flitted through the stands of
grasses growing up from the still waters of the swamp.

"While I will concede to your expertise on women and
apparel, this is purely business. I'm not trying to impress
her; I just don't want to look strange." After a moment's
pause, he added, "All right, all right. Stranger than usual."

He tossed the brown hat up, then changed his mind and,
as if juggling, tossed the red hat after the brown. Only the
brown fell, and he caught it.

"Not because you recommended it," he said sternly to
the water. "But because it looks more conservative,
more . . . intelligent." He set the hat on his head at a jaunty
angle and, standing at the edge of the water, looked at his
colorful reflection. His gold vest reflected the red of the
setting sun and was nicely set off by his dark green velvet
tunic and black cape. The water distorted his brown boots
and red hose.

At least he hoped that portion of his reflection was distorted. "Maybe I should wear my purple trousers. Purple is
a more royal color and might lend more confidence to my
image."

Frogs and toads took up their calls, interrupting the
buzzing insects.

"Oh. Ha. Ha." The odd little man waved a hand, and the
red hose changed into purple trousers. He bent to tuck the
trousers into his boots. "I didn't mean my confidence. I
meant her confidence in me. I want her to trust me; to believe that I will help her. To— Flowers? What the devil
would she do with flowers?"

He paused, listening. The wind blowing through the
trees and grasses could barely be heard over the croaking
of frogs and buzzing of insects.

"Well, they wouldn't do her one bit of good. And they'd
give away the fact that someone had been in her cell in the
night. However . . ." He turned away, extending his hand
toward a nearby willow tree with a flourish. A small hand-
pick and shovel appeared in his hand. "You may have a
point. Perhaps I shouldn't arrive without some sort of gift."

His other hand produced a length of purple velvet ribbon from the air, and he tied it in a bow around the handles
of the pick and shovel.

"There. Nice and yet businesslike."

In his next pause, a splash rippled the water at his feet.

"If she does escape, there is that other girl, Berengaria.

"Would I be going through all this trouble just for myself?

"Let me put it another way, I've spent ten years, and
I'm this close. I'm not giving up now.

"No, I don't expect any gifts from her. Where would she
get them?"

The odd little man walked over to the crystal ball and
stroked it once. He turned back to the water. "That
wouldn't be a gift. That would be a miracle."

He smiled, said, "Wish me luck," and vanished.

Two bulging eyes lifted out of the swamp water to peer at the spot where he'd stood. Sinking back into the water, they, too, disappeared.

❧

BERENGARIA LISTENED AT the door, while outside in the hallway, the wizards argued with the witch and something heavy was shoved against the door. She had cooked supper rather badly, fearing that the meal might have in fact been her princess test. She needn't have bothered. They'd all fallen on the food as if starving. A tray of food had been taken, along with many bales of hay, to a cell in an upper tower. Berengaria spent little time feeling sorry for the other woman claiming to be a princess. She needed to keep her sympathy for herself.

The dusty ballroom was quite empty, except for the highly stacked bed. Berengaria hadn't been able to discover what the exact nature of her test was, and now feared the worst. Alone in a ballroom with the bed, a few tapestries, a single lit candle in a golden candlestick, and lots and lots of dust.

What would a princess do?

That, essentially, was Berengaria's problem. Her knowledge of princesses was limited to bedtime stories and hearsay. Her claim to be the lost daughter of the last king of Perideridia was only one of three competing theories on how the woman who'd raised her, a sharp-eyed people-hating spinster, had come to be in possession of a baby. All three theories rejected any sort of normal conception by the spinster as being too ludicrous to mention. Berengaria hadn't even been allowed to call the woman Mother.

"Agnes Paisley is a good enough name for me," Spinster Agnes had always said. "I won't take some other woman's title."

After Agnes had died, Berengaria wandered the countryside, searching for herself, trying to find some way to prove who she really was. The sleeping castle had seemed a perfect way to discover the truth.

Looking at the stack of mattresses and feather beds and blankets, Berengaria wasn't so sure.

So, what would a princess do?

A ballroom was for dancing, but if they intended for her to dance, wouldn't they have supplied music and dancing partners?

She eyed the bed. They had to mean for her to sleep. Something about the way she slept would prove her princessliness?

Perhaps she was supposed to remake the bed using only the perfect mattress, feather bed, and blanket for a proper princess.

Berengaria approached the bed. The stack was considerably taller than her. When she grabbed a blanket sticking out from the stack at shoulder height to pull it out, she merely pulled herself off the floor.

With as heavy and well stacked as the bed was, she would probably have to climb it and work down from the top to take it apart. She looked around for a ladder. She circled the bed, checked all four corners of the dusty room, even looked behind a few of the heavy embroidered tapestries, but could find no ladder.

That had to be the test. A true princess would climb to the top of the bed and sleep up there, rather than on the floor, ladder or no.

Glad to have solved that mystery, Berengaria again circled the bed, looking for the best face to attempt a climb. The foot of the bed looked to be the best place to climb. The mattresses weren't of exact lengths, but had been evened up at the head of the bed. Because of that, the foot face wasn't even, and so made possible foot- and hand-holds going up.

She reached up, grabbed a pale blue silk blanket, and pulled herself up onto the gilded, sloping wood of the foot-board. She grabbed a soft purple blanket next. It felt smooth as water to her touch. Looking down, she found a spot to put her foot and attempted to raise herself higher.

The mattress gave way beneath her foot, and the smooth silk slipped through her hand. Her foot hit the curved, gilded footboard as she fell, twisting painfully.

Princess Berengaria sat rocking on the floor a moment, trying to cuddle her throbbing foot and ankle, and blinking back tears. Idiot, stupid princes; frivolous self-centered wizards; vicious conniving witches; bugger the lot of them! She'd show them.

Standing straight but careful not to put any weight on her throbbing foot, Berengaria approached the bed again. The blue silk could be trusted but not the smooth-as-water purple. She carefully got back up onto the footboard.

This time, she chose a brilliant yellow silk blanket shot through with bright red, and above all, thick strands of yarn. She dug her toes—the ones on the unhurt foot—in between the mattresses this time, and, though the end of the mattress sticking out did sag beneath her foot, she stayed up.

A thin, pink feather bed became her next grip, but she fumbled with her hurt foot, slipped, and fell again. She tried to keep her feet from getting caught on the footboard again and succeeded. The solid parquet floor of the ballroom slammed into her side.

Berengaria lay still on the floor a few minutes, gasping for breath. Was being a princess really worth all this?

Still, she had to know who she truly was, and the only way to find out was at the top of this awful bed.

Lumbering to her feet yet again, Berengaria used the same soft blue blanket and warmly familiar foothold, and again chose the yellow-with-red blanket. While looking for a place to put her aching foot, she noticed a mattress sticking out farther than the others, just below waist height.

No one could see her, so throwing modesty to the four winds, she hitched her white nightgown up and stuck her knee into the gap. She pulled herself up, stuck her good foot in, and grabbed for a midnight black blanket.

It was smoother than the purple, and she abandoned it for a sturdy, serviceable gray. Funny how her tastes in colors and textiles was undergoing a radical revolution. She found another kneehold, and discovered herself looking over the top. She'd almost made it.

Her left hand continued to grip the gray, while her right tested handholds on several blankets. The best of the lot was the fluffy, nubby raw silk blanket on the top, but without anything to hold it in place, Berengaria knew it would fall down with her. The next best was a thick white silk, only one mattress above her current grip.

Instead, she found a likely spot to wedge her knee, just under her gray handhold. After getting first her knee, then her other foot in place, she tried flinging herself up on the top of the bed. And missed entirely, falling backward instead.

She managed to twist and try to soften her fall with her

hands, succeeding in bruising both arms and knocking the wind out of herself.

"A pox on all witches, wizards, kings, queens, princes, and, most especially princesses!" she moaned to the hard parquet floor.

Was it worth it? Berengaria looked up at the high top of the bed, then she looked at her swollen ankle and reddened arms. She'd make it worth it.

The blue silk, foothold, the yellow with red, foothold, the gray, foothold, the white silk, foothold. Balling her right hand into a fist, Berengaria thrust her fist deeply under the top mattress and grabbed a wad of smooth green silk some way under the mattress. Using that as an anchor, she reached under the top raw silk blanket and downy feather bed to grab the top of the mattress by digging her fingernails into it.

Pulling herself up and swinging her legs over, she managed to get on top of the bed.

Sitting in the center, she laughed hysterically, clutching the blanket over her face to mask her sobs. After a moment's indulgence, Berengaria took a deep, calming breath. Inching to the edge, she looked down at the floor.

Far, far away, it seemed, sat her lonely candle. She inched away from the edge, breathing deeply, and trying not to shake with fright.

Perhaps she should try to sleep now. Yes, that was it. She'd prove herself a true princess worthy of a bed such as this. Yes, she would, if it was the last thing she did.

Berengaria huddled under the warmth of the raw silk covers and tried to curse them soundly for forgetting her pillow. How in the world did they expect her to prove the depth of her princessliness without a proper pillow?

VEVILA STOOD ON the seat of the spinning wheel, industriously gouging out mortar from around one of the stones. Mortar dust clung to her face and powdered the front of her dress. Not that it mattered. With as dusty as the castle was, no one had noticed when they'd brought her supper and the many bundles of straw.

She sneezed occasionally, but kept going. She'd been at it most of the afternoon and evening. She'd gouged out as much as she could on the top and the two sides and was now finishing the bottom. The problem was that the quartz could only reach into the gap a short way, basically the length of the nugget, while the stone she was trying to pry out had to be at least six inches deep.

Her finger scraped painfully on the stone, and she dropped the quartz nugget. Sticking her gashed knuckle into her mouth in an unsuccessful effort to stop the pain, Vevila tried not to feel like a caged animal. The fact that her finger tasted of mortar dust disturbed her. It seemed that everything she saw, smelled, tasted, and touched was mortar dust. She imagined she'd hear the grating rasp of the quartz digging into the mortar for the rest of her life. She sneezed.

Rooting through her small stash of quartz, she tried to find a larger or at least longer nugget, but there was none to be had. Frustrated, she kicked at them.

Standing on the spinning wheel again, Vevila tried pushing against the stone, hoping against hope that she'd removed enough mortar to shift the stone. The stone remained unmoved.

Vevila jumped from the spinning wheel onto the pile of straw. "Foul, stupid, rude, trifling ninnies!"

She flung straw up and around, all over her cell. "Idiots! Idiots! Idiots!"

Finding no release for her anger in words, she began screaming incoherently, flailing with her fists at the straw and the stones.

"Excuse me," a familiar male voice said. "Perhaps I can be of some assistance."

Digging hair and straw out from in front of her face, Vevila peered out at her cell.

Standing in the back corner, well away from most of the destruction, was the odd little man. Tonight he wore a brown felt feathered hat, a gold vest over a dark green velvet tunic, and wildly purple trousers tucked into battered muddy brown boots. He stopped nervously fingering the black cape he had draped over one arm long enough to waggle his fingers at her and smile anxiously.

"You!" Vevila shouted. She rose from the pile dripping and shaking chaff and stalks of straw from her. "I'll pay anything, do anything, if you'll just get me out of here now."

"I'm sorry. I can't do that," he said.

"Can't or won't?"

He winced and put his cape down next to her rolled-up pallet. "I could substitute gold for the straw again. If you'd like. For another favor."

"You're not very helpful, you know that." Vevila folded her arms and frowned down at him. "Who are you, anyway?"

"My name doesn't matter." He waved off her question. "Do you want my help? Do we have a deal?"

Since frowning and threatening wasn't working, Vevila decided to try using her mother's advice on this odd little man. Trying to smile, Vevila licked her lips and approached him. Delicately running her fingers along the side of his face and into his long, soft, curly brown beard, she said suggestively, "Perhaps we can work out a better deal."

The odd little man gently took her hands from his beard and held them firmly in his small, warm hands. Vevila wondered if he could possibly know she'd planned to yank his beard out by the roots if he refused.

"I . . . I . . . I'm sorry. I can't," he said, sounding truly miserable. "Once you've passed this test, I can help you in any way you want, but until then, I'm constrained to only help you pass the test."

"Why?" Vevila squeezed his hands as hard as she could. When he cringed in pain, she abruptly let go of him, ashamed of herself.

"Once you're proclaimed a princess, I can provide any assistance you may desire."

"What is so special about being a princess?" Vevila stalked away to sit dejectedly at the spinning wheel. She looked over at him, still standing in the corner. "So you can only help princesses?"

"Well, no. I can help other people."

"Just not me." Vevila sighed and plucked straw from her skirt. A thought occurred to her. "Is it because of the witch, Urticacea?"

"No. And, maybe, a little, yes."

"Once I'm a princess, I won't need your help."

"Yes." He looked somewhat dejected himself.

Twiddling a piece of straw between her fingers, Vevila said, "So you'll substitute gold for the straw again if I promise you an unnamed favor."

"Yes."

"Fine. Do it."

The odd little man grinned. "You won't regret it."

"Oh, but I already do."

They gathered up the straw again, and he went to work. When he finished, a small pile of gold nuggets lay where the straw had been. He wiped the sweat from his brow with a shaky, tired hand and smiled a very satisfied smile. She noticed that, unlike the rest of the room, he was covered in gold dust.

"Where exactly do you get the gold?" She brushed gold dust from his shoulder, only to find it sticking to her hand. "Do you have your own gold mine?"

"Not exactly. Not my gold mine, no." The odd little man fiddled nervously with the lacing on his vest. "I happen to know a gold mine where the workers aren't happy, and occasionally gold goes missing for one reason or another. It's difficult but not impossible to get around the magical wards and lift judicious amounts."

"So you're one of the reasons?"

He nodded. "Very rarely. If I were discovered . . ." He shrugged and leaned on the spinning wheel's seat. "I'm not very welcome there."

Vevila idly spun the spinning wheel. "Well, I guess that's it until tomorrow night. Assuming I'm still here."

"Yes, I had noticed your escape attempt."

"Really?" Vevila was surprised. "No one else has."

"Yes, well." He paused and cleared his throat. "I thought it showed a lot of resourcefulness and determination. I have no doubt you will succeed if you truly wish to."

"And why wouldn't I wish to?"

"If you stay and pass the test, you will be inarguably a princess. That's something many women wish for."

"I'm not many women."

"No, and thank goodness for that." The odd little man walked back to his cape and picked it up. From the way he picked it up, Vevila could see that something was hidden in it. "I brought you something." He flipped a fold of the cape over, revealing a small hand-pick and shovel tied together with a purple velvet ribbon. He held them out to her. "For you."

She held them a moment, removing the ribbon. "No one ever gave me digging tools before."

The odd little man blushed. "I thought you'd like something useful. And if you scraped your hands raw on the stones, someone would be bound to notice."

"I thought you wanted me to be a princess?" Vevila asked.

He shrugged as he put his cape on, not meeting her eyes. "You should be whoever you want to be." He bowed to her. "Good-bye." He vanished.

"Good-bye," Vevila said to the thin air. She looked at the tools in her hands, a slow smile spreading across her face. Someone else thought she could make it. To wherever and whatever she wanted.

With renewed energy, she stepped up onto the spinning wheel and began digging at the mortar with the pick.

❧❧❧

RUEBERRY SIGHED CONTENTEDLY, his hand rubbing gentle circles on his distended stomach. His dark, heavy robes were stretched and smooth against his belly, with nary a wrinkle beneath his hand. In front of him on the dining room table, the crumbs and crusts of his defeated meal cowered on gilded platters, the dregs of his spiced wine sulked at the bottom of his chalice. At the far end of the dining room table, the steward snored and drooled. Next to Rueberry, Mazigian cradled his head on the table.

Seeing Zenpfennig standing straight and slim, glowering down on them, Rueberry couldn't help grinning goofily.

Some things in life should be savored. Knowing yourself blissfully satisfied with the very same things that bring no satisfaction to another was something to treasure. Rueberry knew that he was no foul-tempered ingrate.

Zenpfennig frowned disgustedly as he looked from Rueberry to Mazigian. "Perhaps we should just rest tonight. Maybe in the morning things will be clearer, and we'll be rested enough to overcome that blasted curse."

Beckoning to them, Zenpfennig left the room.

Looking to Mazigian, Rueberry began hoisting himself out of his chair. "Come on. We'd better stick together. There's no telling where that witch is at or what she's up to."

Mazigian nodded, lifting his head from the table. His bloodshot eyes gleamed with pain-wrought madness. "I desire no more delight than to be under sail and gone tonight."

"Lean on me." Rueberry pulled Mazigian's arm across his shoulders. "We'll get you to bed. Sorry about the headache. You know how Zenpfennig is when he decides to launch a barrage of spells against some scourge."

Groaning in agreement, Mazigian allowed himself to be jostled out of the dining room.

The three wizards settled for the night in a vastly different situation from the previous night. Zenpfennig had found a large, well-furnished set of empty suites they could put to use, where each would have his own room.

More particularly, each would have some space away from the others. Mazigian fell into his bed, and sleep, as soon as they arrived. Rueberry waited patiently on Zenpfennig, unwilling to rudely drop off while Zenpfennig paced the small sitting room outside their bedrooms and lectured.

"We have to do something about that witch. Her curse and this castle are an affront to everything that is magical. To permit her to continue as she's gone on is . . . is . . . disgraceful. The dignity and nobility of magic, the honor and sanctity of humanity, the very essence of everything in nature demands that this foul, disgusting distortion of truth and righteousness be stopped immediately."

Rueberry nodded politely. The flickering light from the candles in the four-pronged candelabra on the low table cast a sinister light on Zenpfennig, highlighting his bearded chin, flaring nostrils and bushy eyebrows but leaving his eyes and cheeks in deep shadows.

"The question is how?" Zenpfennig paused dramatically in front of a dust-covered tapestry, his fists raised. "The answer is right here. Right under our noses, and, like the castle, we can't see it for the vines that she's covered over it. She's keeping us at bay and busy with something else, while she continues her loathsome pursuits."

Stifling a yawn, Rueberry said, "Perhaps it'll all be clearer in the morning."

"Perhaps." Zenpfennig sat on a cushioned bench, raising a cloud of dust. For the first time all day, he appeared weary and fragile, his bony hands draped over his knobby, robe-covered knees. "But we must guard the young ladies. I fear the witch may do them harm."

"Allow me." Rueberry rubbed his belly and concentrated, with his eyes closed. A glow peeked out from between his hand and his body, growing in strength until its light made the candles burning on the low table seem a dim and futile defense against the dark. Rueberry tossed the light away. It split in two and disappeared through the walls, diffusing as it went. Rueberry opened his eyes. "That should take care of it, until an hour after dawn."

Zenpfennig sighed. "You need more flourish."

"No one was here to see except us," Rueberry complained.

⊙⋙⊙

FALLING. BERENGARIA WAS falling. Instinctively, she flung her hands out, searching for something to stop her.

Grabbing onto a piece of hanging fabric, Berengaria managed to stop her fall while wrenching her wrist. She awakened totally when she realized she really had fallen and was now hanging from the side of the bed, near the bottom. She eased herself down, worrying all the way because the bedding hid in the shadow of the candle's light. The candle itself was much shorter than she remembered it, and she shuddered to think what might have happened had she fallen after it had gone out.

She leaned against the stack of old, dusty mattresses, feather beds, and blankets, her face buried in the bedding, wishing she were up on the top, smelling faint traces of spices and lavender hidden in the dust.

Berengaria climbed the bed again. Practice had improved her skills, and she made it on the first try. Huddling once again under the blankets, she trembled in fear of another fall.

❧

PRINCE ALTHELSTAN HAD told the sleeping Jaquenetta all that had transpired since he'd spoken to her last. In his imagination, she smiled down on him as he knelt at her feet. Her understanding and approval, if only imaginary, lulled him to sleep, his head resting gently on her lap.

❧

URTICACEA LAY IN her thin garret bed, in a secret room, sparse and cold and clean, near the princes. She had to do something about all these meddlers, and soon. She had to keep her prince safe from all the evil they represented.

That vixen had somehow turned the straw to gold. Urticacea knew magic had to be involved, but couldn't figure out where it had come from. Vevila wasn't capable of it nor was that idiot prince. The wizards certainly hadn't done it, or they'd be spending all their time making gold.

The castle was turning against her. Urticacea had known it would happen eventually, but hadn't expected it so soon. It had only been a hundred years! There was no hope for it; she'd have to spirit the princes away and let the castle and its occupants fend for themselves.

Not tonight. She was too tired. Too tired. She drifted off to sleep, planning her escape to protect her poor, innocent prince.

❧

IN THE SILENT nighttime darkness of the king's bedchamber, the scuffle of slippered feet on the wooden floor echoed loudly. King Abelardann sat up and pulled the curtains open. He still couldn't see who it was in the absolute darkness, but the sweet scent of lilac and violets let him know it was his wife. He relaxed back against the pillows, moving aside to make room for her.

"I am concerned," Queen Tarax said, as she sat beside Abelardann on the bed.

The king ran his hand up his wife's leg. "We can take care of that."

She leaned down and planted a kiss on his forehead. "I'm worried about Vevila."

"What's she done now?" Abelardann complained. "I thought you said Althelstan would be safe with her."

"Our son is fine. But," she paused, groping for his hand in the darkness. "But the reports I'm getting from the royal wizards, keeping an eye on them for me, are becoming very alarming. About Vevila. They've locked her in a room."

"Not a bad idea." Abelardann could think of several spots in the palace to lock her up, and wished he'd thought of it before.

"She has managed several escapes so far."

"Well, she would, wouldn't she." The king sighed to himself. That was probably why he'd never thought of it; she couldn't be stopped.

"Apparently, though, there's a strange, short man that has been visiting her in her cell."

"Oh?" King Abelardann sat up in the dark. He might not care for the girl, but that was no excuse to allow her to come to harm.

"It's all right," Queen Tarax assured him with a pat on the cheek. "He hasn't hurt her. He appears to be trying to court her."

"Of his own accord?" King Abelardann asked confused, as he lay back against the soft pillows. "That is strange."

"The problem is, no one knows who he is. He hasn't given her his name or said where he's from. And he only appears when none of the others are around. He just does not appear to be the right sort."

"Are you saying he's not the right sort for Vevila, or that he's just not the right sort?"

The queen sighed. "I know your opinion of Vevila, but still. He's not the right sort."

"Our son, Althelstan, is fine?"

"Yes."

"You say this other fellow hasn't hurt Vevila?"

"No, he hasn't hurt her."

"Threatened her?"

"No."

The king shrugged in the darkness. "If he hasn't even threatened her, I don't see how he could be considered a danger to her. Do you still think Vevila can take care of herself?"

"Yes, but this fellow is different! He's giving her tools, not flowers. He acts like he can read her mind." The mattress shifted as she pulled her legs up onto the bed. "Several of the royal wizards have attempted to find out who he is, without success. Wizards! I've sent several knights out to see if they can search out who this fellow is."

King Abelardann shrugged in the dark, knowing she couldn't see him. "As long as you're happy, dear. But keep in mind that reading minds could be handy where Vevila's concerned. In any case, as long as he's not hurting her, it's my uncle's problem. And with seven daughters from Prince Bernard's various marriages, my guess is as long as the fellow doesn't ask for a large dowry, Bernard won't care."

"Vevila is also the granddaughter of King Otto of Regenweald. He may well have a problem with it."

"Then let him take care of it." King Abelardann snuggled deeper under the covers, while throwing them over Queen Tarax. "I have better things to do."

೧ಳ೪

BERENGARIA AWOKE IN pain, feeling as if something large and hard had struck her back. Which, as she felt around her, she realized the floor had. The candle had gone out, leaving only moonlight streaming in through the windows for her to see with. She slowly sat up, feeling the bruises on her back, arm, and head twinge and throb.

In the dusky, dusty shadows, all color had turned to shades of gray. The striations of gray gave her no hint as to which blankets she'd used for handholds to climb the bed. Carefully and slowly, she began climbing, using tactile hints to determine which silks she could use. Avoid the smooth, search for the rough.

The dust tickled her nose, and she sneezed. Her mouth felt dry and tasted filthy from the dust. She wished they'd left her a glass of wine or water or something, though she'd have had to leave it on the floor, so it probably wouldn't have done any good, anyway.

She crawled onto the top of the bed and tried to push tangled strands of hair from her face. Her hair was a mess, her nightgown was a mess. Everything fabriclike, anything with any sort of weave, seemed to gather dust in this place. Kneeling in the center of the bed, she looked around the eerie, moonlit room.

Gloomy shadows gathered in the corners, hinting at sinister or incorporeal occupants. Vines and weeds clawed at the windowpanes and outer walls. Off somewhere far away, an owl hooted.

Berengaria crouched in the middle of the bed, afraid to fall asleep lest she fall off the bed again, yet afraid to stay awake and confront whatever nastiness lurked in the castle. She stretched out until she could grasp the edge of the feather bed, and pulled it back.

Easing herself underneath the feather bed, she hoped she wouldn't see the floor of the ballroom again until morning.

❧❧❧

VERY QUIETLY, THE odd little man stepped out of the shadows of one corner of the waiting room. He timed each step to coincide with the snores of the king and his guards. He carefully approached the sleeping Prince Althelstan and Jaquenetta. Althelstan's head still lay in Jaquenetta's lap.

The odd little man took Jaquenetta's hand and gently placed it on Althelstan's head. Placing his own hand on her shoulder, he said, "Steel, your resolve. Iron, your will. Diamonds, your decisions. Hold to them still. Ask not for mercy. Accept not defeat. You must be triumphant. You cannot be beat."

With the same quiet, timed movement, he eased himself back into the shadows, smiling, and vanished.

❧❧❧

VEVILA WOKE TO find herself curled up most uncomfortably on the seat of the spinning wheel. Some sort of handle thing had been pressed into her cheek. She could feel the mark with her fingertips and knew it would be an angry red.

Stiffly, she got up, trying to stretch her aching back. The tools lay on the floor in plain sight. Vevila picked them up and stashed them on the other side of the spinning wheel. She stretched again.

As she did so, Vevila noticed the door gleamed with a soft, yellow glow. As she watched, it brightened, the colors changing to red, then orange, then purple, then blue. With a flicker of green glow, it winked out. The solid wooden door remained as she'd remembered it.

Cautiously, Vevila reached her hand out to touch the rough wood of the door. The glow had to have been magic, some kind of magic, but what? Urticacea's? The wizard's? The odd little man's?

The door felt normal. Vevila noticed that the wood seemed rougher today. Or perhaps it had always been this rough, and she'd never noticed. It splintered easily, and she pulled a few needles from the door.

If it was the wizards, possibly they'd put a spell on the castle to tax Urticacea.

Or perhaps Urticacea's spells were losing power.

Or perhaps the odd little man had given her the pick not to dig out mortar but to hack through the door.

Vevila reached for the pick, then stopped herself.

No. The others would be arriving soon to collect the gold. Telling time was difficult in her windowless cell, but she guessed it to be perhaps an hour after sunrise. If she waited until the others had come and gone, she'd have more time before they discovered her absence.

Instead, she examined the door. It swung inward but had no handle for an occupant to pull. The door would have been very hard to open from the inside, even without the bar on the outside. The bar merely made it impossible.

However, Vevila calculated that if she applied the pick in the right spots, she might be able to break off the bar's holders on the door. Then, by putting her fingers in the cracks, she could open the door and escape.

But later.

She unrolled her pallet and fell asleep again.

⚭

R UEBERRY WADDLED IN the middle between Zenpfennig and Mazigian, as they headed for the waiting room. Rueberry tried to ignore the nervous rumbling in his stomach. He'd eaten twice as much as usual this morning, to no avail. Not even extra cheese with his bread had helped.

He worried about the princesses under test. He'd had such high hopes yesterday, when they'd found Vevila with the gold, but it seemed even that the tests had to be passed to perfection—Urticacea's standard of perfection—for the woman to be a princess. It was most nerve wracking, and Rueberry had no cake or sweets to console him.

They trod single file up the narrow flight of stairs to the waiting room. Zenpfennig sneered down on the room's occupants contemptuously. Rueberry hurried forward to shake Prince Althelstan's shoulder.

"Wake up. It's morning. Time to check the princesses."

Prince Althelstan opened his eyes and yawned. "Morning already?"

"Yes," Zenpfennig said. "Let's be about our business."

While stretching, Althelstan asked, "Which princess do we see to first?"

They all looked to Zenpfennig, who tapped his gaunt cheek with a long, bony finger. "Princess Vevila first, I think. Then Princess Berengaria."

"Princess Vevila was here first," Rueberry said agreeably.

"And we're more likely to find success there," Althelstan said gloomily. "At least we know what the test is."

Althelstan led the way to Vevila's cell. As they took the bar off the door, Urticacea arrived, frowning and frumpy.

Inside, Vevila slept on her pallet. Against the other wall, where the straw had been the night before, lay a small pile of gold.

"Well done," Zenpfennig said.

Vevila stirred and sat up, sleepily rubbing her eyes. "Morning so soon?"

"Poor thing." Rueberry hurried over. "You've spent all night up, spinning straw. Don't you worry, we'll find you some breakfast and a new dress, and you can just sleep."

Zenpfennig had insisted they leave the wheelbarrows in the next cell, so they hurriedly collected the gold, leaving behind the few quartz nuggets, and left Vevila to sleep.

They paused outside the door to the ballroom where Berengaria had spent the night. Zenpfennig turned to Urticacea, and asked, "So, now tell us what is the nature of this test, that we may know when we enter."

Urticacea shook her wizened head, letting strands of gray hair trail down into her face. "I'll not tell you now; you might let it slip to that vixen and she fool all of us. The nature of the test should be plainly obvious, should she be a princess."

Mazigian, Althelstan, and Rueberry pushed the chest of

drawers away from the door, and Mazigian opened it. Stepping inside he said, "Ho! Who's within?"

The only answer was a soft soprano groan from high above them.

Looking up, they could see a dainty foot attached to a delicate, swollen ankle sticking out from off the side of the bed. Its owner lay underneath a rumpled raw silk blanket and thick buff feather bed.

"Obvious?" said Zenpfennig raising one eyebrow at the stunned Urticacea.

After a moment's blustering, Urticacea called, "Berengaria? Are you all right?"

A loud groan floated down to them.

"Gentlemen," Zenpfennig said to his colleagues, "let's get the poor woman down."

Working together, they levitated her down with the top mattress beneath her, and her tousled blankets half covering her. With her at a more convenient height, they could see a large bruise on one elbow, a goose egg on her head, and that one of her wrists had swollen.

"Good heavens!" Althelstan exclaimed. "What happened?"

Berengaria pushed herself up, unmistakably stiff and sore. "I slept on the bed all night. I don't know what the problem was, but it was awful. Just awful." Tears glistened in her eyes.

Althelstan turned on the witch. "What did you do?"

Urticacea pointed at the bed, her mouth opening and closing repeatedly.

"Yes," Zenpfennig said, frowning down on her. "Something is obvious here. What exactly were we looking for?"

"It was just a pea. One little pea," Urticacea said.

"A pea!" Rueberry might not be the brightest in the

room, but he knew an opening when he saw it. "You put a pea under those mattresses, knowing she might turn out to be a princess!"

"Disgraceful!" Zenpfennig said.

Urticacea again stood mute, opening and closing her mouth. She appeared to wither under the combined glare of the men, huddling into an old, tired, wrinkled woman.

"It would appear," Althelstan said coldly, "that here is a real princess, true and honorable."

The others nodded, with Urticacea joining last and most reluctantly.

Althelstan turned back to help Berengaria up. "Come, you must kiss the princes."

However, they discovered Berengaria couldn't stand. One ankle couldn't bear any weight, and both her arms were too bruised to allow anyone to assist her.

"Poor thing." Rueberry wrapped the raw silk blanket around her. "We'll have to use some healing spells on her."

"Mmm." Zenpfennig folded his scrawny arms across his hollow chest, trapping the trailing ends of his white beard. "She still won't be in any shape to kiss the princes until tomorrow. And we'll have to get her out of this room."

"Definitely," Althelstan agreed, glaring at the witch. "An ordinary room, with an ordinary bed."

"Just one mattress, and no peas," Zenpfennig said. He crooked a bony finger at Mazigian, then pointed to Berengaria.

Mazigian obligingly picked Berengaria up and followed Zenpfennig out. Althelstan wandered after them.

Before Rueberry could leave, Urticacea plucked at his sleeve and said, "I never intended to harm her. One little pea, under all those mattresses. Who'd have thought she'd even notice it? Let alone . . . ?"

Rueberry had no sympathy for her. "You had to have known that if she was a princess, she'd know." He sailed out.

In the corridor, he heard her say, "But under all those mattresses?"

♱

B ERENGARIA LAY IN the small, and above all low, bed. Red velvet curtains hung around the bed, and, she knew from when she'd first come in the room, over the windows, blocking most of the bright sunshine. Here the shadows weren't gloomy. They weren't dark enough for that.

Most of the dust had been chased from the room, so Berengaria knew someone had been sleeping here recently, but she was so grateful to be out of that awful tall bed, she hadn't asked who. Crisp linens had been placed on the bed, just for her. She never wanted to touch silk again, though now that she was a princess, she'd probably have to, it had to be a requirement of some sort.

She was a princess, a real princess. They'd all said so. Berengaria snuggled happily under the covers, glad to finally know who she was. Princess Berengaria of Perideridia sighed contentedly.

Magic coursed through her, making her itch. She'd always thought magic should make you tingle and glow, but the healing spells the wizards had used merely made her itch. Even that couldn't bother her. She'd done it. She'd proved she was a princess. She had everything she had ever hoped for.

Tears filled her eyes and ran hotly down her cheeks. They might have said she was a princess, but she knew she hadn't felt any pea. Certainly not under all those mattresses and feather beds and blankets. Yet they believed she had and proclaimed her a princess.

Perhaps if they didn't know. If she never told the truth, how would they know? The problem was, she'd know.

Berengaria wanted desperately to be a princess. She'd wanted it as long as she could remember. Not just the clothes and the tall pointed hats and the jewels and the dancing and the romancing, she wanted the respect and the dignity and the confidence.

Lumbering footsteps outside the velvet curtains indicated the chubby wizard had entered her room.

"I've brought you some nourishing soup," he announced just before he opened the curtains. He'd set a tray down on a small chest next to the bed. "Whenever you feel up to eating, it'll be right here." He reached over to wipe away one tear. "Don't worry, Your Highness, you'll be feeling better in no time. The curse may have warped Mazigian's speech, but he's still a dab hand with a spell. You eat a little, and get some rest. I have to take some breakfast up to Vevila, but we'll be back to check on you."

He smiled, waved, and bowed before backing out of the room.

A creamy, savory odor filled the room. Berengaria guessed the soup was the sort usually described as thick, hearty, chunky, or some other robust-sounding adjective designed to disguise the fact that it was filled with fat and starch and could probably keep a village of peasants going for a week.

Sure enough, when she'd finally levered herself up and lifted the spoon from the bowl, the soup proved to have the consistency of very thin pudding, with unidentifiable lumps and clumps hiding in the depths.

A cup of steeped herbs sat steaming next to the soup, but, most encouragingly, just beyond that, a full bottle of wine waited.

Hitherto, Berengaria had despised people who drank to excess over their problems. With temptation before her, she felt a new pity for them, an understanding. Still, she couldn't let Agnes down, the only mother she'd ever known.

She'd eat the nourishing soup, drink the medicinal tea, and have only a cup or two of the wine. A medicinal cup. To steady her nerves and give her strength to recover.

❧

IN THE SWAMPY area to the west of a long, blue, triangular lake, an odd little man in a black cape, befeathered brown felt hat, gold vest, dark green tunic, purple trousers, and battered brown boots sat in the crook of the roots of a willow tree on a dry island, staring intently at a clear crystal ball cradled in his hands. He stroked the ball, smiling happily.

"All in all, everything went very well last night," he said. "Now there are two princesses in the castle. Two more than there were two days ago. I put a spell on the strongest-willed person in the castle, to increase their will, which I believe is fighting Urticacea's spell. Unless I miss my guess, the number of new princesses discovered every day is about to reach a critical point." He grinned out at the swamp. "We are close. So very close."

An insect buzzing nearby found its life suddenly interrupted by a hungry frog. The other insects continued buzzing. Far away, a morning bird chirped.

"Well, not today. Vevila still has one more night of spinning straw into gold before she is proclaimed a princess. And Berengaria is in no shape to kiss princes." The odd little man looked back down at his crystal ball for a moment before continuing. "Why should my interference make a difference? They all have to know the only way to turn straw into gold is magic, not spinning. The wizards certainly have no objection. Prince Althelstan already thinks Vevila should rightfully be a princess. Urticacea set the rules. If this isn't what she wanted, she should have made more stringent rules. I have no sympathy for her."

Out on the lake, a flock of snow-white swans landed and sailed across the smooth, pristine blue surface, leaving elegant, sparkling wakes behind them.

"One more day," he said. "Just one more day, and we can fight for what is ours." His fist tapped the crystal ball gently, and he set it aside in the hollow of a convenient root. Standing, he tossed his brown felt hat up to disappear in midair.

Taking off his cape, he said, "As for me, I'm going to get some well-deserved sleep. I'll set the crystal to wake me if anything happens."

He ran one hand briefly over the crystal ball, then lay down on a soft hillock of grass between two roots, pulling the cape over him like a blanket. In the swamp near his feet, a frog croaked mournfully.

"Just one more day." He sniffed the fragrant grasses under his nose. "I promise. One more day, and we'll be swimming in princesses. Nothing can stop us once we've removed the curse. Nothing."

U SING A SQUATTING shoulder lift, Prince Althelstan removed the heavy oak bar from the door of Vevila's cell. Setting the bar against the wall, he opened the cell door. "All right. Do you remember where you found the dress yesterday?"

"No," Vevila said. "Do you?"

In the instant Althelstan opened his mouth to answer, he realized he was being mocked. Vevila stepped out of the cell and started down the hall. Althelstan followed.

"They said I wasn't to let you out of my sight today."

Vevila turned around swiftly. "Do you plan to play ladies' maid to me?"

"No," he said, shocked.

"Then I'll have to be out of your sight at some point." Vevila started back down the hall.

Althelstan decided against trying any more conversation with her. She seemed to be in one of her moods. He wandered behind her as she searched through several rooms, rooting through various chests, stirring up dust and moths and discarding any number of what appeared to him to be perfectly acceptable dresses. She left a royal mess in her wake, but Althelstan decided it wasn't his place to make her clean up or to pick up after her.

What this castle really needed was servants. Not sleeping servants, but actual working servants. He wondered if he should speak to Urticacea about it. Realizing the futility of that, he pressed on in Vevila's tracks.

"Didn't these women do anything except go to parties?" Vevila muttered as she flung several fluffy dresses onto the floor of a large, abandoned bedchamber.

"I don't know," Althelstan said.

"I wasn't asking you." She pulled out some velvet doublets and hose. Holding them up for Althelstan's inspection, she asked, "Think I could wear these?"

"I don't care. But I don't think the witch would approve." He thought a moment. "Or your mother."

"Who cares what they think?" she demanded.

"Does anyone's opinion matter to you?" Althelstan asked.

"No."

"Then why did you ask my opinion?"

Mysteriously, Vevila threw the clothes back into the chest and stalked out of the room. After opening several doors and not entering the rooms, she asked, "Do other people's opinions matter to you?"

"Yes. Usually."

She stopped, with her hands on her hips. "Do you think I'm a princess?"

"Yes. Of course."

"Then let me kiss the princes. Everyone will wake up, and this will be over."

"Well. But. It's just." Althelstan waved his arms, trying to get them to convey what he thought. The words finally came to him. "Urticacea doesn't. The wizards don't."

Vevila leaned toward him. "The wizards believe I'm a princess; trust me. They just want the gold. Even Urticacea believes I'm a princess. She doesn't want anyone, certainly not some princess who wandered in, waking her precious princes to the evil world. She knows if I kissed them, they'd wake up. It's what she fears most."

Althelstan wavered. Vevila sounded so certain, but then she always did. Especially just before she talked him into something that got him into trouble.

"Tomorrow," he promised.

She sighed and walked away.

"Why don't you wear one of the doublets?" he said, hoping a peace offering would help her mood.

"They were several sizes too big."

"Oh."

The next room wasn't as spacious as the one with the doublets, but it was large. South-facing windows framed a rose-colored brass bed. A tall mirror hung on the wall by a tall chest of drawers. Rows of perfumes and spiced oils in bottles stood behind bits of jewelry on a lace doily on top of the chest of drawers. A carved cedar chest rested at the foot of the bed.

While Vevila opened the cedar chest, Althelstan examined the perfumes and oils. The first bottle he opened held captive the scent of lavender. The next released the odor of cloves, the next roses. It took him a moment to notice Vevila watching him.

"What?" he asked.

"I was just wondering if this might not be Jaquenetta's room." She held up a blue and gray dress. "Does this look like hers?"

The dress had simple lines, no lace, and little in the way of frills. Puffy elbow-length sleeves, one gray and one blue, attached to their opposite color on the scooped neckline, and a small silver cord belt hung ready to cinch the wearer's waist. He tried mentally comparing it to the dress Jaquenetta wore now. They both had the same simple lines and few frills. They were both of subdued colors, this one blue and gray, the one she wore a faded rose. But paling colors could be merely the ravages of time, and all the dresses in the castle were old-fashioned.

Althelstan looked the room over again. It could be

Jaquenetta's room. He shrugged, trying to appear unconcerned. "I suppose it's possible."

Her room. He could be in her room. Those could be her
clothes, her bed, her mirror, her perfumes.

"Would you mind?" Vevila asked, holding up the dress
again.

"Mind what?"

"Mind if I wear the dress?"

"Oh." He set the perfume down quickly. "Oh, no. I'll be
outside, waiting."

Vevila wore the blue and gray dress when she emerged
from the room. "I'd like to see her again."

"Who?"

"Jaquenetta." Vevila smiled up at him. "If she's going to
be family, I'd like to get to know her."

"Certainly." Althelstan practically floated off the floor
with happiness. Any excuse to go see Jaquenetta was welcome, and he did so want his family to like her.

In the waiting room, the king and his guards continued
their incessant snoring. Althelstan headed straight for
Jaquenetta. He picked up her hand and kissed it in greeting. Did he imagine it, or did he actually detect a faint trace
of rose perfume on her wrist?

"She is pretty, I suppose," Vevila said. When he
frowned, she added, "I'm not a very good judge of feminine beauty."

Althelstan nodded. "I think she's very beautiful."

"Nice . . . tiara." Vevila idly wandered from sleeper to
sleeper, as if checking to make sure they were still alive.
"Would you mind if I . . ." She pointed at the ceiling.

"What?"

"Go upstairs and have a look around."

"Why?"

Vevila frowned at him, as if he were a simpleton. "I'm going to have to kiss them tomorrow. I'd at least like to re-assure myself that they aren't hideously ugly."

"I don't think they're too bad," Althelstan hedged. He knew the witch and the wizards didn't want Vevila around the princes. He knew they feared she'd kiss the princes. However, he wasn't sure this was such a bad idea. And she could make nearly anything sound so reasonable that he always found himself wondering exactly where he stood on the particular issue under discussion.

"But, as I recall," Vevila edged toward the stairs, "They looked awfully young."

He maneuvered to block her access to the stairs. "Yes. I agree. They did." Althelstan looked over to his beautiful Jaquenetta. "They looked younger than her, but she's sup-posed to be younger than them." It was a puzzler.

"Let's check again," Vevila said in her most reasonable voice, urging him up the stairs ahead of her.

The moment Vevila put a foot on the stairs, Urticacea appeared in the doorway at the top of the stairs above them.

"Where do you think you're going?" she demanded.

"We're checking to see how ugly the princes are," Vevila said, peeking out from behind Althelstan. "And to see who is older, Princess Jaquenetta or the princes."

Urticacea braced her arms on either side of the stairwell and shouted, "The prince is a handsome young man. Good and clean and bright. Not like you. Kissing him would be an honor. And I'm reserving that honor only for the best, a real princess, true and honorable. And you're not a real princess."

Vevila slid between Althelstan and the wall and ran up the steps. "Yes, I am a princess. It's what you fear most, because you know that if I kiss the princes—right now or at any time, they will wake up, and you'll lose your power over them and this castle."

With a startling swiftness, Vevila put her hands against the witch's shoulders and pushed the witch back into the room. Vevila darted past. Urticacea grabbed onto Vevila's dress, and they fell, rolling out of Althelstan's line of sight.

He raced up the stairs to find them rolling on the floor, slapping, clawing, pulling, and screeching.

"Ladies! Ladies!" he shouted.

They ignored him.

"That's enough!" Althelstan leaned down and picked them up, one in each hand. He pulled them apart, slowly but inexorably.

"Ugly, nasty witch!"

"Why, you common little shrew!"

Vevila lunged for the nearest sleeping prince. Urticacea howled and clawed at Vevila's dress.

Althelstan put one woman under each arm and carried them down the stairs to the waiting room. The howling and screaming from the women drowned out the snores of the king and his guards.

"Ladies!" Althelstan wanted to let them go—they were getting rather heavy to carry around—but they hadn't shown any sign that they were calming down. "Ladies!"

"What is going on?" Zenpfennig roared.

The three wizards stood in the doorway to the lower stairs of the waiting room.

The women screeched and yelled various explanations and excuses and deprecations. Althelstan decided not to try to compete with their combined lung power and merely tottered from side to side, so that the wizards could better hear first one then the other of the women.

Mazigian hurried over, hands outstretched toward Vevila. "I'll take this ring from you," he shouted over the din.

Althelstan turned, presenting Mazigian with Urticacea, shouting, "Take the witch."

"Do not draw back your hand; I'll take no more," Mazigian said, as he tried to walk around Althelstan to Vevila. "And you in love shall not deny me this."

Urticacea scratched out at Vevila, who shouted back, "Evil witch! You know I'm a princess."

"Oh yes I shall." Althelstan turned to keep the witch toward Mazigian, ending up spinning in place with Mazigian running in circles.

"I will have nothing else but only this," Mazigian panted as he chased around.

"Bawdy shrew!" screamed Urticacea. "Weedy common wench!"

"Take the witch!" Althelstan hoped that his dizzy breathlessness didn't mar his attempt at a regal order.

Vevila took advantage of the spinning, planted her feet solidly, and pushed Althelstan off balance. She grabbed onto Mazigian to keep herself up, letting Althelstan and Urticacea fall to the floor. She jerked her arm out of Mazigian's grasp and ran for the stairs, with Mazigian in hot pursuit.

Althelstan hurriedly gained his feet, leaving a stunned and breathless Urticacea sprawled on the dusty floor, and ran after them.

Mazigian managed to stop Vevila at the top of the stairs by catching her ankle. She screamed as she fell. Althelstan tried to ease past, while Mazigian dodged the swift, vicious kicks of her free foot, tenaciously hanging on.

"Let me go, you idiot!" Vevila screamed.

"Perhaps we should let her go kiss the princes," Althelstan said to Mazigian. "What could it hurt?"

"Ay, marry," Mazigian said wearily, letting go of Vevila. "I'll be gone about it straight." He slid bumpily down a few wooden steps, resting.

A strange dizzying confusion came over Althelstan. He reached out for the solid stone wall to steady himself, but it wasn't there. He shook off the confusion and found himself standing in the middle of the waiting room; Mazigian prone on the floor at his feet; Vevila nearby, leaning over, preparing to kiss thin air.

"Enough!" Zenpfennig stood in the doorway with arms upraised, frowning severely. Rueberry and Urticacea stood wide-eyed on either side of him. Zenpfennig made a banishing motion at the sputtering, angry Vevila, and she vanished. As Mazigian clambered to his feet, Zenpfennig turned the full force of his frown on Althelstan and Mazigian. "She cannot kiss the princes until after she finishes her princess test."

"Why?" Althelstan shouted defensively, not precisely certain what he was defending himself against.

"We have to know that she is truly a princess." Zenpfennig's frown lessened somewhat, but his smug self-assurance irritated just as much.

"Isn't a princess still a princess even if someone doesn't know she's a princess?" Althelstan asked.

Zenpfennig's gaunt face wrinkled up in furious thought. "What?"

"If a princess goes out in disguise, she's still a princess, right?" Althelstan looked to Mazigian for support, finding only confusion and tiredness. "If a princess meets someone who doesn't know she's a princess, she's still a princess, correct?"

"In some senses yes, in others no." Zenpfennig's wrinkles smoothed out as he put on his senior lecturer's face. "She would still carry her innate princessliness within her, but being a princess is also a job, a profession, if you will. If she is not acting in her capacity as a princess, she is also not a princess. If a princess were to disguise herself as a shepherdess and go out among the common people acting as a shepherdess, then she would in fact be a shepherdess. Since she was acting in the role of shepherdess. She could not, at that point, act in any capacity as a princess without ceasing to be a shepherdess."

It was Althelstan's turn to frown while thinking furiously. "So what you're saying is that the disguised princess was really a shepherdess, but she would return to being a princess when she stopped being a shepherdess."

"Yes, exactly." Zenpfennig sounded like a professor pleased with a particularly bright student.

"But, then coming back to Vevila's case, if she is in fact a true princess, even though we may not know that, if she acted in the capacity of a true princess, she would get the results of a true princess." Althelstan watched as his listeners started working that out in their heads. "In other words, if she's a true princess, even if we don't know that, were she to kiss the princes as a true princess, the princes would wake up. Am I right?"

"No," Urticacea said firmly. "That would make kissing the prince a princess test, not the act of a true princess. Until we know for certain that she is a true princess, we'll just have to wait."

Rueberry shook his head gently. "No, Prince Althelstan is right. Kissing the princes would be the act of a true princess, and the princes would awaken."

"No, no, no!" Urticacea began jumping up and down in

anger. "She can't kiss the princes until we know for certain." She calmed down and, looking slyly at Zenpfennig, said, "She'll just have to spin straw into *gold* one more night, so that we can be certain."

Zenpfennig nodded judiciously. "The princes would only awaken if she is a real, true princess. Otherwise, they won't. We'll just have to wait one more day."

Althelstan shrugged in surrender. "So, where is Vevila? Is she all right?"

"Oh certainly, she's perfectly fine," Zenpfennig said, smiling. "I just sent her back to her cell. She'll be safe there. No problems with that."

"I left the door open and unbarred," Althelstan said.

"I can take care of that." Zenpfennig fluttered his fingers arcanely and circled his arms.

❧

A N ODD LITTLE man sat in the shade of a willow tree, a black cape half covering him like a blanket, as he leaned toward a crystal ball resting in the hollow of an exposed root. He stroked it gently.

"She almost made it there. So very close." He lay back, with his hands behind his head, to stare up through the shifting willow branches at the blue sky. "I wish she had kissed those idiot princes."

In the quiet following his sigh, a splash rippled across the blue waters of the lake, the edges of the wave disappearing long before they reached the island marking the edge between the lake and the swamp.

"She's a very strong-willed woman," the odd little man said agreeably to the swaying branches. "Not your type, I know, but she'll do the job. Others might not."

Insects whined. Far-off birds called to one another.

"Oh, I doubt that. I mean, there's no law that says that just because she kisses someone she has to marry him. Even if the someone she kisses is under some sort of spell." He reached for the black cape, pulling it up to cover himself. He rolled onto his side, snuggling in comfortably. "That's just a convenient way to end all the folktales. Don't worry about it. I doubt she'll want to marry you, either."

Before the insects could resume their humming, the odd little man added, "And don't make any snide remarks. They wouldn't be appreciated right now."

⬥⬥⬥

VEVILA PACED THE length of her cell. The guttering torches cast weird, distorted shadows around the room. She wondered if she should try to escape through the door with the pick or if someone would be along soon to replace the torches. She didn't want her escape noticed too soon.

Then again, she didn't want to languish, forgotten, in a dark cell, either.

Idiots! Why couldn't they see what the evil witch was doing? Why couldn't they understand how easy it would be to end it all? Why did she have to be stuck in a castle whose only conscious inhabitants had straw for brains?

She couldn't blame Althelstan this time. At least he'd been willing to let her go ahead, kiss the princes, and see what happened. The problem was convincing the wizards. All they ever thought about was gold.

The witch had known exactly how to bait that trap.

Sighing, Vevila watched the fire on the first torch fade

down to nothing. She sat on the floor facing the other torches, wishing she'd attacked the door while she had time.

The second torch flickered out, and the third began to fade. Someone was bound to show up sooner or later. The fat wizard, Rueberry, always remembered her meals. She could count on that at least.

Vevila sat in the gathering gloom, holding tight to her pride and nursing vengeance.

❧

RUEBERRY SIGHED AS he carefully placed a bottle of dark wine on the wooden tray. He wasn't sure how this had become his job, other than the obvious fact that he was the only one awake in the castle who remembered to get regular meals.

He picked up a heavy, dark loaf of bread. The crust was nearly rock hard. He'd noticed a definite decline in the quality of the food in the cellars. He always returned to the same shelves—they seemed to refill themselves in his absence—but the food became coarser and cheaper with each trip.

Once he'd found hard cheeses, delicately aromatic and aging beautifully on the shelves; now all that remained was soft goat's cheese, odorous and recently made, too. Still, for a connoisseur such as himself, a well-made and spiced goat's cheese sufficed, though it did make him wonder about how exactly the castle restocked, maintained, and preserved itself.

A few scrawny pieces of dried fruit joined the other food on the tray. Rueberry arranged it as artfully as he could with his limited resources. Picking up the tray, he headed up for the kitchen, where Zenpfennig and Mazigian awaited him.

"What, finished already?" Zenpfennig sneered. "Why, anyone would think you'd just thrown the stuff slapdash on the tray."

Rueberry nearly stopped and set the tray down, but Zenpfennig turned smartly in a miffed whirl of robes, stirring up the dust, beckoning with a gnarled finger. "Come on."

Discovering Vevila's cell darkened, they feared she'd left again. However, once they'd relit the torches, they found her leaning against one wall, fast asleep, though thankfully not snoring. Rueberry settled the tray near her rolled-up pallet so she wouldn't accidentally knock it over in her sleep. They tiptoed out.

"We'll need a high spot for our next attempt. It's time for brute force. We'll pit our wills against hers," Zenpfennig said as they walked down the hall after replacing the bar on Vevila's cell. "The highest room seems to be the prince's sleeping room." He stroked his long, white beard with one bony hand. "Though perhaps that might not be the best place to work from. It's the center of her sleeping spell on the castle, her strongest and longest spell, and as such would be the most likely place to unweave her spell, but it is also the most guarded place here."

Tugging on the dangly portion of Zenpfennig's dark sleeve, Rueberry said, "Perhaps out of the castle, outside even of the surrounding thorns, might be the best place. Somewhere outside of the influence of her strongest spell."

"The idea has merit. We'll try there first." Zenpfennig nodded judiciously, not so much that Rueberry would consider thinking himself as smart as Zenpfennig. Rueberry knew better than that.

Zenpfennig, possibly out of malice, burned the path wider through the thorns and bramble as they left the castle. Though he was careful to burn behind them, so they didn't have to contend with the heat and smoke and soot as they walked.

Standing just beyond the smoldering path and thick green bramble, the wizards paced out their positions. Mazigian stood in the center, facing back down the path toward the castle, with Zenpfennig and Rueberry on either side of him, facing toward him. Simultaneously, they took a deep breath, then assumed a strange stance: eyes closed, arms upraised, fingers spread as if they were pushing against something. All six eyes snapped open at the same moment, and each wizard's mouth drew back in a wild grimace that might have been a grin—or it might not.

A bizarre ululating groan, starting softly, arose between them and became a great roar. The thorny vines and bramble nearest them trembled. The air itself wavered.

"Argh!" Zenpfennig slapped his hands against his thighs. "Her will has become harder than the very stones of the castle, by sheer force of years. The unthinking solidity of blind tradition is on her side."

Mazigian slumped. "So is the will of a living daughter curbed by the will of a dead father."

"At least try to misquote the poxed play!" Zenpfennig shouted angrily.

"We'll have to try it at the height of her power," Rueberry said. "Perhaps if she has to choose between preserving the castle and the sleeping princes, and preserving the curse she put on us—"

"She'll choose the castle," Zenpfennig said. "Come along."

They stood in the open gates a moment, debating which

of the towers had the highest turret. The green vines covering all made the selection difficult. In the end, they decided that the one with the sleeping princes was indeed the highest, but only by a little. Another branching of the same tower had a turret nearly as high.

Rueberry assumed they'd merely hike up to the room, but as they walked through the twisting labyrinth of the castle, he realized the vines weren't the only difficulty masking the exact layout of the castle. They climbed another musty spiraling set of stairs near the waiting room. At the top, they found a tiny antechamber leading to a good-sized, vine-covered balcony overlooking most of the castle and surrounding countryside.

Zenpfennig decided the matter immediately. "This is it." He paced the length of the balcony, ripping vines from their moorings and tossing them aside to hang down like fragrant streamers from the balcony railing. He pointed his long, gnarled finger and said, "Rueberry, there. Mazigian, there. Focus outward, to her spell over the castle, along with the curse. Let's . . . rattle these stones."

The three wizards stood, eyes closed, arms upraised, fingers spread as if they were pushing something. Again their eyes snapped open, feral grins spread over their faces, and a ululating moan rose around them. The vines billowed out, streaming ones fluttering in the nonexistent wind. The air trembled. The roar of their massed wills rolled out away from them, echoing back from other towers and turrets.

A sharp pounding of triumph shuddered through them before fading, and they renewed the force of their spell. Again a bolt of triumph ran through them, only for a moment. The third time, the balcony shook beneath them, throwing them off their feet and breaking their spell.

The three felt a fourth quake and recognized it as some other assault on the castle's spell.

"What was that?" Zenpfennig bellowed. "We almost had it, except for that."

"No," Rueberry said without thinking. "Whatever it is, it's not directed against the whole castle, just a small portion of it."

"Let's find it." Zenpfennig jumped to his feet from the leaf-littered balcony and hurried off into the castle.

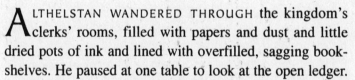

A LTHELSTAN WANDERED THROUGH the kingdom's clerks' rooms, filled with papers and dust and little dried pots of ink and lined with overfilled, sagging bookshelves. He paused at one table to look at the open ledger.

A largish black splotch of ink covered one corner of a right-hand page, all but gluing the quill to the paper. Prior to the ink spot, the writer had made neat, even lines of tiny, scrunched-up scrawlings.

It took Althelstan a moment before he could be certain that this was someone's diary. Not, unfortunately, some interesting someone with a flair for the dramatic and very little sense, who would get into exciting incidents and bold peccadilloes. No, this diary belonged to a hardworking, plodding clerk who found great satisfaction in tables well tallied and minutiae properly recorded.

Flipping a few pages back and sneezing out the resultant dust, Althelstan determined that indeed this clerk defined dull. He started to set the book back down, when a number interrupted the flow of the words on the page.

He looked closely and read, "After six years, His

Majesty despairs of ever finding the key to awakening his son."

Six years! Urticacea hadn't mentioned that little tidbit of information. How many years had passed until the whole castle had been sent to sleep?

Reskimming the diary with all the verve of a younger brother looking for the good parts of his sister's diary for schoolyard publication, Althelstan devoured what information he could glean from the diary. Setting it aside on a freshly cleared spot on the table, he rooted through the rest of the room, looking for diaries and ledgers and clues.

Leaving the room in a terrible mess, except for the neat pile of papers and ledgers he'd carefully placed on the cleared spot on the table, Althelstan stepped back into the other clerks' rooms, intent on documental mayhem.

He found a few more journals of interest in the King's Records Room, and added them to his pile.

It appeared that the princes' sleep predated the castle's sleep by eight years. Long enough for Princess Jaquenetta to catch up and pass her brothers' apparent age.

Vevila was right, Urticacea was an evil, evil witch.

A magical shudder shook the castle. Althelstan steadied his pile of documents. At the second shudder, he picked them up and walked out of the room.

Magic or no, it was time to confront Urticacea with more evidence of her perfidy.

The next two magical quakes didn't even slow Althelstan down as he stalked through the dusty, abandoned halls of the castle, though he did use the quakes to orient himself.

Wherever the quakes were strongest, there he would find the witch.

WHEN VEVILA AWOKE, the torches in her cell were
again burning brightly. Someone, probably the wizards, had brought her a tray of food. This time, they'd left
the whole bottle.

Vevila scooted over to the tray. Once she'd broken the
tough bread crust with her new shovel, it turned out to be
fairly soft, dark, and grainy inside. And it went rather well
with the spiced goat cheese. The wine, however, was kissing cousins with tongue-twisting vinegar. It discouraged
her from getting drunk.

She tried her pick on the soft, loose mortar deep in the
cracks she'd dug around the one stone of her cell. As she'd
guessed, the builders hadn't used as strong a mortar or as
much as they should've in that spot.

After a bit, she took one of the torches from its sconce
to check the depth of her digging. Time and distance were
difficult to gauge in the quiet stillness of her cell.

Uncertainly, she decided that she probably still had a
way to go before she reached the other side of the stone.
Vevila didn't want to wait until tonight, or worse, tomorrow morning, to escape her dreary, confining cell. She
wanted out now.

Returning the torch to its sconce, Vevila eyed the door.
It looked stout and strong, but she knew it splintered if she
pulled at pieces of it. Was the strength an illusion Urticacea
maintained over the castle? Was the castle, in fact, falling
apart around them, held together by the witch's spell?

Time to find out.

Vevila hefted her pick. Both ends had been dulled and
scratched with use against the crumbly mortar, but the
metal looked sound enough, and the handle appeared solid

and strong. Hopefully the odd little man was the sort who only dealt in the best when it came to presents.

He'd given her tools. A lopsided grin stole across her face. He hadn't given her jewelry or fripperies or flowers. She shuddered at the thought of roses. He'd given her something useful. Something potentially dangerous. Vevila couldn't help admiring that in a man. It showed a certain level of confidence and perhaps recklessness. A certain adventurousness that appealed to her.

Dangerous, reckless, adventurous, that was the sort of life she wanted.

Of course, he popped in and out as he pleased, but wouldn't do the same for her. Which was irritating.

The witch was to blame for that, Vevila was sure. She hefted the pick again, swinging it experimentally.

Taking up a position by the door, Vevila swung her pick as hard as she could into the thick wooden door of her cell, at the level of the bar on the other side.

She was getting out of here now!

A loud clang, as of metal on metal, rang out. Wisps and sparks of magic flew out from the door. The castle shook.

Levering the pick out of the door, Vevila watched happily as the wood splintered and tore as easily as old rotted boards. She took aim for the other metal bracket holding the bar on the other side of the door and struck again.

A shudder ran down her arms from the pick. Wisps, sparks, clang, and quake remained the same.

Vevila ripped the pick from the splintery wood triumphantly. She was leaving.

As she watched, a swirl of colored magic smoke writhed over the door. The gashes she'd torn into the door disappeared, leaving only a lingering red smoke and a hint of oak sap in the air.

"Not this time, you whey-faced witch," Vevila shouted as she reared back with the pick again. "I'm leaving now!"

She attacked the door again, digging in deeply with the pick, ripping great chunks from the worm-eaten wood, and screaming.

Again the castle shook. Her arms were jolted violently. But Vevila didn't hear the clanging of metal against metal. Magic smoke covered the door, healing the breaches she'd made nearly as fast as she made them.

The smoke hung heavy and thick in the air, making it difficult for Vevila to see to aim at the door again. She set the pick on the floor, behind the spinning wheel, and stared at the smoke-covered door, thinking.

The peephole opened, but Vevila couldn't see who was on the other side. They obviously couldn't see her, either. Vevila heard some muttering, and the smoke cleared away.

Urticacea's ugly, wrinkled face appeared in the small, square peephole. Her voice was shaky and scared when she demanded, "Who is in there with you?"

"I assure you, I am completely alone," Vevila said regally. "As you quite well know."

"Liar!" the witch shouted. "Either someone is in there with you, or you are practicing magic. And everyone knows royalty isn't permitted to practice magic."

Vevila sneered haughtily at the reddened, scrunched up wrinkles surrounding a bloodshot brown eye in the peephole. "I am alone, and I have never practiced magic."

"You were battering the door with magic." The eye disappeared from the peephole and was replaced with a moving view of portions of the old witch as she jumped up and down. "I felt it. Everyone in the castle felt it. You can't deny it. You're no princess."

Putting her mouth to the peephole to shout, Vevila said,

"I was battering the door with my anger and determination to get out of here, nothing more. It isn't my fault if your spell comes apart at the least bit of opposition. I have never practiced magic, and I am, too, a princess."

"Lying shrew! Vicious wench!" Bony, withered fingers clutched the bottom of the peephole, as Urticacea pulled herself up to shout back at Vevila. "You used magic."

"Lying witch!" Vevila reached out quickly, grabbing the witch's nose and squeezing. "You're a stupid old bat, a has-been witch that can't even hold onto her own spells anymore. You are an evil, wicked, nasty, ugly, manipulative, untrustworthy woman. And none of that is my fault. I am a princess, true and honorable. And you have no right to keep me in this cell."

Urticacea screamed incoherently and batted at Vevila's arm, sticking out of the peephole into the hallway. Vevila had to let go when the witch had moved farther away than she could reach.

"I have every right, you vicious vixen," the witch shouted, while swatting at Vevila's arm. "You come here to this beautiful, pristine castle, bringing your evil, wicked ways, wanting to corrupt my precious princes. I should lock all of you up!"

Pulling her arm back out of the peephole, Vevila said, "Why don't you tell Prince Althelstan that? Or maybe the wizards? I'm sure they'd find your opinions fascinating."

"Wicked, wicked girl!" the witch shouted. "You'll never kiss my sweet prince. You'll never be a princess. You'll never get out of that cell! I'll make certain of it."

"Don't count on it." Vevila clutched the bottom edge of the peephole. "You can hardly maintain the spell to keep the people sleeping in this castle."

"The sleeping spell doesn't have to be maintained," Urticacea sneered. "Once in place, the only thing that can break that sort of spell is the accomplishment of the termination clause." She walked so close to the door that all Vevila could see through the peephole was the top of the old witch's flyaway gray hair. "For you fools, with no wisdom and little understanding, the only way to break the sleeping spell is a princess kissing the prince."

"Then how was it that I could almost shout my way out of this cell door?" Vevila bellowed.

"Keeping the people asleep is one spell. Protecting and maintaining the castle is another," the witch said.

"And you're not up to it, are you? You've spent so much time around sleeping people with no will of their own that you can't handle the least bit of opposition."

"Why, you!"

The peephole door closed, nearly catching Vevila's fingers. She examined her fingers carefully before remembering that the door wasn't as solid and strong as it looked. Balling her hand up in a fist, Vevila punched the peephole door.

Smoke curled up around the arm sticking through the door. Urticacea screamed.

"Let me out!" Vevila shouted.

"Vile, evil girl! You'll never get out!" Urticacea batted at Vevila's hand, landing several stinging blows.

Running footsteps echoed loudly down the hall, above the women's screeching. Vevila heard the thump of a stack of papers on the floor.

"Stop that!" Althelstan shouted. He hauled the witch away from the cell door.

Pulling her arm back into the cell and peeking out, Vevila watched him drag the witch over to a haphazard pile of papers, crushing curls of dust off to one corner of the wall.

"Jaquenetta is a princess!" Althelstan flourished a page under Urticacea's nose. "I have the proof. The princes were asleep for eight years before you put the rest of the castle to sleep. She is the princes' younger sister, even if she looks older, and she is the product of a lawful marriage. So there!"

Urticacea waved a finger at Vevila. "That woman is trying to break down the cell door. She wants to escape."

"Of course she does. She hates being trapped anywhere." Althelstan leaned down to pick up a few folios and some loose sheaves of paper. "I'm here to talk to you about your behavior. Princess Jaquenetta could have awoken her brothers years ago. You put her and the rest of the castle to sleep to prevent her from doing it. That's, that's . . ." He waved the papers through the dust motes in the air. "Wrong. It's wrong. That's all there is to it."

"She's been using magic," Urticacea shouted. "That proves she's not a princess."

"Lying witch!" Vevila hollered back.

"Rubbish." Althelstan barely spared Vevila a glance. "I know for a certainty she can't do magic. Vevila's a princess. That's not the point. The point is you've been exerting more power—political power and territorial influence—than is permitted. It's unlawful and immoral to use magic to maintain political power, but that's exactly what you are doing."

"Vile . . ." Urticacea recoiled from Prince Althelstan. "I'm only protecting my precious prince."

"Precious princes, ha!" shouted Vevila. "You're an evil power-grabbing witch!"

"And Jaquenetta is, too, a princess!" Althelstan waved his handful of documents.

Vevila heard more running footsteps, heralding the appearance of the wizards. Finally, maybe with the witch cornered by all of them, Vevila hoped she'd be able to make the wizards see sense.

"What is going on?" Zenpfennig stood straight, trying to cover his panting.

"Jaquenetta is a princess!" Althelstan bellowed.

"That girl's no princess!" Urticacea shouted. "She's been using magic."

Althelstan again waved his documents. "How could she use magic? She's asleep."

"Not that girl." Urticacea pointed at Vevila's cell door. "That girl."

"Liar!" Vevila shouted through the ruins of the peephole.

"Then how do you explain what you did to the door?" The witch jumped up and down.

"I just hit it. Like this." Vevila pulled back her fist and rammed it into the very solid, hardwood door.

Odd lights played in front of Vevila's eyes, against a deep black background. Her legs could no longer hold her up, and she collapsed to the floor, cradling her hand. A high, loud keening noise rose and fell around her, and it took her several moments to realize she was making the noise.

"Are you all right?" a voice at the peephole asked.

Vevila took a deep breath to stop crying, blinking her eyes to clear them of tears. She rocked gently back and forth, holding her throbbing hand and arm close to her chest.

The door opened, slowly nudging her aside. The three

wizards, Althelstan, and Urticacea all crowded in the doorway, looking down at her.

Blinking up at them, Vevila said, "The last time I hit the door, it just splintered." She looked down at her swelling hand. "I thought it had probably rotted with the years, and the witch was only making it appear strong."

Zenpfennig cleared his throat. "We were attempting to undo her spell on the castle. Perhaps for a short while there, the door would have been old and rotted." Mazigian knocked on the door, and Zenpfennig reached over, stopping his hand. "Now, it's solid again."

"I noticed."

Rueberry placed his hand on her arm, murmuring something she couldn't understand. The pain ebbed away, and her knuckles returned to their normal size. He patted her on the head. "Rest your arm for a bit. It should be okay in a little while."

"We'll check it again when we bring the straw." Zenpfennig looked sincerely concerned. "I do hope this won't interfere with your ability to spin."

As he closed the door, Vevila could see the three wizards nodding earnestly, Urticacea looking smug, and Althelstan waving his documents again. She leaned back against the cool stone wall for a few minutes. The door showed no sign of her recent assaults on it; no gaping holes, no splinters, not the slightest a dent or nick. Even the peephole door was whole and solid and closed.

Her hand and arm were uncomfortably numb, and she felt drained of every last bit of energy and determination. Using her good arm and legs, she crawled over to her pallet, clumsily unrolled it, and curled up, exhausted.

A T THE WESTERN edge of a long, blue, triangular lake, an odd little man sat on a folded black cape covering a hillock of grass growing amongst the roots of a willow tree. He gently stroked a crystal ball.

"That hurt," he said to no one in particular. "That witch must have incredible reserves of will." He stood up, picking up his cape. "Don't worry, though. We'll win in the end. She's up against too much this time."

He walked to the other side of the willow tree, where the shadows were starting their early afternoon growth, and spread his black cape on the ground.

"It will all be over by tomorrow noon." He lay down on one side of the cape, pulling the other half over him as a blanket. "So little time. It's all downhill from now on; like an avalanche, there's nothing that can stop us."

The insects buzzed softly. He closed his eyes.

"By noon tomorrow."

❧

R UEBERRY HAD TO assist Mazigian to put the bar back in place on the cell door, because Althelstan wouldn't stop stirring up the dust with the papers he was waving.

"Jaquenetta is a princess. The princes were asleep for eight years before the rest of the castle joined them." Althelstan thrust some papers at Zenpfennig who, in surprised defense, took them. "She has been exerting undue political influence by means of her magic. She has taken over the governing of this kingdom without the consent of its rightful ruler or its inhabitants. And the kingdom has lost territory, power, and worth, all because of her machinations."

"Hmm." Zenpfennig stroked his long, white beard with

his gnarled fingers. "These are heavy offenses. Have you proof of your accusations?"

"No!" Urticacea shouted, while jumping up and down. "I admit to the eight years between spells, but I do not govern this kingdom, and the kingdom hasn't lost any territory, power, or worth. It never had any of those, except what is in and around this castle. The castle and grounds I have zealously guarded. And I have saved the castle untold amounts in upkeep and maintenance. So there!"

"Well." Zenpfennig looked pointedly at the door of Vevila's cell. "You will have saved that amount only if the castle doesn't rot immediately after the curse is removed."

"It's not a curse! It protects the castle and all within it." Urticacea balled her fists, glaring at Zenpfennig and Althelstan in turn. "And the castle won't rot."

Zenpfennig sneered down at her. "It will if what we've seen this afternoon is any indication."

Urticacea stormed off, muttering.

Turning to Althelstan, Zenpfennig said, "Of course Jaquenetta is a princess. We," he indicated himself and the other two wizards, "have always believed you on that. And we know that Urticacea has evilly manipulated events here." He gently pried the other documents from Althelstan's hands. "However, any documentation that could be useful in a Recondite University prosecution would be helpful."

"You may have them all." Althelstan hurried to get the rest of the documents from where they sat on the floor in the corner. "There's more where these came from. If I find any more, or anything else interesting, I'll bring them to you."

"Thank you."

It was said in such tones of dismissal that Althelstan

turned to go. He glanced back once, shrugged, and walked away. Zenpfennig leafed through the stack of folios, loose papers, and scrolls briefly.

"Perhaps we should have a look around ourselves." Zenpfennig turned and glided down the hall in the same direction Althelstan had taken. "This time, let's look for herbs, magical items, or anything that might turn up. Eh?"

Following him, Mazigian said, "Fish not with this melancholy bait."

"I disagree," Zenpfennig said. "We have tried concentrating our efforts. Perhaps we should diffuse our wagers, the better to find some return."

Rueberry trailed after them, hoping to convince them to detour for a search of the cellars. Instead, Zenpfennig seemed determined to do a systematic search through the entire castle. They picked up bits here and there: a magical amulet, a packet of herbs, an interesting document.

In the clerks' offices, the stacks and stacks of documents, loose papers, scrolls, ledgers, diaries, folios, and books, all covered in and recently mixed with dust, all but halted their rapid progress.

Mazigian looked about them in obvious dismay and murmured, "Come the full stop."

"This will take a while. Perhaps I should go find us some refreshment," Rueberry said to Zenpfennig.

For once, Zenpfennig just nodded in stunned awe. "Yes. Perhaps you'd better. We'll probably be here the better portion of this afternoon." He looked around again. "And tomorrow." He sighed. "And for many tomorrows to come."

U RTICACEA MUTTERED TO herself as she assembled a
few carefully chosen items on the rough wooden
table in her tiny garret room. She placed a stick of green
wood recently torn from a pine tree in the main courtyard—to represent the wood in and around the castle, the
trees, furniture, and doors—next to a small chip of stone—
to represent the stones and bricks of the castle—taken
from the flagstones of the walkway in the same courtyard.
She covered the stick and stone with a scrap of decaying
embroidered tapestry, representative of the castle's various
fabrics. A broken piece of crockery, a tiny shard of glass, a
small scrap of leather, and small lead ring joined the pile.

She sprinkled a pinch of dirt over everything, real dirt
from the yard, not just any old dust floating around the castle. She had no intention of preserving the dust.

A small red rose topped the pile, one petal falling dain-
tily off to rest in the crook of the ring.

Smiling lovingly down at the little heap, Urticacea
thought about the kingdom and people she had known and
protected for so very long. She wasn't about to let everything fall apart the minute her protective spell was broken,
whatever those greedy, misbegotten wizards might think.

Trying not to dwell on the fact that those same wizards
had pointed the problem out to her, Urticacea began her
spell.

❧

A LTHELSTAN CHECKED ON Berengaria. She was sleeping. He returned to Vevila's cell to peer through the
peephole. She was sleeping. Everywhere he went, everyone was sleeping. He couldn't find the wizards, and didn't

want to find the witch. With nothing else to do, he decided to go spend some time with Jaquenetta.

As Althelstan walked down a long hallway, he heard a deep thumping noise. He looked around but couldn't find any source for the sound.

Another deep thump echoed down the hall.

"Hello?" Althelstan shouted. "What are you up to now?"

His only answer was another thump.

He headed off in the direction he thought it had come from. It continued at intervals, allowing him to home in on it. Discovering to his surprise that the noise came from a large gong in the front receiving hall near the main door and gate.

Just as he stepped into the room, a large, matronly woman in a dark black velvet dress shot with silver threads beat the gong again. As the echoes masking his footsteps died away, she turned to frown at him.

"Well, there you are. I've been standing here beating this thing until I began to wonder if there was anyone about this castle at all, other than that fool who should have been terminated long ago for sleeping at his post, if not shot." She dusted her hands off against each other. "This place is in absolutely the worst state I've ever seen." She looked around as if evaluating the worth of each stone and as if disappointed to find them worth so little. "One does what one must, I suppose, but really. I must say you could put forth the effort to keep this place up."

The three wizards and Urticacea entered from different doorways at about the same time. The black-garbed woman glanced over at them and said imperiously, "You certainly took your time about getting here. One of you can go announce me to your king; the rest of you can return to your labors. Or at least," she sneered at the dusty tapestries and benches, "Pick a task, and do it."

"We're not—" Althelstan started to say, but she had no intention of letting him talk.

"Sloth and vice, I daresay." She looked at him with unconcealed loathing. "But that's the only sort of help that can be gotten in these trying times. Still, you should be ashamed of yourself. You could at least pretend to be cleaning, or take an ax out and pretend to be clearing that mess of a garden out there."

"Madam!" Zenpfennig shouted. "I am a graduate of and special investigator for the Recondite University. I do not clean or garden. Even in pretend."

Eyes widening in shock, the black-garbed woman pulled out a black lace handkerchief. She peered intently at Zenpfennig, Mazigian, and finally Rueberry, before she began laying about Rueberry's pointed hat, head, and shoulders with the handkerchief. Rueberry stood in stunned silence while dust flew in all directions. She stepped back to better observe her handiwork.

"My goodness. You are wizards." She held her handkerchief at arm's length and shook it. "Most difficult to tell beneath all that dust." She turned back to Althelstan. "Well, go announce me."

"I am Prince Althelstan of Portula." Althelstan couldn't help dusting his own shoulders off, if for no other reason than to keep the matron in black from attacking him with her black lace handkerchief.

She turned to Urticacea, who sniffed. The witch said, "I'm Urticacea. The prince's fairy godmother."

When the woman turned again to Althelstan, he held up both hands and said, "No. Not mine. She's the evil witch that cursed the castle and put everyone to sleep."

Urticacea started jumping up and down. "I'm not an evil witch! I'm protecting my precious prince."

"Mostly from the likes of us," Zenpfennig observed dryly.

"So it is true that this castle has been put to sleep?"

"Yes, she cursed the castle; everyone is asleep," Althelstan said.

"I'm protecting them," Urticacea shouted.

"And you are?" Rueberry asked before they could go too far on that well-worn tangent.

The black-garbed woman pulled herself up regally. "I am Dowager Queen Dulcamara Umbelliferae Columbiana of Nivalis. Recently widowed." She touched her black lace handkerchief unnecessarily to the corner of her eye. "I have two marriageable daughters, Princesses Stellaria and Gaulthemum. It is on their behalf that I have come here today." She sniffed. "You see, my husband, the late king of Nivalis, had only daughters. On his death, his brother inherited, and unfortunately, he and his brother quarreled most of their lives. Before my dear husband was even buried, my brother-in-law threw us out. Left us to our own devices. We've fallen on hard times. And so, it is for my dear, sweet daughters that I've come here today."

"Very well," Urticacea said. "Bring them in. I'll think of a couple more princess tests to pass them through." She held onto her head as if expecting it to explode at any moment.

"Certainly not!" Queen Dulcamara looked horrified. "I would never subject my daughters to anything so barbaric as a princess test. True princesses are known on sight, not by the use of some foolish test."

"Foolish test!" Urticacea shouted. "How else is anyone to know for certain that your daughters truly are princesses unless they pass a test? Kingdoms come and go. I've never heard of Nivalis."

"Nivalis is a fine, long-standing kingdom, with a great and illustrious history!" Dulcamara sneered down her nose at the witch. "Princess tests are notoriously used by cheats and frauds. Anyone can tell a princess, a real princess, a true princess, by looking at her."

"Poppycock!" spewed Urticacea.

"Don't be ridiculous," Dulcamara said haughtily.

"Well, they can't kiss the prince until they've proven themselves with a princess test." Urticacea folded her arms.

"Whatever are you talking about?"

Urticacea shook her head. "I'm not about to let your daughters in to kiss my prince on just your word that they are true, honorable princesses. No one but a true, honorable, real princess can kiss the prince and wake him up."

Taken aback, Dulcamara said, "I thought it was a princess sleeping in this castle, and princes were gathering to claim the honor of kissing her and waking her up."

"No," Althelstan said and sighed. "There's three princes in the tower that have to be kissed by a princess to wake the castle. We've been trying to sort things out. It's a long story."

"So the only princes here are sleeping?" Dulcamara asked.

Althelstan waved his hand. "I'm not asleep."

"This is so very distressing." Dulcamara fanned herself with her handkerchief. "I came here looking for spare princes. I wanted to invite them to a ball I am having this evening to introduce my daughters to the right sort of society." She leaned confidingly toward Urticacea. "There's so few princesses these days, I'm certain my daughters can make appropriate matches. I've invited all the princes from all the neighboring kingdoms, you know."

Still sputtering, Urticacea said, "Do you plan on testing to make sure they're real princes?"

"You can't be serious." Dulcamara drew back, closer to the wizards.

"A ball?" asked Rueberry hungrily.

"Yes." Dulcamara stepped back toward Althelstan and seemed to remember herself. She waved her handkerchief regally. "Of course, All Are Invited." With her other hand, she pulled a heavy card from another pocket. She held the gilt-edged ivory card out to Althelstan. "I do hope you all can make it."

She flounced out, as Althelstan looked at the card. On one side, elaborate gold calligraphy announced the ball; on the other, plain black ink detailed site and directions.

"Foolish tests!" muttered Urticacea. "Barbaric! Frauds and cheats! I'll show her."

"Now, now." Zenpfennig grabbed her wrists to stop her from throwing a spell. "There's no call for that."

"You heard what she said about princess tests." Urticacea jerked out of Zenpfennig's grasp. "Princess tests have a long and illustrious history. Without some way of testing and weeding out women who aren't princesses, we'd be hip deep in princesses."

Althelstan sighed with longing at the thought.

"Of course," Zenpfennig soothed. "Of course."

"There are prince tests, too," the witch said. "Not as many, and they're not as oftenly used, but they do exist."

"Yes." Zenpfennig stopped himself just short of patting her shoulder.

"How dare she belittle the honorable custom of princess tests." The old witch trembled all over. "She's probably not a real queen. Real queens know about and respect princess tests. Real queens made princess tests to protect their sons." She took a shaky step toward the door. "Nasty upstart woman. I'll give her—"

"Now, now." Zenpfennig deftly caught her arm and steered her back into the castle. "We shall all attend her little ball and see for ourselves if we can know at first glance that her daughters are princesses. That way we can keep an eye on things without actually interfering."

Zenpfennig motioned for the others to follow him. "We'll need some more appropriate clothing. Prince Althelstan, why don't you search for some. My colleagues and I shall prepare a coach and team to take us there." He pushed the witch gently down the corridor. "You should rest up. I understand it takes women time to prepare for these things."

The witch favored him with a withering glare. "I'll check on those other upstart princesses. See if Berengaria needs any more help healing. Or if Vevila needs to be put back in her cell."

"That's the ticket." Zenpfennig smiled hollowly. "We'll all meet back at the receiving room in," he snatched the invitation from Althelstan and examined it, "two hours." He nodded at Urticacea, handed the invitation back to Althelstan, and walked off, motioning for Rueberry and Mazigian to follow.

Urticacea glared at Althelstan.

"I'm not any happier about it than you are," Althelstan protested. "I just want to marry Jaquenetta. That's all I ever wanted, since I first saw her."

She sighed and turned to walk away. Althelstan wondered how it was that she could suddenly look so small and weak and old and tired.

He rubbed the rough paper invitation between his fingers. Why did the wizard expect he would know what appropriate clothes were for everyone? He guessed he'd just get the most elaborate outfits he could find. Remembering what Vevila had said about sizes, Althelstan realized the task would be harder than it seemed.

Too bad he didn't dare go ask her for help.

⟨≈⟩

URTICACEA HOBBLED THROUGH the castle, raising dust, and feeling stooped and weak. More princesses, how could there suddenly be so many more princesses? And why were all of them appearing on her doorstep to pester her prince?

The memory of Prince Althelstan accusing her of undue political influence made her revise her thoughts. It wasn't really her doorstep. The castle and kingdom belonged to King Lazare and ultimately would belong to her precious Prince Lucien. She was merely protecting them in the interim.

Before she left, she'd have to make certain that neither of the two princesses here in the castle could get in to kiss the prince. Berengaria hadn't shown any inclination to get up from her bed today, but it would be just the sort of perverse luck that seemed to have pervaded the last several days for Berengaria to suddenly decide to wander while everyone was out. And Vevila . . . Urticacea shuddered.

That one might not be a witch herself yet, but she managed to bring off an awful lot of magical occasions without the least effort. Urticacea feared what Vevila might be capable of, might accomplish if left to her own devices.

The old witch leaned on the carved wooden door to the

suite the wizards had been using to catch her breath and think things through. They'd stashed Berengaria in one of their rooms. Urticacea wondered if she could use innuendo and insults, implying something untoward between the girl and the wizards, to disqualify Berengaria as a princess.

She shook her head. That would be unfair and dishonorable. Besides, anyone simple enough to believe that a pea could cause injuries and bruising through twenty mattresses, twenty feather beds, and twenty silk blankets would be too simple to understand innuendo. Subtlety was definitely out in Berengaria's case.

Opening the door, Urticacea tiptoed into the suite. She couldn't remember which room they'd put the girl in, and checked an empty bedroom first before locating the right one.

Heavy red velvet curtains sheltered the bed but couldn't mask the even, deep breathing of someone sleeping. Urticacea had become so accustomed to it over the years that she almost forgot to draw aside the curtain and look for the girl.

Berengaria lay in the bed with the covers pulled to her chin, effectively hiding all the bruises. By concentrating and reaching a hand out toward the girl without touching her, Urticacea explored the healing spell and its effects.

The bruises on the girl's ribs and back were fading, her ankle was still giving her trouble, and her wrist ached, but recovery was progressing swiftly. By morning, the whole ordeal would be nothing more than a memory and the occasional twinge when the weather changed.

Urticacea tiptoed out. In the corridor, she paused to take a deep breath and steel herself before heading for Vevila's cell. She needn't have bothered. Vevila slept soundly—so soundly that Urticacea had to enter the cell and put a hand on Vevila's ribs to assure herself that Vevila still lived.

Her prince came next. The witch stared down at the three sleeping figures for a long while. They looked so gallant, serene, and peaceful in their elegant nightshirts with the Chateau-Arbre crest embroidered over the left breast. The coronets encircling their heads drew their honor from the gentle nobility of the young men that deigned to wear them.

She wished they were really young again, the noble little cherubs she had scooped up, fussed over, and made much of so long ago. She wished she could preserve them forever in their perfection, unspoiled, untouched by the evil and cares of the world. If only . . .

No sense wishing for what could never be.

Urticacea went quickly to work, spell-locking the door to the prince's room and setting various wards and guards over them. If either of those pretend princesses tried to sneak up here in the middle of the night, they'd be in for a big surprise.

☙❧

I DON'T THINK we'll find any horses or carriages down here," Zenpfennig said while looking around the pantry cellar disapprovingly.

"No." Rueberry reached for a small ham. "But we'll need a snack."

Zenpfennig sighed. "In my experience, horses are usually found just outside the door, waiting more or less patiently."

"Only if there are servants." Rueberry reluctantly put

the ham back and broke off a piece of cheese to hide in his robes. "Conscious and moving servants."

"There is that." Zenpfennig rounded on Mazigian, waiting patiently in the doorway. "Well, where would you think to find a carriage and horses?"

Mazigian pointed up, and Zenpfennig motioned impatiently.

Rueberry smiled, and held his torch aloft. "Lead on."

Frowning skeptically, Zenpfennig led the way up the cellar stairs to the kitchen.

"Isn't there usually some sort of connection between the kitchen and the stables?" Rueberry asked.

"Sounds unhygienic to me." Zenpfennig sneered down his nose at Rueberry.

"Not necessarily an immediate connection." Rueberry broke off a piece of cheese and popped it in his mouth. "But at least some sort of walkway or covered path. For the servants' convenience."

"Well, it certainly wouldn't be for the master's convenience." Zenpfennig muttered inaudibly about hygiene.

Mazigian tried pushing against the door, but it wouldn't budge. He opened a window, by pushing against a slatted shutter in great need of repair. Lifting his robes, he stepped out and walked into the vines, weeds, and briars beyond.

Zenpfennig refused to lift his robes but was thin enough to sit on the sill and squeeze out with his knees to his chin. Rueberry slowly eased himself out of the opening, first his right arm, then right shoulder, followed by his head and chest. His belly had to be squeezed through, but he was careful about the cheese.

He started to ease his left shoulder through. With his legs on one side of the window and the vast bulk of him unsupported on the other, gravity took over and snatched him completely out of the window. As he reclined in the rising tide of green weeds, his hands instantly sorted through his robes, to discover the fate of his cheese. To his relief, the cheese was unharmed.

Zenpfennig and Mazigian returned to assist him and point out the large, suspiciously stablelike hillock of vines not far away. Zenpfennig burned the blocking briars from the kitchen doorway and a pathway to the stable but stopped short of using fire to burn the vines away from the wooden stable. For that they resorted to brute force, centered mainly around the doors.

There were no horses in residence. Other than standing stalls and the tack hanging on the walls, no evidence remained that there had ever been horses in residence. No piles, steaming or cold. No odor. No loose tufts of hair. Nothing, in short, from which they could definitively decide that here there were horses.

Mazigian rested his green-stained hands against the stable walls, panting. "Where is the horse that doth untread again his tedious measures with the unbated fire that he did pace them first?"

Waving him to silence, Zenpfennig said, "Obviously, all the horses have long since abandoned this place."

"We had a wagon with some oxen when we came here," Rueberry said.

"I'm sure that's been reclaimed by the farmer by now." Zenpfennig tapped impatiently with one gnarled finger on the top rail of one stall. "Most certainly gone by now. In any case, it wouldn't do to show up to this fancy ball in a farmer's wagon." He started for the door. "Perhaps another solution will occur to us."

Outside, they puttered around, trying unsuccessfully to determine if there were any other vine-covered stables by surveying the surrounding weeds. Rueberry, in search of a good place to rest, with some shade, to finish his bit of cheese, accidentally stumbled onto a carriage.

The thing had been originally painted green, which merely assisted the covering thicket. Weeds and bramble grew up between the spokes of its wheels. Vines laced up along the tongue and the brush, growing into and out from a thick layer of leaves and dirt on the seats of the open carriage. A few small, delicate, pale purple flowers dotted the shady areas alongside the hulking mound.

Mazigian made an experimental tug on a long vine, pulling the vine and a good chunk of carriage away from the heap. Dropping that, he investigated another similar lump of weeds and vines, only to discover that the carriage it covered too had also moldered and rotted in the weather.

"It would appear that there are no horses or carriages to be had at all in this place." Rueberry popped the last bit of cheese into his mouth. "I suppose we shall just have to stay here tonight and try to entertain ourselves."

"Perish the thought," Zenpfennig ridiculed. "I said we'd find a carriage and horses, and somehow we'll have to find suitable transportation."

Rueberry sighed. "For really suitable transportation, we'd need footmen and a driver along with the horses and carriage."

A few mice scuttled from the collapsing heap of a third carriage, as Mazigian tried pulling weeds from it. He watched the mice a moment, then grinned up at Rueberry and Zenpfennig, while pointing to the scurrying mice. "Hold opinion with Pythagoras, that souls of animals infuse themselves into the trunks of men."

"Hmm." Zenpfennig stroked his long white beard with his gaunt, gnarled hand. "Perhaps he is onto something."

He motioned to the next weed-covered carriage. "But we need the horses first. Mazigian, scare the mice from that one. Rueberry, prepare yourself. We shall turn the mice into horses as they run."

He nodded at Mazigian, who obediently scrambled over to the next heap of carriage and brush. Mazigian smashed the derelict structure with one blow. Mice scattered in all directions. Rueberry and Zenpfennig threw spells at the small, lightning-fast rodents as best they could.

In the end, six matching dun colored horses milled in confused shock around the demolished heaps of four bramble-covered carriages. Using handy sticks and inventive shouts along the lines of "Off my foot, idiot horse," the wizards herded the horses into the stable and shut the door.

Zenpfennig panted a moment as he leaned against the rough, splintery wooden stable door. "We still need a carriage. What could we use for a carriage?"

"Too bad," Rueberry wheezed, "we couldn't use some of these vines."

"Not the vines." Zenpfennig shuddered. "I wouldn't trust something woven of them. But there must be something else we could use. Can you think of anything close to the shape we're looking for, hollow on the inside, that might work?"

"A loaf of bread?" Rueberry asked.

"Bread isn't hollow."

"True. True." Rueberry smiled. "But perhaps I might find something in the pantry."

Zenpfennig frowned and stood up straight. "While you are fiddling around in the cellars, Mazigian and I shall search out some appropriate servants." He motioned imperiously for Mazigian to follow him and sauntered off without a backward glance.

Rueberry happily returned to the cellars, entering the kitchens through the burned-out doorway. He wandered through the cellars, searching methodically through all the shelves to find something hollow of about the right size.

"Square, roundish, but is it hollow?" Rueberry muttered as he opened a pot of sweet gooseberry jam that was unfortunately far too full for him to empty quickly.

"Hollow, but the shape?" Rueberry squinted at a gourd, as he held it this way and that, trying unsuccessfully to imagine it as a carriage.

He picked up a tin bucket, at first to carry anything he found that might be hollow and the right shape. After a bit, he realized it, too, was hollow and the right shape, though the hole in the bottom might cause problems.

In the end, Rueberry had the tin bucket, a medium lumpy pumpkin, an empty unglazed crock, a silver goblet, a wooden bowl, and a spiced cake that he'd found hiding on a back shelf. He looked outside the kitchen door, but Zenpfennig and Mazigian weren't there.

So he ate half the cake and had to go search out a good wine to accompany it. Zenpfennig and Mazigian still hadn't shown, so Rueberry decided to experiment with transforming the objects at hand into carriages.

As a carriage, the tin bucket looked dented, overused, and showed rust that Rueberry hadn't noticed in the bucket.

The unglazed crock made a fine-looking carriage, until Rueberry tried to step into it, and it crumbled under his weight.

The silver goblet turned into a very elegant-looking carriage, standing high on a thin stem above small, delicately wrought wheels. Unfortunately, there were no steps, and the door to the carriage was too high for Rueberry to reach.

The wooden bowl carriage was sturdy but chipped here and there. It was also wagonlike, making it appear far too plain and common for them to use to take to the ball.

Rueberry eyed the pumpkin. He'd have to make it work. He stepped back into the kitchen and selected a sharp knife. He'd make certain this one came out right.

Whistling happily over his work, Rueberry began carving doors, windows, seats for passengers, a seat for the driver, and a little shelf for the footmen. Most importantly, he carved four small wheels at the base of the pumpkin.

⚬⚬⚬

ZENPFENNIG TRUDGED AROUND the castle, hoping for inspiration and finding none. He didn't want to hitch the horses. He didn't want to drive the carriage. He didn't want to spend the evening acting as a servant to Prince Althelstan and that old witch. It would be far, far beneath his dignity.

Trudging behind him and occasionally making odd noises, was Mazigian. That was an improvement over Mazigian talking to him. Zenpfennig wasn't sure how much more of this curse he could take. All the more irritating because he couldn't find a way to counter and negate the curse.

Using a convenient stick, Zenpfennig beat at the bramble in his way. He'd have to burn a path from the stable to the gate later, and along with whatever ended up happening tonight—with the way things had been going the last several days, there was really no telling what might happen—he didn't want to waste his strength.

Mazigian grabbed his sleeve and said, "A pound of man's flesh, taken from a man is not so estimable, profitable neither, as flesh of muttons, beefs, or goats."

"Eh, what?" Zenpfennig turned back to find Mazigian looking intently and pointing off to the left.

Grazing with every evidence of supreme satisfaction on a large mound of thorny green bramble and weeds, were two nearly identical scruffy, shaggy, brown-spotted, white goats.

"We have not spoke us yet of torch bearers," Mazigian whispered.

"Very good," Zenpfennig whispered back. He drew a deep breath, concentrated, and threw the transformation spell. "Be men, not goats, and serve you well."

Where the goats had been now stood two nearly identical, scruffy, shaggy-haired, surprised youths. One worked his mouth for a moment around the green branch still in it before spitting it out in disgust.

Mazigian stepped forward, gesturing toward the youths, and said, "Prepare you for this masque tonight." With a wave of his hand, the youths were suddenly clean, arrayed in fine, gilt-trimmed scarlet uniforms, with their hair fashionably styled. Mazigian smiled and nodded to Zenpfennig. "I am provided of a torch bearer."

"I suppose they make passable footmen." He waved to the youths and commanded, "Follow us." He led the way back to the stable, where he opened the door and motioned the youths in. "Prepare these horses for tonight. We'll let you know where the carriage is when we find it."

The youths looked at him, confused.

"Prepare the horses." Zenpfennig tried to shoo them farther into the stable, but they just stood, looking dumbfounded. "Bah!" Zenpfennig stepped into the stable, waved at the brushes and tack hanging on the walls. "Clean them up and put that leather stuff on them, so you can hitch them to a carriage."

When the youths still stayed standing near the door, acting stupid, Zenpfennig walked over to loom over them. "Do it, or you shall remain footmen for the rest of your unnatural lives. If you ever want to go back to being a goat, serve me well."

They both bustled forward to hurry about their duties.

"You just have to be firm," Zenpfennig said while shutting the door to the stable. "Now we need a driver. One that will not be as stubborn as a goat." He sighed, surveying the surrounding weeds and bramble. "Any ideas?"

Mazigian grinned, and pointed to a large, orange-striped tomcat sunning itself on the exposed leather seat cushion of one of the collapsed carriages. "Why he, a harmless, necessary cat."

"He'd make the horses run, that's for certain."

Zenpfennig transformed and suited up the cat, who didn't appear to notice any difference, and continued to laze on the seat of the carriage.

"Come here," Zenpfennig ordered as he opened the door to the stable.

The cat moved his head, as if listening to the sounds from the stable. He rose from the cushion, stretching, and sauntered over, apparently more out of curiosity than anything else. He was of an average height but heavily muscled, and walked with an arrogant swagger that didn't disturb his thick mane of burnished blond hair.

Inside the stable, the goat-youths were brushing the horses methodically. When the cat strolled in, the horses became skittish, moving to the back corner, followed quickly by the goat-youths.

Grabbing the cat by the arm, Mazigian quickly steered him out. "Thou art too wild, too rude and bold of voice; parts that become thee happily enough, and in such eyes as ours appear not faults; but where thou art not known . . ."

The cat resisted somewhat but still followed.

Zenpfennig patted the cat on the head. "Come, we'll get you some cream."

The cat followed them happily enough after that.

They found Rueberry carving a pumpkin in the shade of several imaginative carriages by the door to the kitchens.

"Oh. I like this one." Zenpfennig ran his hand up the smooth, cool, gleaming stem of the silver goblet carriage.

"Yes," Rueberry said, "But can you get into it?"

"Hmm." Zenpfennig sighed. The silver carriage looked terribly elegant and extravagant. Exactly to his taste. But getting in it would require him to pull himself up into the door. Most undignified and therefore, unfortunately, unsuitable.

"Who is this?" Rueberry motioned with his knife to the cat.

"Tom. He'll be our driver."

"I see."

"We promised him some cream." Zenpfennig reached down to pick up and examine the carved pumpkin. "Would you please go fetch some?"

Rueberry reluctantly disappeared into the depths of the kitchen, returning shortly with a bowl of cream. He had to hold it while the cat leaned over it and lapped it up with relish.

Leaning back to avoid the splashes, Rueberry said, "We need to transform the pumpkin into a carriage."

"Not here." Zenpfennig looked around at the surrounding sea of weeds. "We'll do it by the stable, where the footmen can hitch up the horses. And we'll burn a path back to the castle door wide enough for the horses and carriage."

On their way back to the stable, Zenpfennig carried the pumpkin, Rueberry and Mazigian herded the cat. The cat wandered back to the exposed carriage cushion to sun himself, while the wizards transformed the pumpkin into a nicely suitable carriage. The outside appeared to be a pleasantly painted pale orange color, and in the right light—possibly pitch dark—no one could tell it had once been a pumpkin.

Zenpfennig wanted to abandon it for the silver-goblet carriage, but was overruled. They started the footmen hitching the horses, retrieved the cat from his nap, and burned a path to the castle's front door.

"Well, we've accomplished what we had to do," Zenpfennig said with great satisfaction. "Shall we see how the others are doing?"

❦

ALTHELSTAN LAID OUT the last of the suits on the benches in the receiving room. All the benches were now covered in a layer of clothing. Silks, velvets, lace, and wool coated every raised horizontal surface in complementing, competing, and clashing colors. He hadn't been certain what the others liked to wear or what they might think would be appropriate, so he'd made trip after trip, trundling down a selection of suits and dresses so that the others could choose what they wanted.

For himself he'd put on a sturdy padded doublet and trousers that he'd packed before leaving home. While very fine and certainly elegant, all the clothing in the castle was at least one hundred years out of date. Althelstan had never considered himself to be the most dapper of princes, but there were limits to his sartorial indifference.

As he leaned against a handy nearby wall for a well-deserved breather, the wizards wandered in the front door, leading a brawny, arrogant lout dressed in a scarlet and gold uniform.

"Who is this?" Althelstan stood up straight, trying not to appear tired and grumpy.

"Tom, our driver," said Zenpfennig.

Tom, having found a mirror, stared and pawed at it in absolute fascination.

"Got lucky and found him wandering the countryside, did you?" Althelstan asked.

"By the stable," Zenpfennig said. "Found some footmen, too. They're hitching the horses to the carriage."

Jealous of the wizards' easy good fortune, Althelstan gestured to the clothing lying around the hall. "Choose what you will, gentlemen."

Mazigian seemed drawn to several choices, unable to make up his mind. Rueberry was too busy keeping track of the wandering Tom to really look the selections over. Zenpfennig eyed the clothing with undisguised distaste.

"I think we'll wear our own clothing." Zenpfennig shook some of the dust from his robes. "They'll need to be cleaned, of course." He grabbed the shoulders of his robes and, with a barely audible mutter, shook them. His clothes were instantly clean, crisp, and mystically decorated with spangly bits.

Zenpfennig grabbed the harried Rueberry's shoulders and performed the same magic on Rueberry's robes. Mazigian followed suit only after much prodding from Zenpfennig.

"So where is the witch?" Zenpfennig asked.

On cue, Urticacea entered the hall, wearing a dress that probably hadn't seen the light of day since her youth, possibly some two hundred years earlier. It rose up her neck to half conceal her chin in frothy lace, and dragged the ground, sweeping dust up into the pleated hem with every step. In between the collar and the hem, the dress had the collapsed, leaky-balloon look of an eighty-pound woman in a hundred-forty-pound dress. The lace on the ends of her sleeves hung past her fingertips, and she constantly pushed them up her scrawny arms.

She glared at the gaping men.

Althelstan rallied and said, "Very, uhm, nice."

Tom walked over, leaned down, and began rubbing his cheek against her shoulder. Alarmed, Urticacea began trying to push him away, unsuccessfully.

"Oh, don't mind him," Zenpfennig said. "Just scratch his belly, and he'll go away."

"What?" The old witch pushed Tom with both hands, but he merely continued rubbing his face against her hands.

Zenpfennig waved one hand airily. "Scratch him behind his ears if you prefer. He just wants a little attention."

"I'll bet." But Urticacea did start scratching behind Tom's ear, and Tom held still, angling his head to make sure she got the right spot.

"We'll need to bring Princesses Vevila and Berengaria supper before we leave," Rueberry said as he left the room.

"The straw!" Zenpfennig motioned for Mazigian to follow him as he hurried after Rueberry. "We almost forgot the straw for Princess Vevila."

Althelstan looked around the room at all the fancy clothes he had carefully placed on the benches. He decided it would be the better part of wisdom not to mention how no one had appreciated all his hard work.

The room was silent, other than the odd, satisfied sighing sound Tom made. Althelstan watched the tiny Urticacea tiptoeing, with her fingers hidden in burnished blond hair, scratching behind the brawny man's ear.

His eyes met hers, and he decided that, truly, the better part of wisdom would be in not mentioning this scene, now or ever.

❦

RUEBERRY RUMMAGED THROUGH the cellars. Unexpectedly, most of the shelves were empty, rather than being replenished. The food that did remain was coarse, hard, and in many cases beginning to spoil. He'd never seen the pantry in this condition. Dust had begun to collect on the shelves. Rueberry had come to expect this to be the one dust-free place in the castle.

He ended up making up two trays with coarse bread, wine, and strips of dried meats. He apologized to both Berengaria and Vevila for not having food more suitable to their princessliness when he delivered the trays.

Zenpfennig and Mazigian arrived with the last load of straw as he was apologizing to Vevila. Zenpfennig hustled him away, anxious to get out of the castle and to the party.

❦

VEVILA SAT CHEWING methodically on the dried meat, while glaring balefully at the pile of straw beside her. The wine was better than the previous bottle, and she'd downed about a third of the weak, sweet wine.

So the others were going to a ball. Vevila grinned wickedly. She had no intention of being in her cell when they returned. Idly, she considered various revenges she could wreak before she disappeared into the night.

In the end, Vevila decided to wait on revenge. She could only perpetrate minor offenses here at the castle, and she did want to be long gone before they returned. Better to escape and live to revenge another day.

She retrieved her pick from its hiding place behind the spinning wheel and attacked the mortar around her chosen stone with renewed vigor.

Tonight. It would all happen tonight.

☙❦❧

B ERENGARIA SAT ON the edge of the soft, red velvet bed, staring morosely at the simple meal the kind wizard had brought her.

She was a fraud. A complete and utter fraud. No princess she, she couldn't even pass a simple princess test without lying, cheating, and deceiving. She hadn't felt that pea. She hadn't even known about the stupid pea until the witch had mentioned it.

Yet they'd all accepted her as a princess. They'd actually believed she'd been bruised and injured by a pea under twenty mattresses, twenty feather beds, and twenty silk blankets. Berengaria wondered at the sensitivity of true princesses. To be so easily hurt had to make life very difficult for them.

Why, she'd slept on the ground under the stars without pain or problem. A true princess undoubtedly was far too delicate for such hardships.

The old village herb woman had been right. Berengaria

could only have been the result of an evil liaison of the devil. She was far too sturdy, strong, and worst of all, a liar, to be a princess.

The only thing to do was leave now, tonight, before morning came. Before she could disappoint Prince Althelstan, the wizards, and Urticacea.

Berengaria collected her things into her battered brown bag and left the suite.

Two turns farther into the castle, and she was good and properly lost.

☙❦❧

AT THE WESTERN edge of a long, triangular lake, where the soft ground and still water mixed into a swamp, in the shifting, sheltering boughs of a willow tree in the center of a small island in the swamp, stood an odd little man, alternately conjuring and unconjuring various articles of clothing. A spangled purple cape was briefly considered before being tossed up to disappear into thin air.

"Yes, what I wear tonight is very important. Tonight is my last chance. It has to go right. Everything must be perfect." He shook his head over a small, scarlet cap before flipping it into nothingness. "It will all be over, however it goes, by noon tomorrow."

While the odd little man considered and rejected several more articles of clothing, the insects hummed and the birds called their late-evening songs. The sun barely peeked over the mountains in the west.

"The problem is that sometime before noon tomorrow, I will undoubtedly run into Urticacea. I'm not looking forward to facing her down." The odd little man shuddered and tossed a sturdy black leather doublet onto a crystal ball nestled in the hollow of one of the willow tree's roots.

"She will undoubtedly unmask me, denounce me before everyone. I need to secure my position before that." He frowned for a moment before continuing to conjure clothes. "I want to appear to be humble and less threatening than I am. Not only for Urticacea but also for Princess Vevila. But I don't want to encourage anyone to think I'm weak and easily dismissed."

He considered a pair of black woolen trousers, holding them up to compare with the black doublet already chosen. "They're sturdy, but it wouldn't be very colorful."

Croaking frogs punctuated the humming and buzzing of the insects. A bare flare of sun hung at the top of the mountain to the west.

"Perhaps it would be best." He tossed the trousers on top of the doublet. "After all, I'm working, not making a fashion statement. You can't get more basic than black."

In moments, the odd little man was dressed all in black, except for his battered, muddy brown boots. He walked to the edge of the island to peer down at his reflection in the still swamp water. The sun disappeared behind the mountain, leaving only the red and violet reflections off the clouds to light the lake.

The odd little man shook his head. "Too much black."

He pulled his hat from his head, and it vanished. With a twitch of his wrist, a white beret with a short white plume appeared in his hand. He set it on his head and looked at his darkened reflection.

"Better."

The insects buzzed, birds called, frogs croaked.

"And to make certain no one thinks to take advantage

of me." The odd little man conjured a white baldric with a sharp steel sword. He put it on and smiled at his reflection.

After adjusting his white hat, he looked off at the swamp. "Wish me luck. It'll all be over soon."

☙❧

I N A LARGE rented mansion in a small fashionable resort town not far from the vine-covered castle, a thin young woman in a stained and tattered dress dashed up the rickety back stairs to her garret room. Behind her, a large, matronly woman in a dark black velvet dress climbed the stairs slowly, with the creaks and groans of the old wood drowning out her huffing and puffing.

The large woman paused before closing the door to the small garret room. "You're not to make a sound the entire evening. Do you understand? Not a peep. Should you attempt to make a scene of yourself, I will have you thrown out into the gutter without a cent, without a reference, without anything. Do I make myself clear?"

"Yes, ma'am." The young woman huddled on her thin, hard bed.

"Good."

The door slammed shut, and the young woman heard the clicking of the key turning in the lock and the clatter of the bolts sliding into place. She waited as the echoes of heavy footsteps on the stairs faded farther and farther away.

She turned to the wall beside her bed and pushed the right spot on one warped board. She caught the board as it fell toward her and laid it aside on the bed.

After easing herself through the gaping hole to the dark, stale stillness of the attic beyond, she felt around for the candle and matches. The lit candle cast a small circle of light into the gloomy depths of the attic.

A short walk brought her to the unlocked door to the attic. Beside the door hung a slinky white lace and satin dress, with pins still holding some of the lace in place. The young woman examined it critically.

The skirt was all wrong. Real ball gowns had yards and yards of fabric so that they swirled and lifted when the wearer turned. She hadn't had that much fabric, having to make do with the scraps from her stepsister's satin and lace petticoats. This dress would never swirl.

"Can't be helped," the young woman whispered to herself as she picked up the needle and thread from the small kit on the floor by the dress.

She quickly tacked the lace in place, then tried the dress on. It was tight, she'd have to take shallow breaths, but it would do. The slippers she'd made from her stepsister's cast-off soles and more lace. Looking down, she hoped no one would notice.

A sparkling tiara she'd found forgotten in an abandoned, nearly empty costume box in the attic went on her head next, and she piled her dark hair around it to disguise its true nature. Lastly she pulled on a pair of white lace gloves she'd made, wishing she could see what she looked like.

Wishing, ha. Wishing had gotten her nowhere, which was why she'd taken matters into her own hands. She might as well have wished for a fairy godmother to do all this for her, take care of her, and keep her from evil.

RUEBERRY LEANED CONTENTEDLY into the spongy cushions of the pumpkin-carriage. The sumptuous pale orangey interior had ample room for the wizards, witch, and prince to spread out on facing semicircular seats. The windows had no curtains, but a small candle placed in each window gave them more than adequate light. On the whole, he was rather pleased with himself and particularly proud of the seed-shaped seat cushions.

The horses trotted off at a near gallop, while Tom entertained himself with the reins and whip, and the footmen clung for dear life in back. Before they left, Zenpfennig had spent time explaining to Tom where to go for the party, but Rueberry secretly guessed that Zenpfennig had really magicked the directions into Tom's mind.

The carriage's occupants rode for a while in the gathering dark without talking. Rueberry couldn't tell whether that was because they were tired or because no one wanted to start a potentially malignant conversation.

Althelstan, seated next to the witch on the front-facing seat, glared reproachfully at the wizards. Zenpfennig had kindly offered to take the rear-facing seat, and Rueberry wondered if Althelstan had actually not known that the rear-facing seat would be jolted less or if he was just now finding that out. Perhaps Althelstan merely didn't care for his seat partner. Urticacea frowned democratically at everyone.

With surprising suddenness, the creaks and jolts of the rutted dirt road were replaced with the ticking of the wheels and the clapping of horses' hooves on cobblestones. The ride smoothed out and speeded up. On the other side of the window candles, brick and wood houses flew past.

Zenpfennig lifted his staff to poke a depression in the soft roof above them. "Slow down, you maniac."

The carriage continued at speed until abruptly swinging into a curve and stopping.

The footmen jumped off the back and opened the door. Urticacea and Althelstan exited first, followed by the wizards.

They stood at the bottom of a long, white marble staircase leading to a brightly lit mansion. At the top of the stairs, two liveried guards stood staring incredulously down at them. As they climbed the stairs, the guards exchanged glances.

"Only princes can enter," the guard on the right said.

"I'm a prince," Althelstan said.

"They're not." The guard on the left nodded at the wizards and Urticacea.

"They're my retinue," Althelstan said haughtily.

"None of the other princes brought a retinue," the right-hand guard said.

Althelstan sniffed and held his nose at a snooty angle. "I am not responsible for the vagaries of other princes. A true prince would never traipse about without a proper retinue. And I certainly have no intention of allying myself with a house that doesn't respect correct princely decorum." He turned to leave. "You can tell your mistress that."

"No. Wait! Wait!"

Pausing, Althelstan lifted one eyebrow and looked over his shoulder at the guard.

"I was just surprised none of the other princes brought their retinues." The guard waved toward the open door. "You can all go in."

They tromped in, Althelstan in the lead, the wizards fol-

lowing, and a miffed Urticacea bringing up the rear, muttering, "What they need here is a clever prince test."

The house had obviously been rented for its potential
for holding parties. The front door opened onto a large balcony entryway in front of a steep, white marble staircase
leading down to a large ballroom. The balcony was level
with a field of fully stocked and glowing chandeliers.
Smoke clouded the high ceiling above. Below, at the foot
of the stairs, a line of well-dressed young men stood waiting for the privilege of speaking to the Dowager Queen
Dulcamara, who would pass them on to someone who
couldn't be seen around the chandeliers. Other young men
milled about the tessellated floor of the ballroom, but
mostly they flocked around the buffet and ambushed servants wandering with trays of drinks.

A white-and-brass-liveried servant nodded at the newly
entered company, whispered to Althelstan, and shouted,
"Prince Althelstan of Portula and friends."

Nobody looked up. No one appeared to notice them.
They walked down the stairs to stand at the end of the receiving line. And wait. And wait. And wait.

Others arrived after them. Ahead of them, some prince,
standing and talking to the queen as if no one else was
waiting, laughed in a manner reminiscent of a horse snorting.

Rueberry surveyed the room, trying to figure out why
the whole scene seemed wrong. It wasn't until he saw the
strange young man off in a corner dancing a jig out of time
to the orchestra that he realized that the only women present were the queen, her two daughters, and Urticacea. The
young men were milling about and eating all the food on
the buffet before Rueberry could even get there, because
there was little else for them to do. Obviously, the queen

didn't want any rivals to outshine her daughters, but Rue-berry thought this bordered on the ridiculous.

To amuse himself, he tried counting the princes to see how many were present. Pleased with himself, he leaned toward Zenpfennig. "There are sixty-four princes here tonight."

"I counted fifty-seven," Zenpfennig said.

"Seventy-two," Prince Althelstan muttered. "I know each and every one of them." He gestured to a few standing close to the buffet and said, "Princes Oleksander, Gustaf, Ramon, Josep, Wilhelm, Thanos, and Kenji. They don't even need a princess; their fathers will let them marry anyone they want." He nodded to the dancing fool in the corner. "I know what Jean-Paolo is doing here. His family can't pay anyone enough to marry him."

"I wonder why," Zenpfennig said dryly. He frowned at the orchestra, sheltered under the balcony and very far away from the buffet. "So, are the princes expected to dance with each other?"

"Probably supposed to take turns with the princesses, once the receiving line is gone." Althelstan shook his head. "Although a few of these fools . . ."

Urticacea looked extremely disturbed.

They shuffled forward, as the next prince moved on past the queen and her daughters. Eventually, it was their turn.

"Prince Althelstan," Queen Dulcamara said, as Althelstan bowed over her hand. She smiled at the wizards. "Great wizards, and uhm . . ." Her smile froze in puzzlement over the witch.

"Urticacea," the witch said.

"Yes." Dulcamara gave the word several extra syllables. "My lovely daughter, Princess Stellaria." She mo-

tioned to a tired-looking, thin young woman, whose bright
gold gown leeched all color from her face. The girl curtseyed; Althelstan bowed. "And my sweet, dear girl,
Princess Gaulthemum." Another tired, washed-out young
woman in a silver dress curtseyed; Althelstan bowed.

"Aren't they beautiful." Dulcamara beamed at the
young women, who tried to stand straight and smiled
crookedly.

"Lovely," Althelstan said, on what Rueberry could only
assume was automatic.

"As you can see, they are true princesses." Dulcamara
sneered down at Urticacea. "No princess test is needed
here."

Zenpfennig put a restraining hand on Urticacea's shoulder. "We won't detain you further." He began pushing Urticacea away from the other women. "You have so many
guests to greet."

Rueberry helped Zenpfennig herd the witch away from
the queen and her daughters, mostly so that he could steer
the group toward the buffet. Not that difficult a task, as
most of the group seemed to have the same idea, and no
one wanted to wait until the starving horde of rumbling
princes had eaten all the goodies.

"Princess tests have a long and honorable history," Urticacea muttered.

"Of course." Zenpfennig offered her a nearly decimated
tray of sweets from the buffet. "But not everyone has the
same customs. We must respect others' quaint, if obscure
and uneducated, folkways."

Urticacea took the tray and began stuffing sweets in her
mouth. Rueberry selected another tray, this one with the
sad remainders of a variety of meats, and began filling it
from the buffet.

Mazigian munched on a fan-sized piece of lettuce he'd pulled from between two empty silver platters. He looked around at the milling princes. "There be land rats and water rats, land thieves and water thieves."

"Pretty accurate assessment." Althelstan snatched a full glass of sparkling white wine from a passing servitor. "We'd better eat while we can."

❧

THE END OF the pick no longer reached far enough into the cracks around the stone to dig into the mortar. Vevila traded the pick for the flat shovel. She thrust it into the gap and began to scrape, scrape, scrape away at the remaining mortar.

Dust coated her hands and face and sprinkled down the front of her dress, muting the blue and gray into one dun color. She'd become accustomed to the grit in her mouth, but she had to stop every occasionally to wet her throat with some of the sweet wine.

Coming back from one short wine break, Vevila leaned against the shovel she'd left in the gap. It suddenly gave and broke through with a grinding, snapping sound. Luckily, the handle prevented it from slipping through all the way. She quickly broke through on all four sides. The mortar in the far corners she couldn't get at with either the pick or the shovel, no matter how she tried.

Impatient with herself and the stone, Vevila grabbed the pick and began striking the stone near the top right corner. On the fifth hit, the corner moved forward a bit.

Slowly but surely, she worked each corner loose, then inched the stone forward. Once the stone was halfway out, hitting it with the pick became impractical, so she started pushing the stone forward.

Sweat beaded on her brow as she pushed, leaving dark tracks where it mixed with the mortar dust and ran down her face. Sometimes it seemed to Vevila that the stone would never move; sometimes it jerked forward so fast that she was certain it would fly directly across to hit the wall on the other side of the corridor.

In the end, the stone tottered, tilted, toppled, and fell like a stone. The thud of its landing echoed down the corridor and shook Vevila's cell. For a moment, it sounded as if the stone had screamed, but Vevila decided it had to be her imagination.

Vevila stared at the hole and the bit of corridor she could see in stunned glee. She'd done it. She really had escaped.

All she had to do now was to climb out of her cell and walk away. Nothing could stop her. She was free.

She grinned maniacally, reached into the hole for the other side, and began to pull herself up.

✧

BERENGARIA TIPTOED THROUGH the dusky, dusty, mysterious corridors of the castle. She clutched her battered brown bag tightly, ready to swing it at any ghost or monster that accosted her.

The sleeping inhabitants disturbed her. The way they snored and sighed under a thick covering of dust, the cobwebs that blew in the breeze of their every breath, somehow they all seemed to stare at her, with their eyes shut. All seemed to accuse her of her inadequacies. Berengaria could almost hear a dreamlike whisper, "You are no princess!"

Somewhere in the castle was another princess. The wizards and Prince Althelstan had mentioned her. Althelstan's cousin, if Berengaria recalled correctly. They had said she was locked in a cell in a tower. Berengaria desperately wanted to find her and talk to her.

If nothing else, maybe she knew the way out.

Turning the corner, Berengaria discovered another set of stairs. This one spiraled up, with several torches lighting the way.

The castle was laid out so strangely, mostly vertically. Staircases guarded the end of every corridor and sometimes surprised you in between. There were spiral staircases, straight staircases, and square staircases, narrow ones and wide ones, short ones and long ones, deep ones and ones that she could only take on tiptoe because they were so shallow.

She started up the stairs. If Vevila was in a tower, up was possibly the right direction. At the top of the stairs, the flickering light of two rows of torches illuminated a gloomy, windowless stone hallway. Berengaria quietly stepped into the hallway.

"Hello? Is anyone down here?"

A stone fell straight down in front of her.

Screaming, she turned and dashed back to the stairs. Tripping halfway down, she rolled across the lower corridor into a small, dark, balcony alcove. Berengaria lay there a moment to catch her breath, clutching her battered brown bag to her chest as a shield.

When her breathing slowed and she could hear around the pounding of her heart, the sound of eldrich voices and strange cries drifted down from the corridor upstairs.

Huddling as far back into the dark as she could, Berengaria swore to herself that if she ever found the way out of the castle, she would tell the truth about being a princess, and never, never cheat again.

~❦~

THE INTERMINABLE RECEIVING line had ended, and the orchestra picked up the pace. Unfortunately for the hostesses, none of the princes seemed inclined to take the hint and ask the wilted, overdressed princesses to dance. Jean-Paolo had the dance floor to himself, waving his arms and legs about and covering a good third of the empty space with leaps and pirouettes.

Althelstan ignored Mazigian's nudging and nodding toward the princesses. Neither of them compared to his beautiful Jaquenetta. And, though Althelstan would never admit it, he was beginning to see the sense in Urticacea's princess tests. He doubted either of those two wan, faded wenches huddling together in the corner were princesses. They just weren't arrogant enough.

Whatever other faults Vevila might possess, she could always be counted on to bring supreme confidence and regal conceit to any endeavor. Althelstan couldn't see Jaquenetta withering under the glare of duty. Hadn't she gathered with her family and closest friends to awaken her brothers in the face of Urticacea's disapproval?

Gaulthemum, in the shining silver dress, clutched her sister Stellaria's hand, and they leaned together for some furtive whispering.

A moment's study convinced Althelstan that he'd never seen such pinched-up, crabby faces. Frown lines already showed on the girls' foreheads. He wondered if this was

Dulcamara's sole proof of royalty. The problem was that the girls weren't so much ugly as homely and socially foolish. The oldest's face had a long, horsey look, and the youngest's a decidedly pointed chin.

Mazigian finally quit pestering Althelstan and walked over to Queen Dulcamara. Althelstan couldn't hear what Mazigian said to her, but she looked very startled before she allowed him to lead her onto the dance floor.

A few of the princes were eyeing the princesses. Before they could find pillowcases to put over the girls' heads to make socializing easier, a troop of servants arrived with a variety of filled trays for the buffet.

Althelstan pulled Urticacea out of the way of the stampede just ahead of the lead prince. She clung to his arm, eyes big and round, staring at the incredible amount of illegal elbowing and shoving at the buffet.

"This is no place for decent folk," she said.

"Well, no," Althelstan said. "It's a royal ball."

Urticacea looked up at him. "So, do you think the girls are princesses?"

He sighed. He hated to admit the truth to her, but the truth was rather obvious. "No. I don't think they're princesses."

"Obviously not." Zenpfennig stepped up beside them. "Still, one must do one's duty. Hm?" He stared significantly at Althelstan.

A whistle caught their attention, and they turned to find that Rueberry had somehow bribed or robbed a servant of several trays. He'd appropriated a corner with several chairs, which now held the trays. He waved the little group over.

"Isn't this rather rude?" Zenpfennig whispered fiercely when they'd reached Rueberry.

"Only if they notice." Rueberry grinned smugly. "And they won't notice."

Zenpfennig arched an eyebrow but said to Althelstan, "Go get us a tray of drinks, would you."

Althelstan secured a tray of drinks but nearly dropped them when the doors at the top of the stairs banged open.

At the top of the stairs stood a vision of loveliness and majestic elegance in a dress designed to display its wearer's charms rather than her wealth. Her dark, shiny hair was piled atop her head, spilling over a sparkling tiara. While the liveried doorman dithered around her, she floated down the stairs, the fingers of one gloved hand barely touching the handrail.

Althelstan shook his head as the princes charged to the foot of the stairs, shoving and kicking and punching and pushing in an effort to be the first there.

In a stunning somersault leap, Jean-Paolo beat the crowd, landing on the last step with a flourish. He bowed to the princess and escorted her to the dance floor.

She remained serene through her time with Jean-Paolo. It wasn't long. A third of the way through the tune, Prince Oleksander cut in and was himself routed by Prince Thanos.

In the corner, Princesses Stellaria and Gaulthemum glared cattily at the interloper and whispered fiercely to each other. Their mother abandoned Mazigian on the dance floor to join her daughters' verbal dissection of their party crasher.

"Well, throw her out," Stellaria whined loud enough to be heard above the orchestra.

Dulcamara's response couldn't be heard, but Althelstan could guess what it was. The invited princes looked likely to follow the woman if she was bounced out.

Excusing himself from his little group, Althelstan accosted Jean-Paolo by the buffet table. "So, who is she?"

Jean-Paolo shrugged and grinned goofily. "She wouldn't say. But she has a voice like an angel's. I could listen to her forever. If you expect to speak with her at all this evening, you'd better get over there." He nodded to where the gaudily clashing princes surrounded the dance floor in a more or less orderly mob.

"I think not," Althelstan said. "She's not for me."

"You prefer those shrinking violets?" Jean-Paolo glanced now to the hostesses snarling at each other in the corner.

"They're not for me, either." Althelstan picked up a stray olive. "I've already found the woman I want to marry."

"I thought your father hated Vevila." Jean-Paolo threw three olives into the air, dodging about to catch them in his mouth as they fell.

"Not Vevila."

Mumbling around a mouthful, Jean-Paolo said, "You think she's forgiven me for that incident with the fountain and the tree?"

"Not Vevila."

"Oh well." Jean-Paolo shrugged equanimitably. He broke off a large portion of bread and the leg of a pheasant and turned to go back to the milling princes. "See you later. I intend to get another dance with the mystery princess." He jigged off, clearing a large space in the line of princes for himself.

Althelstan returned to his small group in the opposite corner of the room.

"I don't think their party is going very well," Urticacea cackled.

"It's a smashing success from a certain point of view," Althelstan said.

"Perhaps if someone would just show proper decorum," Zenpfennig said. "If one prince would show the respect and duty due to our hostesses, the others might follow his example."

Avoiding Zenpfennig's gaze, Althelstan pretended not to understand his meaning. "I doubt it with this lot."

"Or those 'princesses,'" Urticacea said.

"We should probably go," Althelstan said uneasily.

"No we shouldn't." Urticacea quickly sat down on a nearby cushioned chair and propped her feet up on top of an empty tray on the next chair. "I want to stay and see what happens. I haven't had this much fun in ages."

Looking to the wizards, Althelstan found no help. They, too, seemed enthralled with the disaster taking place before their eyes. Mazigian seemed somewhat sympathetic but said, "The lottery of my destiny bars me the right of voluntary choosing."

Althelstan contented himself with a pile of sweets from the buffet. Dulcamara glared at him for his perfidy. That he could have withstood, but her daughters looked pleadingly at him, nearly on the brink of tears. He couldn't stand by and watch them be humiliated.

He walked over and asked the eldest, Stellaria, in the brilliant gold dress, to dance. Instead of the warm, welcome reception he expected, she sniffed and reluctantly said yes.

She appeared to be merely tolerating his unfathomably whimsical desire to dance, as he escorted her through the milling princes and onto the dance floor. She kept a proud, snooty expression on her face and danced mechanically and inattentively.

"The weather has been very nice lately," Althelstan said as she stepped on his left foot for the second time.

"Sorry," Stellaria muttered automatically, while continuing to glare at the mystery princess.

Later, he tried, "Very interesting country this, pretty and mountainish, don't you think?"

"Sure."

Trying to turn them in circles as they danced, Althelstan hoped to get her attention away from the other woman. Her scowling gaze never left the beautiful, laughing princess. Even though to do so would mean her head turning completely round twice on her neck, which Althelstan knew was impossible, yet he could have sworn she'd managed it.

"You also think she's fascinating?" Althelstan squeaked as Stellaria accidentally kicked his right shin.

Stellaria turned her glare on him, and he instantly regretted ever trying to get her attention. "No. She's not fascinating. She's a mannerless twit."

"So, why are you staring at her?"

Confusion briefly appeared on her long, horsey features. "I could swear I've seen her somewhere before." Her face resumed its accustomed nose-in-the-air, something-smells expression.

Althelstan sighed. "I know I haven't. When I started this quest, I thought I knew every existing princess on sight, and the only unmarried one was two-year-old Princess Caryl. Now, single, marriageable princesses seem to be coming out of the woodwork."

"Oh?" Stellaria snarled. "We're coming out of the woodwork, now, are we?"

Before the conversation could deteriorate further, the song ended, and the orchestra's leader indicated they would be taking a short break. Althelstan breathed a pri-

vate sigh of relief and escorted Stellaria back to her waiting mother and sister. After requesting the next dance with
the younger sister, Gaulthemum, Althelstan hurried back to
the corner his "retinue" had taken over.

"What do you think of 'Princess' Stellaria?" Urticacea
sat in her small, cushioned chair like a wizened old queen
surrounded by her favorite courtiers. Zenpfennig stood,
leaning against the wall somewhat behind Urticacea, patronizing all and sundry with his disdain. Mazigian and
Rueberry sat next to each other in chairs on the other side
of the witch, with Rueberry on the end so he could have
the servants at his beck and call.

"I don't think she's very happy with their party
crasher." Althelstan grabbed a full glass of sparkling white
wine from a tray Rueberry had liberated from a passing
servant.

"I should think not," Zenpfennig said, looking at the
mystery princess in the manner he might use for a slug on
his dinner plate.

Urticacea cackled with glee, and Zenpfennig frowned
deeply at the back of her head.

"I'll be dancing with the younger sister," Althelstan said
around wine sips. "Then, unless any of you plan to dance
with the princesses, I think we should leave."

Zenpfennig put his hand to where his heart would be,
assuming he had one, and said, "We're wizards. We certainly can't dance with unmarried princesses."

"But rich, widowed, used-to-be-Queens are perfectly
acceptable dance partners for wizards." The witch laughed.

"Mazigian was merely doing his duty to his hostess."
Zenpfennig stood up, no longer leaning against the wall.
"Nothing else."

"For my love, I pray you wrong me not." The way

Mazigian said it made the witch's glee subside. She nodded in silent apology.

The sound of instruments being tested warned Althelstan that the orchestra was returning from their break. He stalked away from the corner to claim Gaulthemum for the next dance.

"Isn't she just the ugliest woman you've ever seen?" Gaulthemum asked, while watching the mystery princess as Althelstan escorted her onto the dance floor.

"Well—"

"And that dress. That's just obscene, don't you agree?" she twittered.

"Actually—"

"The nerve of her, crashing our sweet little ball like that." Gaulthemum's homely, pointy-chinned face stared insipidly up at his as they danced. "Definitely not the sort of behavior a prince looks for in a potential wife. As I was telling sister, the princes came here tonight to find a wife, not some bubble-headed plaything with no manners, no sense of propriety. . . ."

Unable to squeeze a word in edgewise, Althelstan quit trying. He listened to her ramble on, giving him her opinions on everything from the mystery princess, to the house they'd rented for the ball, to the problems of finding good servants these days, to how all this fine weather merely gave everyone the sneezes.

He didn't want to nod at her; heaven knew she didn't need any encouragement, and he didn't want to leave the impression he agreed with her. However, he found his mind wandering, his attention drawn elsewhere, anywhere, and his head seemed to be ready to bob on automatic every time she drew breath.

"So nice to finally meet an intelligent and discerning

prince." Gaulthemum fluttered her thin, short eyelashes at him. "Men are so much more attractive when they are mature, polite, and . . ." Her rare silent pause drew his attention. "Strong."

A sudden sick feeling invaded the pit of his stomach, but Althelstan kept his smile plastered on his face. He knew his smile was slipping, crooked, and forced, but it remained on and hopefully masked his thoughts.

Gaulthemum licked her lips, like a tiger eyeing a meal. "I hope you won't take advantage of my silly girlishness in confessing that I think you the handsomest man in the room." Her eyelashes fluttered again over her weak, watery eyes. "I've had a crush on you since the first moment I saw you."

The general applicability of her words left him in no doubt that she'd prepared her compliments ahead of time. Trying to hide his repugnance, Althelstan opened his mouth to assure her of her safety, but got no farther.

"Of course I can trust you," she babbled. "A prince like you, anyone can tell from just a glance that—"

Althelstan was spared whatever came next by the end of the song. Gaulthemum smiled and giggled at him as he escorted her back to her mother, and she waved her fingers as he hurried to the safety of the far corner. He felt much more comfortable in the company of the ugly witch and the three argumentative wizards.

"I think it is time for us to go," Althelstan said.

Rueberry nodded after looking over the bleak, empty buffet and the forlorn, bare trays stacked around them. "Time to go."

By common, unspoken consensus, they did not take their leave of the hostesses. Not that the hostesses noticed them sneaking up the stairs quietly, hunched down in single file, glancing furtively back. Dulcamara and her daughters were far too busy glaring at the princes and whispering about the mystery princess.

A cool, fresh night breeze welcomed them to the dark outside. The door's guards lounged in an alcove, smoking their pipes and ignoring everything else.

The pumpkin-coach, horses, and footmen waited patiently, but Tom, the cat-driver, was nowhere to be seen.

"Here, kitty, kitty, kitty," Rueberry caroled.

The door guards glanced over, interestedly.

"'Kitty, kitty, kitty'?" Althelstan asked, confused.

Mazigian clapped him on the shoulder and whispered, "Mock the lion, when he roars for prey."

"What?" Althelstan looked to Zenpfennig for an explanation.

"Tom was a cat." Zenpfennig waved his hand in a flourish, and a limp, odiferous fish appeared in his hand. Holding it at arm's length, he offered it to Rueberry. "Here, try this."

A strange mewling cry out of the darkness presaged Tom's appearance. His rumpled clothes, disheveled hair, and smug grin told everyone he'd had a better evening than they had. Tom swiped the fish from Zenpfennig's hand and leapt gracefully up onto the driver's seat, grabbing and snapping the whip.

The rest of the party piled in quickly, but Zenpfennig and Mazigian still had to drag Rueberry in as the carriage lurched forward, pulled by the desperately frightened mice-horses. Althelstan and his "retinue" all settled silently into the cushions, except for Urticacea, who occasionally cackled evilly.

꧁✦꧂

QUEEN TARAX WRUNG her hands and paced the small, sumptuous, green receiving room. "Of all the wizards and all the knights I've put on this, none has been able to bring me the name of that strange, small man."

"Is Vevila still safe?" King Abelardann didn't bother looking up from his scribbling of a draft proclamation.

"Yes."

"Is she still locked up?" He tickled his nose with the feathered end of his quill while trying to think of a word to substitute for *tax.*

"For now, but she is trying again to escape." Queen Tarax stopped pacing on the opposite side of her husband's plain cherrywood writing table. "I'm worried about what might happen between her and that strange man. We don't know who he is; we don't know what he wants; we don't know anything about him!"

"Weren't we going to let Otto of Regenweald worry about her?" Abelardann pushed back his wooden bench and put the quill back in the inkpot. He couldn't write properly worded proclamations while she gabbed at him.

"My dear! By the time he got involved, she might have come to harm. We can't allow that."

"He's small?" When his wife nodded, Abelardann asked, "Obviously smaller than her? Much smaller than her?"

"Yes. He's much smaller than her."

"Hmm." Abelardann stroked his chin, and glints from his many rings sparkled his eyes. "But you say so far he's treated her well."

The queen nodded.

"And you said he gave her something. Something she wanted."

"Tools."

"He sounds smart enough to know better than to cross her." Abelardann grinned. "And if not, she's big and strong enough to put him through the wall. We shouldn't be worrying about this. Vevila is perfectly capable of taking care of herself."

The door burst open.

"Your Majesties!" A young guard in studded leather armor bowed and saluted. "The wizards sent me. There's been a development."

"What?" King Abelardann inquired mildly.

Queen Tarax pulled on his sleeve. "I set the court wizards to watching over Vevila, along with Althelstan. Something's happened. Hurry."

❧

GETTING UP INTO the hole was only the beginning, Vevila discovered. The jagged, serrated surface of the mortar still clinging to the sides of the hole scraped and tore at her arms and face and dress. Her struggles convinced her she'd obviously been eating far too well and not getting enough exercise in the last two days. After the initial pull to get her up into the hole, she eased her shoulders and chest through the small opening to the corridor by wiggling uncomfortably across the tight tunnel.

The dress had also been a bad choice. The puffy sleeves snagged on the remaining mortar and tugged the dress tight against her shoulders, giving her a few moments' problem. The wide, flaring skirt, sliding and fluttering against her ankles, gave her legs much-needed mobility for climbing and running but bunched up around her thighs when she tried to slip through.

Dangling down the wall in the corridor, over the fallen rock, Vevila twisted around to examine her stuck hips.

Torches resting in their sconces lined the walls. The ones on either side of her hips provided her with an excellent view of the strained blue and gray fabric and a few rips.

By pushing with her hands against the cool stone walls to lift herself up, she managed to lean first to the right side on one hand, to pull some of her skirt out of the tunnel, then the left.

"May I be of some assistance?" a familiar voice asked.

Vevila lost her one-handed balance on the stone and fell against the wall, slamming her chest and head.

"Oh dear. I'm very sorry." The odd little man climbed up on the stone and reached up to cradle her head in his hands. After the leeching chill of the stone wall, his hands felt very warm. "I didn't mean to startle you."

She turned her head to look at him, and the plume in his hat tickled her nose, causing her to sneeze down on his face.

"Sorry," they both said at the same time.

He let go of her head with one hand, using it to pull his hat off. And Vevila suspected he covered wiping his face with removing his hat. His brown, curly hair rippled up as he pulled the hat off, then sprang back in all directions, like schoolchildren fleeing their teachers at the end of the day. He lifted his face to look up at her, grinning broadly.

"May I be . . ." His eyes widened, and he dropped his gaze. "Of some assistance?"

"Certainly." Pushing against the wall, Vevila started to raise herself again, and without looking, he moved his grip to her shoulders to assist. "I seem to be stuck."

"Would you like me to turn the straw into gold for another favor?" he asked. "You could go back in, I could turn the straw into gold, and in the morning, they'll declare you a princess and let you out."

Straining around clenched teeth as she worked more of her dress free of the craggy tunnel, Vevila said, "I'm not going to be here in the morning." She put one hand on his shoulder to get better leverage. "I'm not the sort of person who can be locked up in a cell and expected to stay put."

"Of course. I understand." The odd little man flailed one hand about to find her elbow without actually looking up. "I'm the same way myself. But—" He groaned as she put her other hand on his head and pushed, but didn't try to stop her merely braced himself. "There are certain advantages to being a princess. I thought you might want to consider them."

"There are no," Vevila's hand slipped off his head, and she grabbed both his shoulders to pull, "advantages to being a princess."

The sound of shredding fabric and their muffled cries accompanied her tumble from the escape tunnel. The odd little man nicely cushioned her descent as he slipped from the fallen stone onto the cold stone floor of the corridor.

"I don't want to be a princess," Vevila announced to the breathless, pinned little man beneath her. She tried standing up and collapsed, sitting on the fallen stone. "I have no intention of sticking around here until morning to face that nasty old witch, those idiot wizards, or my pathetic, soon-to-be-revenged-upon cousin," she snarled, gathering her anger and adrenaline for flight.

The odd little man slowly and stiffly regained his feet. He leaned against the far wall of the corridor and sighed in a discouraged way. "I appreciate your feelings, and I won't stand in your way."

"I wouldn't let you stand in my way!" Vevila jumped to her feet and stalked quickly down the corridor. She stopped at the top of the stairs and turned to glare back at him running to catch up with her. "I wouldn't let anyone stop me."

"I know that," he said quietly, nearly meekly. "And I wouldn't try."

Vevila stopped at the bottom of the stairs and looked back at him, really looked at him. Several steps behind her, his face was at the same level as hers. He held his white plumed hat dejectedly in one hand, and his long brown hair curled loosely around his head and face. He was dressed all in black, except for the hat and the white leather baldric holding a short sword.

He'd turned straw into gold for her, given her the only good company she'd known the last two days, and cushioned her fall when she escaped. The least she could do was thank him.

"Thank you for helping me." Vevila pointed up. "Escape and all, but I really must leave here now, before they return. I've had it with their silly princess test."

The odd little man nodded and waved off her thanks.

She started walking, took two steps, and stopped. "I don't suppose you'd know the way out?"

Running his hand through his hair, the odd little man seemed to consider his options. He smiled and nodded. "Yes. I know the way out. Follow me."

He took two steps and stopped. "I don't suppose you'd like to go have a try at kissing the princes?"

"That would really burn their porridge." Vevila grinned. "But no. I just want out of here. Now."

Leading the way, the odd little man said, "Just thought

I'd check. You could prove you were a princess, get your revenge, and still leave here, all in one fell swoop."

They started down the next set of stairs. Vevila wondered at the sound of footsteps behind them but assumed it to be an echo or a trick of the acoustics.

"No," she said. "I'd really only get revenge on that ugly old witch that way. Althelstan would be very pleased with himself, and the wizards wouldn't mind at all. No. I want to get them all." She brushed aside a stray cobweb that hung down in their path. "It'd be nice to get them all in one fell swoop, but I don't think it'll be that easy."

"One never knows." He pointed to a door down the corridor. "That is the main receiving room. The front door is through there."

The strange decorating scheme in the main receiving room made them both pause. Curiosity made them investigate.

Picking up two doublets and a dress draped less than artistically across a bench, Vevila said, "Why would someone cover all the benches and tables with clothes?" She dropped them back where she'd gotten them. "What's been going on here?"

"No telling. It's a very strange castle." He fingered a velvet tunic. "Though this is stranger than usual."

"Doesn't matter. I'm leaving."

Vevila expected inky blackness, eerie bramble, and queer lonesome animal noises to greet her outside. She certainly didn't expect to see four horses pulling an astoundingly enormous carved pumpkin with a mrowling maniac holding the reins and cracking the whip. She quickly stepped out of the way of the speeding coach, back toward the castle.

"What have we here?" the witch's voice screeched from the pumpkin.

"Vevila!" Althelstan cried as he stepped out of the pumpkin. "I thought we'd left you locked in your cell." He turned back to the wizards as they, too, stepped out of the enormous orange contraption. "Did you forget to bar the door?"

"Of course not." Zenpfennig loomed over Vevila. "How did you get out?"

"I dug my way out." Vevila folded her arms and refused to allow the gaunt wizard to intimidate her.

"Resourceful girl," Rueberry murmured.

"She was trying to sneak up and kiss my sweet prince!" the witch declared. "Found out you couldn't, didn't you."

"I have no idea what you're talking about," Vevila sneered. "I was trying to leave. I'm sick of your stupid princess test."

The old witch opened her mouth to say something more to Vevila, then suddenly turned to the castle door. "Who's in there? Come out this instant!"

The odd little man stepped out, his hand on the hilt of his sword. His eyes glittered in the dark with animosity.

"You!" the witch screamed, pointing one crooked finger at the odd little man. "You filthy monster. What are you doing here?"

"Searching for a princess," he said.

Oh? Vevila tried to pretend she'd never seen him before, the dirty rotten scoundrel.

From behind him, Berengaria stepped out of the castle door. "I was following them out."

"They were together?" the ugly old witch asked.

"He knew the way out," Berengaria explained.

"Ha!" the witch shouted, turning on Vevila again. "Consorting with lowlife villains, are you? What did you give him to get you out of your cell? Not a princessly sort of thing, eh dearie?"

Berengaria moved to the protection of the wizards, looking scared. Althelstan kept looking anxiously from Vevila to the witch to the odd little man. Only the wizards looked calm. Mazigian patted Berengaria on the arm reassuringly.

"I dug my own way out." Vevila stood as regally and sneered as majestically as she could. "I dug with the quartz where the mortar was thinnest and pushed one of the stones out. That's how I got out. He was in the corridor and offered to show me where the front door was. And I didn't promise him a thing for it. I've made him no promises tonight at all."

"Do you know who he is?" the old witch shouted.

"No idea," Vevila said.

"He is Rumpelstiltskin," the witch announced. When this was met with shrugs of indifference all around, she began jumping up and down. "Haven't you ever heard of him? He used to be the younger prince of Tragopogonia. But he and his brother took up evil, black magics, killing their own father and nearly destroying the kingdom. Luckily, their uncle stepped in, banished them, and saved Tragopogonia."

The odd little man toyed with the hilt of his sword. "You lie, wicked crone!"

"Everyone knows about you." The witch shook her crooked finger at him. "Everyone has been warned about you. Everyone is on their guard against you."

His hand tightened on his sword, but other than that, the odd little man didn't move. He didn't even appear to breathe.

"Well, I haven't heard of him," Althelstan complained.

Glaring at the witch, the little man said, "Liar."

The witch glared back. "He's a notorious adventurer, powerful wizard, and dangerous rebel. Deny it."

"There are records of a Rumpelstiltskin in the Recondite University," Zenpfennig said.

Mazigian shrugged. "I would she were as lying a gossip in that as ever knapped ginger, or made her neighbors believe she wept for the death of a third husband. But it is true."

"I am what I am," Rumpelstiltskin said. "But you are a presumptuous, meddling harpy."

"Villainous miscreant!" the witch shouted back at him.

"Mangled strumpet!"

"Puny varlot!"

"I'm leaving," Vevila said.

The witch grabbed her arm before she could take a step. "You've been consorting with base, reprehensible villains while we've been gone. I don't believe you escaped that cell yourself. I don't believe you remembered to spin the straw into gold, and I don't believe you're a princess. And we'll prove it now."

Vevila struggled in the witch's grasp, but the old gnarled fingers dug into the flesh of her arm. Of course the wizards, Althelstan, Berengaria, and Rumpelstiltskin followed behind, blocking her escape route.

Cackling, the witch led the charge up the stairs. "You've failed, girl, failed completely and utterly. And that's all you'll ever be: a failure."

The fallen stone checked everyone's forward progress.

"As you can see." Vevila prodded the stone with her slippered toe. "I dug around the mortar and pushed the stone out, then crawled through."

Zenpfennig lifted a torch from its holder and very gently, very cautiously, ran his hand along the inside of Vevila's little tunnel. Arching one eyebrow, he rubbed his fingers together, and specks of grit fell to the floor. He tilted the torch toward the tunnel and tiptoed, trying to peer in. "She's definitely been digging."

"All right," the witch said grudgingly. "So she dug her way out. She still didn't spin the straw into gold, and she still isn't a princess."

Mazigian and Althelstan removed the bar from the door of Vevila's cell and opened the door.

Gold nuggets lay scattered across the floor, as if strewn like seeds on a ripe, plowed field.

Numbed with shock, the witch let go of Vevila and stared at the gold with her mouth open.

Rumpelstiltskin winked up at Vevila, passing one finger over his lips in a hushing motion, while no one was watching. Vevila didn't know whether to be furious or relieved. She settled for saying, "I didn't have time to gather them up into a neat pile. Sorry."

Moving to stand beside Berengaria, Rumpelstiltskin pulled gently on her sleeve. "What's going on?"

Berengaria shrugged. "Princess Vevila passed her princess test. Something about gold, I think."

Althelstan patted Vevila on the shoulder. "Neat or not, she passed the test. I believe that she has proven herself to be a true and honorable princess."

The old witch slowly collapsed to sit on the floor, shaking all over.

"Definitely. Vevila is truly a princess." Zenpfennig stood beside Althelstan and waved for Mazigian and Rueberry to get the wheelbarrows.

"A princess," the old witch whispered. She picked up a

nugget of gold to examine. "She spun straw into gold." The witch's voice was high and strained. "She's a princess."

"Well, come on," Althelstan tugged on Vevila's arm. "Go kiss the princes."

"Wait!" shouted the witch, holding up one hand.

"Now what?" Althelstan sighed disgustedly.

The witch turned her head to face Althelstan. Tears ran down her pale, wrinkled cheeks, and she looked pleadingly at him. "Wait until morning. Please. What are a few hours? Let my sweet prince have one more night of rest before you force him back out into the wicked, cruel world. Please."

"It has been a long night," Rueberry said. "And once the castle is roused, I doubt we will get any sleep."

Everyone looked to Althelstan, who looked at Vevila. "Should we wait until morning?"

Vevila knew if they waited, the witch would find, or try, some way to get out of it. But really, what difference would it make, at least to her? Vevila didn't care if the castle continued sleeping or woke. She didn't care about the sleeping princes. The wizards had what they wanted; the witch was already unhappy.

That left Althelstan, who'd readily agreed to locking her up, who was stupid enough to think that straw could be spun into gold, who hadn't helped her one bit.

She smiled and said, "I see no harm in waiting until morning. We could all use a little sleep before we wake the castle."

Everyone trooped out of Vevila's prison cell, even Vevila. This so confused Zenpfennig that he tried to usher her back in.

"There's a hole in the wall, remember?" Vevila pointed to the fallen stone. "I'm not staying here."

As they all walked through the flickering light of the torch-lined corridor, Rumpelstiltskin grabbed Vevila's hand and whispered, "I can explain everything, if you just give me a chance."

"Not now," Vevila whispered back.

Zenpfennig's hand descended on Rumpelstiltskin's shoulder. "If you would be so kind, we'd appreciate a professional word with you before you go."

Vevila's hand tingled as the odd little man let go of it, but she was too tired to give it much thought.

The company parted at the stairs, some going up, others down. Vevila planned to lose the others and keep walking right out the front door. But strangely, at the first empty bedroom they passed, she entered, lay on the bed, and fell fast asleep.

⟨✦⟩

THERE, YOU SEE, my dear." King Abelardann leaned back in his seat, away from the large crystal ball sitting in an elaborate fretwork holder on the table in front of him. "Vevila is perfectly capable of taking care of herself."

Queen Tarax leaned back in her own seat, a rough straight-backed wooden chair, unconvinced. The undecorated room held only two rough pine chairs, a rough pine table, and the large, elaborately displayed crystal ball, along with the king, queen, two dark-robed court wizards, and a single quiet guard by the door.

"What of that spell he put on her at the end?" Queen Tarax asked the shorter wizard.

The wizard unfolded his arms and shrugged. "A simple

sleep spell. It will do her no harm. It was to last only a few hours, not even an entire night."

"But why?" Queen Tarax asked.

The king patted his wife's arm. "Because, as anyone who knows her at all, she had no plans to sleep. Vevila was going to march right out of the castle into the night, right into trouble. Far better for her to leave during the day. Much safer. He obviously is concerned over her welfare."

"What do you know of this Rumpelstiltskin?" the queen demanded of the wizards.

"Rumors, such as the witch spoke of," murmured the tall wizard. "He is a powerful, untrained wizard. He has a reputation as an adventurer, a radical. He was a prince, though it's never been clear who did what to whom in the revolution that followed his father's death. And he can be dangerous."

"Though," the king mused, "in this case he does appear to be on our—or rather, Vevila's—side."

The wizards exchanged a look and nodded agreement.

"I didn't like the idea of our son going off on this ridiculous quest." Queen Tarax folded her arms and wrapped about her a mood King Abelardann recognized all too well. She was about to very nicely and humbly make demands. "I'm afraid things may have gotten out of hand. I know you think Vevila can handle anything, but she is only a young girl when all is said and done. I truly fear this Rumpelstiltskin may pose a serious threat to our son, Althelstan, and our cousin, Vevila. Please, for my peace of mind, do something to protect them."

King Abelardann stood. "As you wish."

BERENGARIA OPENED THE door of her bedroom just enough to peek out. The wizards were gathered with the stranger, Rumpelstiltskin, in the parlor, effectively preventing her ignominious retreat. They'd escorted her to the room she'd abandoned earlier, apparently assuming that she wanted to go back to sleep.

Either that or they didn't care what she thought or wanted.

Somehow Berengaria felt certain real princesses weren't treated that way. At least Vevila, who was a real princess, wouldn't have tolerated it.

Sighing, Berengaria closed the door. She was no princess. She wondered that they hadn't noticed yet. Though with Vevila around, maybe it just didn't matter anymore. After all, they only needed one princess to kiss the sleeping princes. Her situation was immaterial now.

She sat on the edge of the bed, expecting to cry, but the tears never came.

A pox on them all. She was as important as any of them. She was. She'd show them. That was what a real princess would think.

Remembering her earlier vow to tell the truth about her princessliness, Berengaria flopped back on the bed. She might as well sleep. She couldn't do anything else right now.

Lying on the bed, staring at the red velvet canopy above her, Berengaria debated the various merits of being a princess versus being unflinchingly honest.

❦

ZENPFENNIG HELD THE door as Rueberry entered their suite, overburdened with what he'd plundered

from the pantry. Zenpfennig whispered, "Shall we start a
fire to stop a fire?"

"You mean set a thief to catch a thief?" Rueberry whispered back. Zenpfennig nodded. Rueberry remembered
when they'd first tried getting rid of the spell, speculating
that someone else not formally trained yet knowledgeable
and skilled might know of a way to break the spell. It
couldn't work any less than any of their previous attempts.
Though consorting with wild wizards went against everything Rueberry believed to be good.

Rueberry arranged the last, distressed, scraps of dried
fruit and lopsided stale loaf of bread on the low table in the
parlor. Zenpfennig had appropriated the large cushioned
couch, though he might be regretting the puffs of dust
raised with his every move. Nothing was effective against
the dust in this castle. Mazigian stood guard by the door.
Their hazardous guest sat on a plain wooden chair next to
the couch, trying to appear calm.

Zenpfennig tried, and started, several openings, aban-
doning each in turn. Finally he said, "We would appreciate
a professional consultation. If you don't mind."

"About what?" Rumpelstiltskin said suspiciously.

"A curse," Zenpfennig said.

"Oh." Rumpelstiltskin relaxed, even accepted the glass
of strong, thick, dark liquor Rueberry offered him. "Tell
me about it."

As Rueberry poured the other glasses, Zenpfennig explained the curse on Mazigian and themselves. Rumpelstiltskin listened attentively, asking only for several
repetitions of the actual words of the curse. He nodded
thoughtfully as Zenpfennig listed all their attempts to remove the curse so far. Everyone was silent for a moment.

Turning to Mazigian by the door, Rumpelstiltskin said, "But you can sometimes modify the quotes?"

"Pray thee, take pains to allay with some cold drops of magic," Mazigian said desperately, "my skipping spirit, lest, through my wild behavior, I be misconstrued in the place I go to, and lose my hopes."

"There are some changes there." Rueberry took a seat on the other plain wooden chair opposite the strange newcomer. "What he's saying is that he wants your help. And both mys should be thys, and magic should be modesty. The changes he makes usually make the quote more fitting to the circumstances or more understandable."

Rumpelstiltskin stared off, thinking for a moment, and murmuring, "Speak as you want, you never shall, your tongue will always your thoughts befoul. Unsimple quotes stand in the stead, of what it was you wish you said. The words of the bard of another place, dropping trippingly from your face. Until you've learned humility, respect for others, and docility. The better part of valor is discretion, educate yourself upon this lesson." He shuddered. "It's a good strong curse. She's plainly had a great deal of practice at cursing." He looked around, as if taking in the whole castle.

"Do you have any new ideas on the subject?" Rueberry asked, hopefully.

"The obvious cure is the release built into the spell. 'Until you've learned humility, respect for others, and docility.' Any chance of that?" Rumpelstiltskin said.

Mazigian grimaced. "Talk with respect, and swear but now and then, wear prayer books in my pocket, look demurely, nay more while grace is saying, hood mine eyes thus with my hat, and sigh, and say 'amen'; use all the observance of civility, like one well studied in sad ostent to please his grandam, never trust me more."

"No," Zenpfennig translated.

"I could have a go at a straight removal." Rumpelstiltskin swirled the liquor in his glass. "But you've already tried that. Urticacea has had a long, long time to develop her will. And it sounds as if she laid this one down near the peak of her powers."

"Her will has been waning, hasn't it," Zenpfennig mused as he stroked his long, white beard.

Rumpelstiltskin set his glass down on the table. "I don't think that'll help. Both this curse and the castle spell are very close to things she holds dear and were infused with their force at the onset. I think both would remain, even if she were to die or leave."

The other three all stared at Mazigian, who shifted his weight from foot to foot nervously.

"Well." Rumpelstiltskin climbed down from the chair. "Let's see what we can do."

~❧~

ALTHELSTAN KNELT AT Jaquenetta's feet, taking her limp, warm hand in his to kiss. "Urticacea declared Vevila a princess. Tomorrow morning, she'll kiss your brothers, and you will be released from this curse."

"It's not a curse!" Urticacea hobbled into the room. "I've managed to keep her quiet and out of trouble for almost a hundred years. That's not a curse. That's a miracle."

He patted Jaquenetta's hand, then stood up. He rested one hand on Jaquenetta's shoulder. "Well. However you choose to term it, it will be gone tomorrow morning."

"Hmph." The old witch hobbled to the stairs. "Go to bed. Morning will come soon enough."

"Good night," Althelstan said automatically. He leaned down to whisper into the sleeping Jaquenetta's ear. "Not much longer, my darling."

The inhibiting presence of the witch in the upper room prevented Althelstan from resuming his accustomed chat with Jaquenetta. He resented knowing the witch to be so close and probably listening in over the snores of the king and his guards. He missed his evening talk with the sleeping girl.

Instead, he roamed the room, but there was little to see and nothing to do. He wished the witch would leave, and wondered what was keeping her so long upstairs with the sleeping princes.

Finally, Urticacea made her slow, faltering way down the stairs. She looked up in surprise to see him still standing by Jaquenetta.

"Are you still here?" she asked. "Why are you hanging about, boy? Go to bed."

"You should go to bed, too," Althelstan replied unable to think of anything else.

"That's where I'm going." She tottered across the room, pausing halfway to the down staircase to turn back to him. "Well, aren't you going?"

"In a little bit."

Her beady eyes narrowed, and the wrinkles in her face deepened suspiciously. "What are you planning on?"

"Nothing."

She shook one crooked finger at him. "You're acting mighty suspicious. What . . ." Her gaze fell on the sleeping Jaquenetta. "You! You were planning on taking advantage of her in her sleep!"

"I would not!" Althelstan protested.

"Ha!" the witch shouted. "Why else would you be standing around here, waiting for me to leave? You evil minded—"

"Now see here." Althelstan moved protectively in front of Jaquenetta. "I would never harm her. I'm not like that."

Urticacea shook her head and frowned. "I don't trust any of you lot. This is an evil, evil world, and you are an evil, evil boy." She headed back to sit on the bottom step of the stairs going up. "And I'm not leaving these unprotected people alone with you."

"You're wrong; I'm not evil!" Althelstan shouted. "And maybe I shouldn't leave these unprotected people alone with you."

"Ha! You could easily prove me wrong just by walking out of this room and leaving her alone until morning." Urticacea cackled. "But you wouldn't, because I'm not wrong."

Unsure how to answer her, Althelstan said, "Good night!" and walked out down the steps.

He couldn't be certain, but he thought he heard her say, "I thought he'd never leave."

❧❦

BRILLIANT STARS GLITTERED and twinkled on the reflective surface of a long, triangular lake in a dark mountain valley. The tops of the eastern mountains were rimmed with a thin line of color as a false dawn invaded the sky. Morning birds called to the sun to hurry up, while drowsy night owls settled in for a good day's sleep.

Under a willow tree on an island at the swampy western edge of the lake, an odd little man suddenly appeared near a crystal ball nestled in a hollow formed from the tree's roots.

Rumpelstiltskin sighed. "That went better than I expected." He turned to the crystal ball. "Where's the princess?"

As he approached the ball, a large, bumpy, glistening frog jumped up at him.

"What?" He grabbed the crystal ball, running his hands over it caressingly, growling softly to himself. "Perfidious female. I should have known I'd never get a wink of sleep tonight."

Kneeling on the soft, dewy ground, he placed the crystal ball back in its root-hollow resting place. "I have to rouse the castle. I—" He paused, looking out at the fog drifting over the swamp. "Of course, I . . . Well, no, I didn't tell her yet." He paused again. "Don't be ridiculous. I remember what I'm doing all this for. Taking on Urticacea is merely a side benefit I intend to leave to someone else."

He stood up, straightening his baldric and cap. "To accomplish our goals, we need three things: first, magic; second, a princess; and third, allies. I've already acquired the first, and I think I can get two and three in one fell swoop. If you will just trust me and stop criticizing my every move."

The odd little man took a deep breath. "When I return, I'll bring a princess with me. I swear it."

❧

URTICACEA COULD HEAR her bones creak and pop over the rattle of the wheelbarrow. She determinedly continued putting one foot in front of the other and pushing. She felt light as a feather, as if any stray breeze might blow her away. Her willpower was draining fast.

Thankfully, she only had to get the last prince up onto the rough, straw-filled wagon; then she wouldn't have to expend any more magic to get him safely away. The oxen would pull the wagon for her; all she had to do was guide them.

In the fading darkness outdoors, the farther reaches of the castle, vines, and bramble all merged into dun, featureless gray. Nearby, the stones, leaves, branches, and stems took on eerie properties, revealing and hiding themselves in a ghostly fashion. A soft sighing, almost a snore, came from a gray-coated guard by the gate.

Next to the large carved pumpkin carriage—abandoned by horses, footmen, and driver—stood the wagon the wizards had used on their trip to the castle. They hadn't had the sense she'd had to put the oxen and wagon somewhere safe. She'd hoped to send them packing in it but didn't mind putting it to use as an escape vehicle.

Pushing the wheelbarrow next to the wagon, she breathed a sigh of relief. She was nearly done.

A foreboding sense of doom fell over her. Something or someone was trying to rouse the unenchanted inhabitants of the castle. Still, she had a chance if she could get out of the surrounding bramble before she was discovered.

Levitating the prince made her tremble and sweat. She held on, determined, until she had him up beside the other two sleeping in the straw in the wagon bed.

She didn't dare pause to catch her breath but couldn't stop herself from leaning on the side of the wagon before beginning the monumental climb to the seat. She made it. She'd made it! She lifted the reins. . . .

A dark carriage pulled into the gate, nearly running into

the oxen. The horses on the strange carriage reared and screamed. The oxen placidly backed away toward the castle, giving the strangers more room.

The driver calmed the horses, and a large, loud, irritating woman in a ball gown descended from the carriage.

"Good gracious!" the self-styled Queen Dulcamara shouted. "Whatever are you doing?"

Urticacea wished for a bit of will, just enough to curse the vexing baggage before her. Unfortunately, she didn't have it in her.

"Get out of my way," Urticacea said strongly, trying to be quiet at the same time.

The idiot woman's daughters descended from the carriage, still in their party finery. They clung to each other, whispering and pointing.

The sound of running footsteps from the castle let Urticacea know she wouldn't make her getaway. She was trapped.

❧

"WAKE UP!" ALTHELSTAN screamed. "She's getting away!"

Vevila blearily opened her eyes. Why was she in a tall oak bed, under soft, silky, dusty blankets? Why wasn't she far, far away from the vine-covered sleeping castle? Hadn't that been her plan?

"Quickly, come on." Althelstan grabbed her arm and began dragging her out of the bed. "That adventurer went to wake the wizards. We've got to get to the front gate and stop her."

"Stop who?" Vevila grabbed onto Althelstan to steady herself as she slid off the bed. "What adventurer?"

"We have to stop Urticacea. That odd adventurer fellow, Rumble-something, he discovered her. She's stealing the princes from the castle."

She ran next to him through the corridors and stairways of the castle. Realizing only as they ran into the wizards and Berengaria and Rumpelstiltskin in the corridor outside the receiving room, that she'd been roped into assisting to stop what she wanted to happen.

"What are you doing at this hour?" demanded Dulcamara of the witch.

The witch yelled back, "What am I doing? What are you doing dressed like that at this time of the day?"

Dulcamara looked past the witch and walked over to the others emerging from the castle. "Our ball was a complete disaster!" she wailed, holding out one hand toward Althelstan. "Those other princes only danced with that horrid gate crasher. I had hopes that perhaps sweet Prince Althelstan might have happy memories of the time he spent with one of my daughters. Or . . ." She turned to hold her other hand out toward the wagon. "That my daughters might have the opportunity of kissing the princes and getting husbands."

Zenpfennig frowned down most severely as he towered over the witch sitting hunched in the wagon. "And what were you doing?"

Folding her arms, the witch silently and defiantly glared at Zenpfennig.

"In this shameful and perfidious act you have betrayed your claimed position as the prince's fairy godmother and revealed yourself truly as an evil witch," Zenpfennig scolded. "To stoop this low to maintain your power over him is both unworthy of your magical abilities and a gross

disregard of the basic respect due the princes as living be-
ings. This egregious violation—"

"Ha!" The witch jumped off the wagon, away from
Zenpfennig toward the dark carriage. She flung open the
door. "Who is that, lurking in here?"

Reaching in, the witch grabbed a cowering, fearful
young woman in a plain, rough dress and head scarf and
pulled her out of the carriage.

"That's merely my daughters' maid." Dulcamara
sniffed, not even looking toward the pair.

The witch snatched the scarf from the young woman's
head, and long, dark, shiny hair spilled down the young
woman's back in thick curls. Grimacing, the witch said,
"Looks like we found the mystery princess gate crasher."

"Her?" Dulcamara stalked over to Urticacea and the
maid. "She's no princess." Dulcamara grabbed the young
woman's chin, tilting and turning her face to catch the light
better. After a thorough examination, Dulcamara made an
exclamation of disgust. "So, you thought *you* could catch
a prince. Obviously, they knew you for the slattern you
are."

Stellaria and Gaulthemum snickered and whispered to
each other behind their hands.

The maid wrenched herself from both the witch's and
Dulcamara's grasp. Shaking and flushed with fury and em-
barrassment, she snarled, "Dowager Queen Dulcamara?
What a joke." She turned to Zenpfennig. "She's a liar, and
no more than a duchess." Pointing to the huddled sisters,
she added, "And they're merely a duke's stepdaughters.
They're no more princesses than I am." She bowed her
head, blinking back tears glistening in her eyes. "I'm the
duke's true daughter. They forced me to act as their maid
after my father's death."

"You would be?" asked Zenpfennig.

"Lady Amelanchier Ceneritious." The girl curtseyed. "My father was Milton Ceneritious, duke of Camassia."

"You're not any of you princesses!" the witch shouted with satisfaction.

Watching the spectacle with rapt fascination, Vevila jumped when Berengaria brushed against her arm while stepping around her.

"I must confess," Berengaria said in a small, high, trembling voice, while keeping her gaze on her feet, "I never felt the pea beneath the twenty mattresses and twenty feather beds and twenty silk blankets. I had trouble climbing up the bed and kept falling off in my sleep, and so I was bruised and injured when you found me in the morning."

Vevila suddenly found herself the object of everyone's intense scrutiny. Putting her fists on her hips, Vevila pulled herself up as tall and straight as she could in her dusty, ragged, plain dress. "Don't you, any of you, dare look at me like that! I have as much or more royal blood coursing through my veins as Prince Althelstan. And I passed my princess test."

She glared haughtily, trying to pin the ugly old witch with her stare. "I am a true, honorable, and noble princess. I always have been, and you know it!"

"Then please kiss the princes." Althelstan bowed her toward the wagon, before looking at the others in the courtyard. "I am constrained to marry only a real princess, and not my cousin, but perhaps, since my sweet cousin isn't interested in marrying any of the princes, perhaps they might be willing to marry some of these lovely young women, who've gone to such lengths to prove themselves princesses." He smiled at the nonprincessly young women.

Everyone nodded approvingly except for Vevila and the evil witch. Frowning, Vevila opened her mouth to speak.

"Wait!" Off to one side of the courtyard, in the early-morning shadows, leaning against the castle wall, idly picking leaves off the vines, stood Rumpelstiltskin.

"Now what?" Althelstan shouted.

"I'd like a word with Princess Vevila." Rumpelstiltskin motioned for Vevila to join him. When she refused, he added, "About a favor."

Reluctantly, Vevila joined him in his shadowy corner, away from the others. "What?"

"I want to call in my three favors," he whispered.

"Two favors," she murmured.

"First, I want you to exact promises of unnamed favors from everyone else here before you kiss the princes."

Vevila glanced back at the shriveled, seething mass of glowering witch. "I don't think I'll get one from the witch."

"Not her, no. But all the others. Yes?"

"Isn't that like wishing for more wishes?" Vevila just barely prevented herself from pointing out that he should require her to grant him those favors.

"It works." He shrugged.

"Fine. Fine."

"Second, I want you to kiss a frog. A particular frog. I'll show you which one."

"A frog!" Vevila hollered. "A slimy frog?"

Making hushing motions with his hands, he said, "It's not that bad."

"You're not the one kissing the frog."

"It can't be any worse than kissing those three." He motioned to the wagon.

"You're kidding. Right?" she asked.

"Just touch your lips to the frog. Okay? A tiny moment of your life. You're not lowering yourself all that horribly, and no one needs to know about it."

Why not? Vevila mused. There were probably any number of princes who would have nothing to do with her if they knew she'd kissed a slimy amphibian, simply as a favor to an odd, dangerous little man. Though it would leave her to scare off the very strange princes who found that attractive.

"Fine, I'll do it."

Across the courtyard, the others tried to overhear while yet appearing to be otherwise engaged.

He hunched farther into the shadows by the castle, parting the thick, green, climbing vines. "Third." Looking scared and hopeful, he asked, "I want you to marry me."

"Oh no." Vevila shook her head and her finger at him. "I owe you only two favors, not three."

"I changed the straw into gold three times," he protested.

"You did that third time on your own," Vevila said. "I never asked for that. I never promised you anything for it. In fact, I specifically said I didn't want you to do it. You did it anyway, on your own recognizance. I'm not responsible for what you do because you want to. I only have to fulfill bargains I make, not ones someone else assumes for me."

"But think of all the fun and excitement you'd have," he said fiercely as she walked away. "Think of the adventures. We'd make a great team!"

Vevila kept walking. She walked to the rear of the wagon and leaned against the side, plucking straw from the bed and dropping it on the weed-covered ground.

"None of you believed that I was really a princess. You

forced me to pass through a princess test. You locked me in a cell for three days. You didn't let me go to the ball last night. You haven't treated me at all properly."

Picking a particularly long piece of straw, she pointed it around at all of the others. "I want each of you to promise me a favor that I can collect at some time in the future when I need it."

"I'm certain I speak for everyone," Zenpfennig said, "when I say that after what we've been though here together, we'll all be doing favors for each other in the future. Helping each other out. Not just out of remembrance for all that we've endured together but out of true friendship."

"True friendship doesn't lock someone in a cell." Vevila stepped away from the wagon. "I want to know that I can go up to each and every one of you, if I need to, and get a favor from you." She stared at Zenpfennig. "Without negotiating a price or a return favor." She glared at Althelstan. "Without cajoling or flattery or begging." She nodded to Dulcamara. "Without fear that time or failing memory or dishonor would cause you to refuse me." Her gaze rested on Berengaria, then slipped to Mazigian. "I want each of you bound to this promise, to this future favor."

Zenpfennig shook his head. "I don't think all that is necessary."

"I do." Vevila took another step away from the wagon. "After what I've been through, I don't think it's very much to ask for awakening the castle for you." She opened her hands to take in everyone in the courtyard. "I won't be getting anything out of it. After you forced me to spend three days in a cell, I'm not about to sacrifice myself for your gain."

"That's a true princess for you," the old witch muttered.

Slowly they all capitulated, except the witch. Each

promised, upon their word, a future favor to Vevila. She very carefully listened to how each one said it, making a few change what they said to keep them from weaseling out later.

Climbing up onto the wagon, Vevila crawled over the sleeping princes, disturbing loose straw and velvet doublets. Grasping each of them by the collar, in turn, Vevila lifted the princes' heads and gently and quickly kissed their dusty, stale lips.

As she hopped from the wagon, grateful to be away from the fetid ripe stench of teeth unbrushed for almost a hundred years, Vevila realized that Rumpelstiltskin had been right, kissing a frog couldn't be any worse than kissing those three. She didn't want to know how he'd come to know whereof he spoke.

The three princes blinked, yawned, and began to stretch. The wizards hurried forward to help the princes up, while Dulcamara huddled with her daughters and stepdaughter. A tear ran down Urticacea's cheek. Althelstan turned and ran back into the castle.

One of the three princes picked up some straw, looked at it, then around at his brothers and the wagon and the wizards, then up at the clear blue sky above them.

"Eh, where am I? What happened?" he asked. His brothers echoed him.

Dulcamara and her daughters and stepdaughter moved to put themselves between Berengaria and the wagon. As Berengaria shifted around to see what was happening, the sisters elbowed and pushed her back out of the way.

Rumpelstiltskin tugged on Vevila's sleeve. "About the frog."

"Now?" she asked.

"Sure. Yes. Now." He glared up at her. "I'll take you

there now, and we'll get it over with as quickly as possible."

"Take me there?" Somehow it hadn't even occurred to Vevila that he might be expecting to disappear with her.

Berengaria stepped up beside them, her face a mask of sorrow and fear. "May I stay with you?"

"Certainly." Vevila linked her arm with Berengaria's. There might be safety in numbers.

As Rumpelstiltskin lifted his arms, preparing his spell, Rueberry shouted, "And where are you off to?"

"We have to see a frog about a man," Rumpelstiltskin shouted. "We'll be back."

He dropped his arms, and suddenly Vevila found she and Berengaria and the odd little man were standing on a small island at the swampy edge of a large lake nestled in a mountain valley. Pale green, leafy willow branches gently waved above and around them. A small, shining crystal ball, nestled incongruously in the hollow of an exposed root, the only made thing in this pristinely natural setting.

All around them, insects droned, birds flew and chattered, and the strange, slimy things that lived all or most of their lives in the water swam or oozed. The heavy, wet, vital odor of the myriad living and decaying organics in the swamp thickly perfumed the air. Vevila was grateful her feet didn't squish into the ground as she walked.

"Where are we?" Berengaria whispered frantically to Vevila. Vevila shrugged.

"Over here," Rumpelstiltskin said from where he'd walked to the edge of the water on the other side of the crystal ball. He leaned down, murmuring something Vevila couldn't hear, and picked something up.

When he turned around, she could see he was holding

an extremely large, slimy green, bumpy ugly frog, and smiling.

Maybe kissing a frog was worse than kissing three young men who'd lacked access to perfect hygiene for the last one hundred years. Vevila knew she was about to find out.

"Aaaah!" Berengaria shivered and ducked behind Vevila to cower and cling to Vevila's dress.

Vevila walked toward Rumpelstiltskin, against Berengaria's horrified resistance. "Oh, keep it away from me. No, no. Don't get any nearer."

Rumpelstiltskin held the frog up as high as his arms would reach. The ugly, glistening thing quivered in his unsteady two-handed grip. Its eyes bugged out of its head, and it croaked. Its flippered back legs scrambled against the odd little man's wrists.

Taking a deep breath and steeling her nerve, Vevila leaned forward. She extended her lips as far from her face as she could get them, and they touched the frog.

Surprisingly, the frog was no worse a kisser than several suitors she'd allowed to get this close. The frog's kiss had that same drooly feel as kissing a teething baby, without the well-chewed bread crumbs to wipe off after.

Leaning back, relieved and happy that it hadn't been worse, Vevila opened her eyes to find a tall, dark, and handsome man standing in front of her. His violet wool tunic strained across his broad shoulders, a gold coronet circled his brow, and his strong arms encircled her as his smoldering eyes gazed down on her.

"Gentle lady, lovely princess. You have freed Us from that miserable spell, and We shall marry you."

It was worse. All things considered, Vevila preferred the slimy frog to the prince that wanted to marry her. She reached behind her, feeling for silks and velvet, and pulled Berengaria around to thrust into his arms.

"But." The new prince looked confused. "You kissed me."

"You don't want her, remember?" Rumpelstiltskin stepped between the new prince and Vevila and pointed to Berengaria. "You tell everyone this princess kissed you, and you make it sound good and convincing."

The new prince shifted his confused stare from Vevila to Berengaria and back, over and over. "But which is which?"

Rumpelstiltskin lifted one hand to Vevila. "Princess Vevila. She's the one with the gold and the spinning wheel."

"And the pick and shovel," the prince said.

Nodding, Rumpelstiltskin raised his other hand to Berengaria. "Princess Berengaria. She's the one with the tall bed and the pea."

"Oh yes. We remember now." The prince smiled down on Berengaria.

"My brother, Prince Ravendelfort of Tragopogonia," Rumpelstiltskin said, finishing his introductions.

"King Ravendelfort," Ravendelfort corrected.

"King Ravendelfort," Rumpelstiltskin said quickly. "He was enspelled by our wicked uncle, who then stole the crown. Ten long years ago. We were cast out, and our uncle, Swinburne, has been spreading lies about us ever since."

Berengaria shyly looked away from Ravendelfort. "I'm not really a princess. I didn't feel the pea, you know."

"Of course you're a princess," Vevila exclaimed disgustedly. "If I say you're a princess, and they," she waved her hand at Rumpelstiltskin and Ravendelfort, "say you're a princess, then you're a princess."

Shaking her head sadly, Berengaria whispered, "I don't know. I don't think it works that way."

"Of course it does." Vevila flung her hands up, frustrated. "If everyone says you are, then you are."

"If you were to marry a prince, you'd be a princess." Ravendelfort lifted her chin to force her to look into his eyes. "Perhaps you'd prefer to be a queen."

"Oh." Berengaria stared at him, her blue eyes wide.

"After all, you did release us from the curse."

"But . . ." Berengaria started to point to Vevila.

Ravendelfort turned her back to face him. "No."

"Oh."

Rumpelstiltskin tugged on Vevila's sleeve and inclined his head toward the other side of the willow tree. "Let's leave them alone for a bit."

In the cool shade of the other side of the willow tree, Rumpelstiltskin leaned against the trunk of the tree, folded his arms, and, while staring at the ground, said, "Thank you."

"Just returning the favor."

They both stared at the deep blue lake. Insects droned, and a pair of swans glided by.

"You could have refused. Kissing a frog is fairly disgusting."

Vevila leaned down to pick up a rock and throw it into the lake. "Well, I've always heard that a princess must keep her promises."

"You saw how she acted." Rumpelstiltskin motioned over his shoulder without looking back. "She wouldn't have cared what I'd done for her. I don't think I could have gotten her to kiss him."

Glancing over her shoulder, Vevila saw that Berengaria and Ravendelfort were no longer talking. "You could now."

He glanced back and grinned. "Let him have a few minutes of peace and happiness. Soon enough we'll be battling our wicked uncle for Tragopogonia." He sighed and pulled his hat from his head. His fingers forlornly brushed the wilted plume. "It'll be close. Afterward . . ." He looked up to Vevila.

"Yes?"

"Afterward, I'll have to find something to do with myself." When Vevila frowned, confused, Rumpelstiltskin added, "Right now he needs me to regain his kingdom. But then I'll be a liability. He couldn't keep me around, not hardly. He'd have to introduce me to people as 'Our brother the Wizard-Prince Rumpelstiltskin.' Even if he convinced Tragopogonia to accept me, the other kingdoms would turn on him."

"I never understood that." Vevila watched a flock of birds skittering and looping through the air on the other side of the lake. "What's so wrong with being both royal and magical?"

Rumpelstiltskin shrugged. "Too much concentration of power. No one minds if you have one source of power: military, political, magical, economic, or whatever. But when someone starts combining them—say, magical and political as in a wizard-prince, or if, say, a very rich general became king—and people tend to get upset. They're afraid you'll go crazy, and . . ." He stepped out from under the willow branches, spread his arms, and in a very deep, booming voice said, "Decide to Rule The World!"

Birds flew off into the sky from everywhere around them. On the opposite side of the lake, the flock scattered.

The insects ceased their droning, and in the silence, his voice echoed back from the far side of the calm, blue lake.

"What are you up to now?" Ravendelfort demanded.

"Shouting." Rumpelstiltskin turned, and Vevila could see the mischievous glint in his eye.

"Well, we need to get going." Ravendelfort led Berengaria around the willow tree. "But we aren't dressed properly. Please do something about that."

The odd little man waved one hand negligently at Berengaria and Ravendelfort. Her dress became a frothy confection of white silk and lace, very becoming for a bride. His wool tunic transformed into dark leather and gleaming chain mail under an ermine-trimmed velvet cloak. The coronet on his head became a great shining bejeweled crown.

Vevila found herself the object of Rumpelstiltskin's scrutiny. She looked down at the rips and wrinkles a day's worth of her wearing could impose on unsuspecting cloth. The beginning of another hand waving caught her attention. "No!"

Too late, he'd already waved his hand. Strangely, nothing happened. Rumpelstiltskin found this odd, also, and tried waving again. Nothing happened.

"Hmmm." Brushing his hands down himself, Rumpelstiltskin transformed his clothes into a less imposing, less sparkling version of his brother's. He smiled grimly back at Vevila. "Shall I, or would you prefer to do it yourself?"

"What?"

"Your clothes."

"What?"

"Do you wish to wear that back to Chateau-Arbre?"

"What?"

"The sleeping castle. Or would you prefer something else?"

Ravendelfort tugged on Berengaria's sleeve. "We should leave them alone for a moment." He led her away to the other side of the willow tree.

"This is fine." Vevila shook her ragged and rumpled gray and blue skirt and glared at Rumpelstiltskin. "And I am not a witch."

"You're a natural. Untrained, but definitely powerful." Rumpelstiltskin grinned. "I could train you."

"I don't think so."

"Tut tut. What would Zenpfennig say?"

"I don't care."

His grin subsided into a serious expression. "Actually, we could use some help in our upcoming battle with our uncle. Would you be interested?"

Puzzled and more than a little interested, Vevila asked, "How exactly could I help?"

"You're smart. You're quick. You're good in a fight. You've become very resistant to magical attacks and could probably pick up magic spells easily. You're exactly the sort we want on our side when we go up against Uncle Swinburne." He extended his hand to her. "Would you consider it?"

"There is, of course, the small matter of the fee you'll be owing me."

"Fee?"

Vevila folded her arms. "I want a favor."

His eyebrows danced up and down his forehead. "A favor?"

"A favor as in a good deed," Vevila said, trying not to smile or laugh. "Not as in your favors."

Shrugging and grinning, Rumpelstiltskin said, "My favors, as in good deeds I perform, are all I *can* offer."

"Let's not mangle the language too much. I think we understand each other. Do we have a deal?"

"Deal."

They shook on it.

Rumpelstiltskin sighed. "I still think we'd make a great team. You and I, explorers and adventurers, courted by kings and armies, feared by bandits and pirates. Notorious. Rich. Legends in our own time."

"Time to go," Vevila shouted to get Ravendelfort's and Berengaria's attention.

An exasperated sigh escaped the odd little man's lips before he started on the spell to take them back to the castle. Vevila knew he'd only dropped the subject temporarily.

☙❧

ALTHELSTAN RACED THROUGH the castle, not even pausing when he heard the screams and shouts from the dining room. Groggy nobles and muddled servants wandered aimlessly through the corridors and rooms. They looked stunned and haggard. The only time the awakened people looked the least bit alert was when they jumped to get out of his way.

Up the stairs, through the corridor, and up more stairs. He raced into the waiting room, only to find it completely empty.

"No!" he shouted.

Voices drifted down from upstairs, and Althelstan ran up to the princes' old room. Everyone from the waiting room milled about. He shoved past one of the king's guards to get to the object of his affections. He barely noticed the guards begin to pull their swords and the king wave them back. She stood before him, walking and beautiful and rumpled and frustrated.

"Princess Jaquenetta," he breathed, barely daring to actually speak her name.

"Who are you?" she demanded imperiously as he approached her with hands outstretched.

He bowed. "I am Prince Althelstan of Portula. I found the castle and brought my cousin here to kiss your brothers. I . . ." He couldn't think of anything to say that he wanted to say in front of all these witnesses.

"So your cousin wants to marry the prince?" the king asked.

Barely glancing back at him, Althelstan said, "Oh no. She doesn't want to marry the princes. I'm not sure what she wants." His gaze drank in her bright eyes. "I . . . Your beauty has captured my heart."

Forcing a smile, Jaquenetta said very slowly, "Where are my brothers?"

"Out in the front courtyard." Althelstan hooked his thumb over his shoulder to point at the staircase. "The witch was trying to kidnap them before Vevila or Berengaria could kiss them."

"Berengaria?" said one of the other noble gentlemen.

"He can explain on the way." Jaquenetta grabbed Althelstan's wrist and towed him down the stairs. "Start at the beginning."

"My father decreed I could only marry a real princess," Althelstan said as they rushed through the waiting room. "So with the only real princess, the only one meeting his criteria that is, being two years old—"

"Skip that part," Jaquenetta ordered as she towed him

down the dusty corridor. "Will you look at this mess!" Althelstan started to stop, but she kept him moving. "Start at where you found the castle."

He started again. He reached the part where they'd returned from the ball to find Vevila leaving the castle with Rumpelstiltskin when Jaquenetta pulled him out into the courtyard.

❧

THE OTHER TWO princesses disappeared with that awful short man, so Dulcamara urged her daughters and stepdaughter forward toward the princes. Here was an opportunity for the girls, if only they wouldn't do something incredibly stupid. Perhaps the girls could snag these princes before their sleepy befuddlement left them.

"Poor thing," Gaulthemum said, taking one prince by the arm to lead him to a vine-covered bench. "It must be very confusing for you to wake up here after a hundred years."

"A hundred years!" he exclaimed.

"Oh, yes. The witch cursed you so that you slept until awakened by the kiss of a princess." Gaulthemum paused to look shyly away and blush.

A bit contrived but not too bad, Dulcamara decided. At least Gaulthemum could be counted on to make the effort.

Amelanchier led the second prince to the bench and stood behind him, massaging his shoulders. He sighed and moaned contentedly.

The witch tried to step up to the third prince. He yelped and backed directly into Stellaria, who was still trying to figure out what to do to get his attention.

"Not to worry," Stellaria said sturdily, interposing herself between the prince and the witch. "I'll keep you safe."

"No one's safe around her," he whispered.

Dulcamara forced out a laugh, hoping it sounded naturally amused. "What Your Highness needs is a wife. Everyone knows a wife will protect you from all other women."

The groggy prince looked at Stellaria. "Are you married?"

For once, the girl was quick on the uptake.

"No, Your Highness." She half curtseyed while holding onto his arm and leading him away from the witch. "I'm perfectly available." She batted her thin, short eyelashes at him. "I'd be honored to marry you."

"Oh, good." He tottered over to join his brothers on the bench, dislodging Gaulthemum so he could sit. He looked at the brother Gaulthemum was dithering over. "I'm getting married."

The brother pouted. "What about me?"

"I'll marry you," Gaulthemum said.

Grinning, he turned back to Stellaria's prince. "Guess what? Me, too!"

They both looked at the third prince, who stretched his neck and said, "A little to the left. Oh yes. That's the spot. Right there. Wonderful."

"Well?" the middle prince said.

"She's a keeper." The third prince sighed, smiling.

"I'll keep you, too," Amelanchier leaned down to whisper in his ear.

Dulcamara grinned delightedly. Even if Amelanchier's prince weaseled out in the end, two out of three wasn't bad. "And pray, what are your names?"

Holding up one finger, Amelanchier's prince said, "Un."

The middle prince, Gaulthemum's, held up two fingers. "Deux."

Stellaria's prince held up three fingers. "Trois."

"How . . . dynastic." Dulcamara looked nervously to the wizards, but they were still draped over the wagon, watching her and her daughters with amused, indulgent expressions.

At least she'd have no trouble from them. The witch was turning a very unhealthy shade of purple. Several persons unknown had emerged from the castle to stare. Dulcamara wasn't certain who they were or what they might try to do.

An odd howling sound came from beside the gates. One of the unknown persons milling about the courtyard peered around Dulcamara's carriage and screamed.

Several of what Dulcamara thought were servants went running around the carriage. Moments later, a huddled mass of them came back, carrying what appeared to be a howling statue of a royal guard, made of some unknown white gray material.

They paused beside the door to the castle, waiting while running footsteps of several varieties from the inside of the castle echoed around the courtyard.

❧

THE COURTYARD LOOKED much like it had when Althelstan left. Except for the strange tableau of servants carrying a very loud statue by the castle door. They scurried off into the castle as soon as the door had cleared. The princes were now fully awake and sitting up on a bench, surrounded by Dulcamara and her daughters. The wizards were still on the wagon, about where Althelstan remembered them climbing up to help the princes. Urticacea stood alone, radiating fury and frustration.

Jaquenetta released Althelstan's wrist when she spied the princes. "Lucien!"

No sign of recognition could be seen in the princes' faces as she ran to them. However, looking at her, they also saw the other nobles and the king emerge from the castle.

The princes stood as one.

"Father," one prince said. The others echoed and bowed with him.

King Lazare completely ignored all that and hauled all three of his sons into a tight embrace. They were soon surrounded by the other castle denizens.

Dulcamara and her daughters withdrew. The wizards walked around to stand by Althelstan. Urticacea remained aloof and angry. Happy jabbering chatter filled the courtyard. Althelstan wondered if he'd soon wish for the snoring back.

Eventually, Jaquenetta separated herself from the crowd around her brothers. She nodded to Dulcamara, and asked, "So which of these young ladies kissed my brothers?"

"None of them," Althelstan said before Dulcamara could get more than a syllable out. "My cousin, Princess Vevila, kissed your brothers." He looked around the courtyard. "Where is she?"

"She left with Rumpelstiltskin," Rueberry said. "He said they had to see a frog about a man. Made no sense to me."

"You let her leave with that, that, dangerous adventurer?" Althelstan sputtered horrified.

"Oh, he's not all that bad." Zenpfennig sniffed. "He's

probably just a victim of rumor, hearsay, and innuendo. Quite a nice fellow, once you get to know him."

Rumpelstiltskin, Vevila, Berengaria, and what could only be another prince appeared suddenly in the far corner of the courtyard.

"There she is." Althelstan waved his hand to Vevila.

Jaquenetta approached Berengaria. "Thank you, Your Highness, for delivering my brothers. You shall marry him."

The other prince put his arm around Berengaria. "This one is already spoken for."

"Not me." Berengaria motioned to Vevila. "Her."

Everyone stared at Vevila. Althelstan had to admit that standing as she was in a courtyard full of people dressed in their very best, she didn't appear particularly princessly. Her hair tangled and frizzed like a magpie's nest on her head. The wrinkles and scratches on her dress leant her no distinction. The glaring, frowning, and defiant posture didn't help, either.

"I'm sorry." Jaquenetta walked to stand in front of Vevila. She paused for a startled look down at Rumpelstiltskin, before returning her attention to Vevila.

"I'm the only true princess here," Vevila snarled. "So I have to do all the work."

A quick smile of understanding glinted on Jaquenetta's face. "Thank you," she repeated. "One of my brothers will marry you."

"Excuse me," Dulcamara shouted. "But they've already engaged themselves to my daughters."

Vevila patted Jaquenetta's arm. "They want to marry those girls. That's fine."

"No, it's not!" Urticacea shouted.

A moment of silence followed, which Althelstan couldn't help breaking with, "Now what?"

Urticacea glowered at him before facing her long-time adversaries, Jaquenetta and the king. "The princes are in truth only one prince. He must be rejoined in himself before he can marry anyone. Thus there can be only one princess to marry them."

Dulcamara seethed, and her girls gathered nervously around her, but they said nothing. The princes looked troubled and murmured among themselves.

"As you say," King Lazare said, nodding to Urticacea.

"I will rejoin them." Urticacea raised her hands to the princes, and waved them in ornate arcane patterns, speaking in a language Althelstan didn't know.

Nothing happened.

She tried again. Again, nothing happened.

Flexing her fingers and appearing distraught, Urticacea muttered, "It's a simple release. Why isn't it working?"

Another attempt failed.

Zenpfennig stepped forward, motioning back toward his colleagues. "Perhaps we can be of assistance?"

"No," one of the princes said. "We don't want to be rejoined."

"We always agree on everything," the second said. "We've one mind and one personality, but we have become accustomed to having three bodies."

"We like being in three places at once," the third prince said. "We'd rather be separate and each have our own wife. That would be three times the fun."

Urticacea stared, horrified, at the princes. "You don't want to be rejoined?"

They shook their heads.

She shook all over, terrified and appalled and overwhelmed. She opened and closed her mouth, with no sound coming out, though Althelstan could see she wanted to scream. She suddenly turned and ran behind Dulcamara's carriage, out through the path in the overgrown bramble.

Mazigian grinned and waved at her retreating back. "Adieu! These foolish drops do somewhat drown my manly spirit: adieu!"

"Hush. Stop that." Zenpfennig covered his face with his hands. "It would appear the curse has not worn off with her disappearance."

"So you, too, are cursed by her," the king said.

"That is the very defect of the matter, sir," Mazigian said as he bowed.

"Do you think she will be coming back?" Dulcamara shooed her daughters toward their fiancés. "Perhaps we should get them married as soon as possible?"

"I, too, wish to marry as quickly as possible," the prince standing behind Rumpelstiltskin said. He smiled at the king. "Then we must speak of alliance."

"Agreed." King Lazare waved to his sons. "We'll get you safely married and in a few months have a second wedding to celebrate."

"Celebrate what?" one of the princes asked.

King Lazare surveyed the courtyard. "Celebrate the reclaiming and cleaning of the kingdom."

❧

VEVILA HADN'T INTENDED to follow on to the chapel with the rest of the castle's inhabitants. She intended to leave; to run far, far away from here. Yet there she was, near the front of the chapel, between Rumpelstiltskin and

Althelstan, watching Zenpfennig, Rueberry, and Mazigian officiate as the three Prince Luciens married Amelanchier, Stellaria, and Gaulthemum, and King Ravendelfort married Berengaria.

The vines and weeds and bramble had broken through the floor of the chapel, growing not only in and around the patterned floor where seats once had been but up the walls and across the ceiling. Pale red, yellow, and purple flowers dotted here and there throughout the chapel, endowing the chapel with a sweet, delicate scent. Servants worked feverishly as Zenpfennig droned on, pulling down vines, pulling up weeds, and clearing the chapel. They left the flowers alone, to provide some sort of festive wedding atmosphere. But Vevila could only think what odd wedding decorations the frantic servants made.

Rumpelstiltskin suddenly grabbed her arm and shouted, "An army approaches."

"What?" Prince Ravendelfort asked.

"Who?" King Lazare asked.

The wizards' eyes unfocused for a moment. Rueberry whispered, "He's right."

"From a nearby kingdom. And they're very close." Rumpelstiltskin put his fists to his temples in concentration. "Abelardann. Does that name mean anything?"

"My father," Althelstan said.

Vevila winced. The subtle shifting of stances and expressions around the room told her that Althelstan had just exposed both of them as possible hostages.

Althelstan, apparently not as oblivious as Vevila had assumed, said, "Why would he march here with his army? He has no policy of aggression or acquisition."

A sort of frantic confusion broke out through the chapel as servants ran about under King Lazare's orders to prepare to meet the army. Seven liveried soldiers surrounded Althelstan and Vevila, swords drawn and pointed.

"You idiot," Vevila muttered to Althelstan.

"They'd have figured it out soon enough, anyway," a voice from closer to the ground said.

Vevila looked down. Rumpelstiltskin hadn't moved from his spot beside her and seemed blithely unconcerned about the sword point near his nose.

He grinned up at her. "Could be fun."

Chateau-Arbre's full, small contingent of soldiers marched into the chapel, fanning out around the walls, and preparing bows and arrows. One soldier was dripping wet, with soapsuds still clinging to his hair. His armor seemed to consist mostly of some hardened cement around his torso and limbs. He walked stiffly, since the armor on his legs and arms seemed to have little in the way of joints.

Dulcamara and her daughters huddled back behind the wizards with her daughters' fiancés. King Lazare stood with his arms folded, facing the entryway and waiting. King Ravendelfort seemed torn between allying himself with his brother or with King Lazare.

Berengaria pushed her way through the soldiers to stand behind Vevila. "This is ridiculous."

The clank of armor and thump of boots sounded from the corridor.

A neatly, if antiquely, dressed servant entered the chapel and announced, "King Abelardann and the army of Portula seeks an audience with King Lazare about the woman known as Princess Vevila."

"There you are," Abelardann boomed, pointing his sword at Vevila. "You've worried Queen Tarax into a state." Fifteen of Portula's best soldiers filed in behind him. However, none had their swords drawn, and none looked particularly ready to fight.

King Lazare motioned for his soldiers to stand down. If Abelardann noticed, he hid it well.

The Chateau-Arbre soldiers parted, leaving no one between Vevila and Abelardann. Abelardann spotted Rumpelstiltskin, and his sword point found a new target. He strode forward, hollering, "And you there. What sort are you exactly? And what are your intentions?"

"Hello, Father." Althelstan bowed.

"Hello, Son." Abelardann didn't take his eyes off of Rumpelstiltskin. "Your mother sends her love. We can talk after I take care of this."

Althelstan prudently stepped back out of the way, beside King Lazare.

"I'd like to call in my favor now." Vevila grabbed Rumpelstiltskin, putting him in front of her as a shield.

"Oh? What?"

Feeling him tremble under her grasp didn't help her confidence. "Save me from him. I don't want to go back and marry a prince. You owe me a favor."

The sword's point touched Rumpelstiltskin's chest, directly in line with his heart. King Abelardann towered over them, scowling down at the odd little man. "Well?"

Rumpelstiltskin held up one finger. "One minute." He turned his head to look up at Vevila behind him. "Technically, I don't owe you a favor, since you haven't fulfilled your side of the bargain yet."

Her fingers dug into his shoulders.

"However, if I do this for you, then you will owe me, possibly giving me greater leverage in your repayment."

"Rumpelstiltskin," Ravendelfort said warningly.

"On the other hand, we do need allies, and he did bring his army."

"Your answer?" Abelardann growled.

"The problem, sir, is," Rumpelstiltskin said, again holding up one finger, "if I must choose, which of you is the stronger ally: you with your army or her?"

They exchanged a long look. Looking down from above, Vevila saw Rumpelstiltskin mouth, *Her.* Abelardann nodded.

Very gently and carefully, Rumpelstiltskin pushed the point of the sword away from his heart and toward the ground. "The best solution would be one in which each of us gets what we really want without anyone having to surrender any point."

"Agreed." Abelardann almost smiled. "Do you have a solution?"

A loud sigh traveled through the room, as everyone let out the breath they had been holding.

"Let me be certain I understand what everyone wants." Rumpelstiltskin pointed to Vevila. "You want your freedom. And adventure."

"Yes," Vevila said.

He turned next to King Abelardann. "And you want her happily married to a prince?"

"Yes," Abelardann said.

"And I want to get my brother on the throne of Tragopogonia. For that we'll need allies and assistance. After that, he'll still need allies, and I'll need to be moving on." Rumpelstiltskin patted Vevila's hands, still on his shoulders, and smiled up at King Abelardann. "There may be a way. If you will ally with my brother, as King Lazare has agreed to, I will see if I can convince Vevila to marry a prince here and now. Then you won't have to worry about her ever again."

Narrowing his eyes in suspicion, Abelardann said, "That I'd be interested in seeing."

Taking Vevila's hand in his, Rumpelstiltskin turned to face her, his face reddening. "One more time. Will you marry me?" He continued before she could answer, "If you marry me, you will marry a prince, making your relatives happy; and your life will be filled with adventure and excitement, and I can teach you to use your magic."

The point of Abelardann's sword touched Rumpelstiltskin's back. "You marry her? I'm not at all sure of that. After all, you're . . ." He paused, looking down on the much shorter man. His free hand made a motion as if to call attention to Rumpelstiltskin's height, but he seemed to think better of it. "An adventurer."

"Some princes sleep." Rumpelstiltskin motioned to the Luciens. "Some are frogs." He nodded to Ravendelfort. "Others . . ." His hand brushed down his chest. "Have different problems."

He smiled up at Vevila. "What a team we'd make." His expression turned sad, and he said, "Unfortunately, I'm afraid it's me or him."

Vevila closed her eyes so she couldn't see Abelardann glowering at her. All the complaints of all her relatives still rang in her ears. She sighed and opened her eyes to face Rumpelstiltskin. "Fine. I'll marry you. But you owe me big for this." At least life wouldn't be boring.

"Sure, sure." Rumpelstiltskin grinned.

The occupants of the chapel reassembled themselves into a wedding party. Abelardann insisted on escorting Vevila and Rumpelstiltskin up to stand beside the other four couples. And he remained behind them, with his sword at the ready. Though Vevila was never sure who he planned to skewer if they didn't keep their end of the bargain.

Zenpfennig finished his lecture. "Remember that as you take these vows, you are promising each other to love, honor, and cherish each other for the rest of your lives. To keep each other through sickness and health. To hold to each other for better or for worse. In token of this, you may now exchange rings."

Rueberry waddled over to stand in front of Lucien Un and Amelanchier. He smiled indulgently at them. "Do you both promise this?"

"We do." Un reached over to slip a ring on Amelanchier's finger. She leaned against him and slipped his ring on.

Next, Rueberry asked Lucien Deux and Gaulthemum, "Do you both promise this?"

Gaulthemum giggled and Deux giggled as they tried to slip the rings on at the same time. "We do."

Stellaria and Lucien Trois stood serious and dour, as Rueberry approached them. When asked, they responded with a quick and solemn, "We do."

They each put their own ring on. The only way to tell they were happy was by watching them clasp and squeeze hands afterward.

Appearing satisfied with this, Rueberry stepped over to the next couple. He nodded, nearly bowing, to King Ravendelfort and Berengaria, before asking for their pledge.

King Ravendelfort responded with a deep, loud, and very royal, "We do!" drowning out Berengaria's soft soprano. The two exchanged rings with a ceremoniously royal flair.

Vevila nervously watched Rueberry approach them. A quick glance down showed her prospective groom to be nervously fiddling with the collar of his chain mail. A stirring behind her brought King Abelardann, with his sharp, drawn sword to her attention.

"Do you both promise this?" Rueberry asked innocently.

"We do," they said swiftly, both glancing back at the grim King Abelardann.

There was a moment's hesitation, before Rumpelstiltskin said, "Oh. The rings."

He looked around, but no one had any to offer. With a wave of his hand he pulled two gold nuggets from thin air.

"Excuse me." He grabbed Vevila's hand, and, before she knew what he was about, shoved the nugget onto her finger, making a perfectly sized ring. The shock traveled up her arm.

"Ouch."

"Sorry." He handed her a nugget, held out his hand, and closed his eyes. He winced as she pushed the rock against his finger. Suddenly it slid on easily, as if made just for him.

Rueberry returned to stand by Zenpfennig.

Mazigian stepped forward, smiling, and said, "You that choose not by the view, chance as fair and choose as true! Since this fortune falls to you, be content and seek no new. If you be well pleas'd with this and hold your fortune for your bliss, turn you where your lady is and claim her with a loving kiss."

As the other couples embraced, Vevila stared down at Rumpelstiltskin. He seemed unwilling to push the issue. She tried to remember what it was he'd said. Some princes sleep, some are frogs, others . . .

Leaning down, Vevila kissed him. Of all the various types of princes she'd kissed today, his kiss was the nicest. His breath was sweet and fresh, and his lips completely free of slime or drool.

She stood back up and glared down at him. "I thought you said you were cursed."

Backing away, with hands held up in surrender, he said, "I didn't actually say I was cursed. I merely implied it."

He tried to put Abelardann between him and Vevila, but Althelstan's father merely sheathed his sword and stalked away, muttering, "She's your problem now. I need to speak with your brother."

"I was cursed," Rumpelstiltskin said hastily as Vevila advanced on him. "But, this," he waved his hands to indicate his short stature, "is fate's little joke. The curse I was looking to get rid of was loneliness and boredom."

"Oh, I predict your life is about to be very interesting," Vevila said. "I can flat guarantee the next several minutes will be full of incidents and occasions."

Vevila had hold of his collar before he could even turn to run. "You are going to be telling me the truth, the whole truth, the unwarped truth, the unmagnified truth, the undecorated truth, and nothing but the truth from now on."

"Yes. Oh, yes." Rumpelstiltskin nodded vigorously.

"I don't want you putting any spells on me," she said. "And I don't want you using spells on anything or anyone else around me in order to manipulate me."

"Agreed."

Letting go of his collar and standing up, Vevila said, "And you'll start by telling me if you ever have used any spells on or around me to manipulate me."

"I don't think this is the time." He edged away from her, eyeing the knot of men forming around his brother.

She folded her arms and growled.

All in one breath, he said, "I put a sleep spell on you last night, because I needed you to stay here, so you could kiss my brother and free him from his curse. Other than that, I swear I've never put any spells on you or used spells to manipulate the situation you were in. Except perhaps to assist you." He took a deep breath. "I really need to get over there and make sure Ravendelfort doesn't do something stupid."

"Not to worry, you could always threaten them with me." Vevila strolled slowly in Rumpelstiltskin's wake. "And in any case, it's his kingdom now."

Off in one corner, Dulcamara congratulated her daughters and their fiancés. It was a little private party almost.

In another corner, Althelstan stood waiting patiently, watching his father and King Lazare negotiate with King Ravendelfort. Jaquenetta was nowhere to be found. Berengaria held tightly to Ravendelfort's hand silently, while Rumpelstiltskin gently nudged his way into the conversation.

Around them, all servants worked frantically, trying to restore order to the chaos that the castle had become.

Reminding herself that she was a bystander no longer, Vevila went to join the kings' negotiations.

❧

ZENPFENNIG REACHED AROUND Kings Lazare and Abelardann to pat the soon-to-be King Ravendelfort's shoulder. "You have your brother and these good men to assist you. We shall be returning to the Recondite University to make our report. Undoubtedly, someone will be along to investigate your uncle's wrongdoing. Do you need any other assistance from the Recondite University?"

"Thank you," Ravendelfort said sincerely. "Thank you all. We look forward to the university's inquiry into the circumstances of Our uncle's reign, and assure you and the University of Our full cooperation."

As Zenpfennig herded his colleagues out, Rueberry complained, "But they're bound to have a feast to celebrate. We'll miss all the fun."

"With what? You've emptied the larder. We need to get back to the University and submit our reports. It's vitally important." Zenpfennig grabbed a passing servant as they walked out into the courtyard. "We need a carriage prepared and brought around."

The harried youth looked up from his armload of weeds to survey the vehicle-filled courtyard. "Which one is yours?"

Rueberry opened his mouth, and Zenpfennig clamped a gnarled, bony hand over it. "The silver one on a tall stem, around the other side of the castle. See to it."

Huddling with the other two wizards after the servant had left, Zenpfennig said, "We must transfer the gold into the carriage magically, after it is brought around, and take it back with us to the University as evidence."

Mazigian looked very enlightened, nodded, and said, "Ay, ay, three thousand ducats."

"The kings have more important things to think about." Zenpfennig arched an eyebrow at Rueberry. "We shouldn't worry them over some paltry bits of gold nor that upstart wizard-adventurer. This once, I think, we would be wise to use the power of our wills instead of our muscles."

The youth soon returned, guiding the lead carriage horse and keeping the reins from the driver, who mrowled down at him. Under his other arm he carried a ladder and a promisingly large basket.

"He jumped up there when I went to bring it 'round." The youth began setting up the ladder. "Queer sort. Is he your driver?"

"Yes." Zenpfennig sneered haughtily down on the youth, discouraging further conversation.

Mazigian clambered up the rickety wooden ladder to the ornate silver door with no problem. Zenpfennig followed at a more dignified pace, allowing Rueberry to slowly and nervously ascend.

By the time Rueberry reached the top of the ladder, the floor of the shiny smooth carriage was covered in gold nuggets, making the footing in the interior even more treacherous. Zenpfennig leaned tiredly against the door frame and said, "We'll be taking the ladder with us."

The youth lifted it up, and Mazigian pulled it into the carriage and shut the door.

With his staff, Zenpfennig struck the side of the carriage, creating a high, pealing, bell-like sound that echoed back from the castle. "To the Recondite University, driver."

The driver caught the reins as the youth tossed them up, and with a loud, "Mrowl," startled the horses, and got the journey off to a fast and rocky start.

☙❦❧

ALTHELSTAN STOOD IN the corner as the kings discussed various trade and alliance treaties between the three of them. He understood why the odd Rumpelstiltskin would concern himself with such matters, having devoted the last ten years to getting to this point, but he didn't understand why Vevila felt compelled to continually disrupt the proceedings with her unwanted comments.

All around them, servants busied themselves, clearing cobwebs, cleaning dust, pulling weeds, and repairing broken fixtures. A few even plied the working nobles with what drinks and food they had scrounged from the nearly empty larders. Althelstan waved off an offer of sweet wine.

Jaquenetta had left the conference early—and to Althelstan's mind in proper princessly form, quite unlike Vevila—to see to the restoration of the castle.

The kings were all smiling and shaking hands. Althelstan guessed the meeting was breaking up. Time for him to see to his business.

"Sires," he said bowing to them all. "Father, King Lazare, I wish to request the hand of the fair Princess Jaquenetta in marriage."

"Well done, Son," his father said.

"As long as she has no objections, you have Our blessing," King Lazare said.

"Wait." Vevila held up one finger. "I thought he had to marry a real princess. Isn't it true that there is no evidence to prove that Jaquenetta is a real princess?"

Furious, Althelstan glared at Vevila. After all he'd done for her! After carrying tons and tons of straw up to her cell, and helping her find dresses, and all he'd done to see that she was declared a real, true, honorable princess. How dare she do this to him!

King Lazare looked around nervously, as if expecting the witch to show up.

King Abelardann shook his head. "Perhaps We were a bit hasty with that proclamation."

"In that case . . ." Vevila began to twist the gold wedding band off her finger.

"The proclamation is fine, Father." Althelstan pushed the strange, short man toward Vevila, and turned his back on them both. "I know all about princess tests now. I'm certain she'll pass."

Behind him he heard Vevila chuckle.

Without bothering to turn around and glare at her, Althelstan motioned toward the kings. "Shall we find the fair princess and see if she can be persuaded?"

They found Jaquenetta in the main dining room, staring in horror at a scum-covered puddle. The fragrant bough of roses, stuck by thorns into her sleeve, couldn't mask the strong, moldy odor that had so long reigned supreme in the room. Her right hand clutched a short length of vine, and her left hand held a rotted length of purple velvet that might possibly have been curtains once.

"Fair Princess," Althelstan began, falling to one knee beside her. "I am Prince Althelstan of Portula. Your beauty has captured my heart, and I beg you to marry me."

Her head turned, and she stared at him with the same look of openmouthed horror she'd used on the putrid puddle. Her eyes blinked twice, and, like someone coming out of a trance, she said, "Where would we live?"

"Portula, of course." Althelstan stood, reached for her hand, removed the rotting velvet, tossed it on the floor, and placed her slender, cool hand between his. "I'll be king someday."

She tossed the vine away and flung her arms around his waist. "I'll marry you. So long as you take me far, far away from here."

Putting his arms around her—careful of the roses—and glancing at his father, Althelstan said, "There is one little thing. You have to pass a princess test."

"A princess test?" Jaquenetta pulled away from him slightly.

"Oh, don't worry. It's nothing much." Althelstan patted her back and tried to pull her close again. "You just have to spin straw into gold, or be able to feel a pea through twenty mattresses and twenty feather beds and twenty silk blankets, or—"

"What?" she shouted, and tried to squirm out of his embrace.

King Abelardann placed a calming hand on her arm—careful of the roses—and said to Althelstan, "I think perhaps we should leave the choice of test up to your mother."

"Spin straw into gold?" King Lazare said, dumbfounded.

With the tiniest shake of his head and holding up a restraining hand, King Abelardann said, "I'll explain later. When we're alone."

Althelstan wasn't sure what his father meant, but he had no doubt that Jaquenetta would pass. He smiled down on her. "Fear not. You'll like Queen Tarax. And I know she'll like you."

"How can you be certain?" she asked.

He whispered in her ear, "You're not Vevila." He slid his lips across her soft cheek to her warm lips and kissed her.

❦

AFTER THE FEAST and the dancing and the merrymaking, after most of the celebrants had gone to bed, King Abelardann and King Lazare retired to a small parlor on the second level of the inner south-southwest tower.

"About Princess Jaquenetta." King Abelardann eased

himself into a large, cushioned chair and put his feet up on the conveniently placed footstool.

"Yes, We should warn you about her." King Lazare flopped into the matching chair next to Abelardann's.

"Warn Us?"

"Yes. She's a very headstrong girl, but she means well. She works hard, can read and write. She's very intelligent, actually, but she's somewhat opinionated and, well, obstinate."

"Oh that." Abelardann shifted to get himself more comfortable on the soft, inviting cushions. "We all survived Vevila, and no one could be as stubborn and opinionated as her. What We wanted to talk about were these princess tests. She'll have to undergo one, because of that damned proclamation, but don't worry, We'll see she passes. Anything rather than see Our son marry Vevila."

King Lazare settled back in his chair, eyes closing and opening, as if fending off sleep. "Oh, We don't know about that. Sometimes the kingdom is better off with a strong woman beside the king."

❧

VEVILA LEANED INTO the strangely seed-shaped cushions and poked one finger into the soft, spongy walls of the orange carriage. "Something odd about this."

"Pretty good job, I thought." Rumpelstiltskin eyed the inside of the carriage professionally.

The brilliant morning sun streamed in the open windows of the gently rocking carriage. Outside the windows, the countryside rolled by as the horses steadily lessened the distance between them and Tragopogonia. A faint, pumpkiny scent increased with the heat. On the front-facing seat, across from Vevila and Rumpelstiltskin, sat Ravendelfort and Berengaria, leaning against each other, sleeping.

Rumpelstiltskin seemed lost in thought, slumping down in his seat and staring at the door of the carriage. After a moment, Vevila thought she heard him mumble, "Speak as you want, you never shall. Your thoughts . . . hmm. No. That wouldn't work."

"What?" Vevila asked.

"Sorry." Rumpelstiltskin sat up and sighed. "I was just thinking about the wizards. They asked me for help with the curse Urticacea put on them. But I couldn't figure it out."

"What was the curse?"

He quoted, "Speak as you want, you never shall, your tongue will always your thoughts befoul. Unsimple quotes stand in the stead, of what it was you wish you said. The words of the bard of another place, dropping trippingly from your face. Until you've learned humility, respect for others, and docility. The better part of valor is discretion, educate yourself upon this lesson."

A moment's thought was all Vevila took. "That doesn't sound so hard to break."

"Really?"

Uncertain if he was angry or amused, Vevila shrugged. "All he has to be is humble and respectful."

"I thought of that one," he said defensively. "The other wizards said they couldn't imagine him humble or respectful or docile."

Vevila nudged him in the ribs. "Don't be silly. The problem isn't him, it's them."

"What are you babbling about?"

She laughed. "The only way I could kiss the princes was to be proclaimed a princess, remember?"

"Yes." He sounded even more defensive and fierce than ever.

"So what makes a woman a princess?" she demanded.

Rumpelstiltskin folded his arms and glared at her. "I don't know anymore."

"From my experience, it seems that if everyone says she's a princess, then she's a princess, regardless of where or how she started."

"I don't see what princesses have to do with the wizards' curse."

Pinching her hand to keep from laughing again, Vevila said, "If everyone else said he was humble, respectful, and docile—regardless of his actual behavior—then he would be humble, respectful, and docile. And the spell would be broken."

He sat for a moment opening and closing his mouth. Finally, he stopped and grinned, lifting his hands to start a spell. "We have to get word to the wizards!"

Vevila grabbed his hands in hers. She leaned down and whispered, "No. They're wizards, and heading for the Recondite University. They're smart; surely they'll figure it out. And you are a wild, barbarous wizard. They don't like that sort of thing at the University. It might be trouble for you to get too close to there." She held on until he subsided.

"You're probably right." He looked to his brother, sleeping on the other bench. "And we need to prepare for Tragopogonia."

"Very true. Very true."

Eyes narrowing, Rumpelstiltskin stared at her. "Speaking of the truth, would you really have divorced me if King Abelardann had done away with his proclamation?"

"And marry Althelstan?" Vevila shuddered. "Never."

"Then why did you threaten to?"

"Oh, that. I wanted revenge on Althelstan for locking me in that cell. It isn't much, but delaying his marriage was the best I could do. They'll still get married; he'll just have to wait until she passes a silly princess test."

"Revenge? That was all it was, just revenge?" Rumpelstiltskin thought that over a moment. "You were revenged on Urticacea when you kissed the princes and woke them. On Althelstan when you delayed his marriage. And on the wizards when you stopped me from giving them the answer to removing the curse."

"I don't know what you're talking about."

"You owe me big."

Vevila turned from watching the spring-green countryside rolling by outside the orange frame of the window. "What?"

"You wanted revenge on all of them for locking you up, didn't you." He pointed at her. "Admit it."

Pointing back at him, she said, "And you could have gotten me out of that cell the first night, couldn't you. You kept me in there to suit your own purposes, because you needed a princess." When he didn't respond, she added, "I'm right. And you promised you'd tell the truth about all the times you manipulated me. You liar."

"I didn't lie!" He pushed her finger from his face, trapping it between the soft cushion of the carriage bench and his tightly squeezing hand. "You asked me to tell about every time I used a spell, on you or around you, to manipulate you. That time I deliberately didn't use a spell to manipulate you."

"Ha!" Vevila shouted. "Weasel wording won't help you this time, you little wretch."

They fumed in silence, while a mile's worth of pastures and fragrant orchards rolled past.

"So, I suppose you want revenge on me now," Rumpelstiltskin said.

"Yes," Vevila growled.

He shrugged. "Could be fun."

She turned away so he wouldn't see her smile.

※

A LARGE, CARVED pumpkin carriage rolled down the thin, brown, dirt, ribbon road through forest and field. Off in the distance, another quite ordinary carriage, surrounded by a small army, rolled much more slowly over larger dirt roads in a different direction. Even farther away, a tall silver carriage rocketed along, making its own path through forest and field.

Near the triangulated center of these vectors, a tall stone castle, made up of towers and turrets, emerged from under a hundred years' worth of magically growing vines and weeds, through the valiant efforts of servants and nobles alike.

Not far from the shouts and hustle around the castle, a solitary man marched into the dusky shelter of a deep forest. His face was a bright, scrubbed red, and his hands still wrinkled from a long soak. Behind his ears a whitish sort of gray plaster clung in small bits. He muttered something about never working as a gate guard again, and fearsome denizens of the unknown depths of the forest fled in panic from his path.

※

A ND THEY ALL lived happily ever after.